ADVANCE P
MURDER IN THE MALOO

"A raucous and ribald glimpse into Shanghai's cacophonous late nineteenth century. Paul Bevan's welcome translation of *Murder in the Maloo* reveals a city of strivers, adventurers and grifters in a take-no-prisoners emerging metropolis."
— Paul French, author of *City of Devils and Midnight in Peking*

"Fists fly when Ma Yongzhen, the legendary strongman from Shandong, turns up in Shanghai, and ruffles the feathers of Scrofulous Bai. Paul Bevan's translation is slick and thoroughly entertaining — a fascinating insight into old Shanghai and the city's gangland culture."
— Helen Wang, award-winning translator

"Vibrant and warm, Paul Bevan's nimble translation *Murder in the Maloo* brings a host of colourful characters from the Shanghai underworld to life. The addition of a meticulously-researched essay provides historical context and extends a friendly hand to English-language readers who may be meeting with popular Chinese Republican fiction for the first time. A truly excellent work of literary translation and scholarship."
— Elizabeth Emrich-Rougé, University of Cambridge

MURDER IN THE MALOO

A TALE OF OLD SHANGHAI

Attributed to
Qi Fanniu and Zhu Dagong

Translated with an Introduction and Essay
by Paul Bevan

EARNSHAW
BOOKS

Murder in the Maloo: A Tale of Old Shanghai

Attributed to Qi Fanniu and Zhu Dagong

Translated by Paul Bevan

ISBN-13: 978-988-8843-65-7

FICTION / Historical

Cover image: Detail from, "Ma Wang Shi, Shandong Ma Yongzhen, diao pangzi, hongni guankou," SOAS Library, CWP 38

EB214

Published in Hong Kong by Earnshaw Books Ltd.

For my Mother and Father.
Long will they be missed.

CONTENTS

Translator's Introduction 1

Cast of Characters 9

Murder in the Maloo: A Tale of Old Shanghai 11

"Ma Yongzhen's Shanghai," an essay by Paul Bevan 174

A Note on Language 205

Changes to the Text 210

Appendix: Original Preface to Murder in the Maloo 217

Bibliography 220

Acknowledgments 226

About the Translator 229

INTRODUCTION

Murder in the Maloo: A Tale of Old Shanghai is a story about Ma Yongzhen, who journeyed from Shandong Province in northern China to the cosmopolitan city of Shanghai, to make his fortune in the worlds of horse trading and the martial arts. The book was written in the early 1920s by two authors, Qi Fanniu and Zhu Dagong and is set in the years 1878 and 1879. According to the information provided by the authors in the main text, they each wrote one half of the book. However, their exact contributions are harder to assess, as it seems that Zhu Dagong was responsible for editing the whole book and Qi Fanniu left him alone to take charge of that task at an undefined point in the writing process.

The "maloo" of the title, refers to the Chinese word, *malu* 馬路 (literally "horse road"), translated in this book as "avenue". For the foreign residents of Shanghai in the 1870s, "The Maloo" referred specifically to the biggest of the "avenues", Nanking Road, but there were in fact six avenues (malu) situated in the center of the International Settlement of Shanghai. All of these were named after Chinese cities, for example, "Foochow Road" or "Kiukiang Road", but were also known to the locals by a series of numbers—in the case of Foochow Road, *si malu* 四馬路 (Fourth Avenue). This numbering system is still occasionally used by locals today. The area in which these avenues are located is central to the action of much of the book, particularly when it comes to the many visits to restaurants and teashops that are so crucial to the story.

The English title chosen for this book is taken from a newspaper article in the *North-China Herald* that appeared soon after Ma

Yongzhen's death, "The Murder in the Maloo". The original Chinese title of the book, as published in 1923, was *Ma Yongzhen yanyi* 馬永貞演義 (Ma Yongzhen: An Historical Romance). There is nothing wrong with the original title, except that it does not sufficiently explain to an English-language readership of the twenty-first century the true nature of the book. Hence the change to *Murder in the Maloo: A Tale of Old Shanghai*. The story is very loosely based on fact. Ma Yongzhen was an historical figure who was murdered in Shanghai in 1879. My translation of the sequel to this story, *The Adventures of Ma Suzhen*, was published by Palgrave in 2021. These two books stand as self-contained works of fiction, and are indeed quite different from one another in both content and approach. Both are adventure stories written in the period when so-called "Mandarin Ducks and Butterflies" fiction was at the height of its popularity. *Murder in the Maloo* concentrates on the protagonist's quest to become top dog as a gangster in the horse trading and martial arts circles of Shanghai. Its sequel, *The Adventures of Ma Suzhen*, takes a rather different approach, with the fictional female protagonist fighting against inhumanity and injustice while on the road from Shandong to Shanghai, with the ultimate goal of taking revenge for the murder of her brother.

The Ma siblings became central characters in the 1923 play *Ma Yongzhen* and in a film made by the Mingxing Film Company, *Ma Yongzhen of Shandong* four years later. Almost entirely unknown to an English-speaking audience, these heroic siblings are widely known in Chinese-speaking communities around the world. This is largely due to the more recent dissemination of their stories in adventure films that have appeared in profusion, particularly in the 1970s.[1] All these films are in the "martial arts" mode, and were made by well-known film studios, including the acclaimed Shaw Brothers Studio. The 1923 play, according to newspaper reports and reviews of the time, laid a particular emphasis on comedy and this is reflected in this translation of the book.

The preface to the book was composed by one Chen Dongfu (n.d.), and is written in a complex and involved form of literary Chinese of the sort typically used for such formal dedicatory purposes (see page 217). It is on the theme of the Ma clan's lineage, and includes many historical and literary allusions. This style of writing is notably different to that found in the story itself. Much of Chapter One is set in 1878, the year the historical figure Ma Yongzhen arrived in Shanghai, but to begin with, its general format and the type of language used, gives the impression that it is introducing an earlier, albeit historically ambiguous period. As the chapter progresses, it settles down into a less formal, but still somewhat antiquated style of language, of the type commonly used in the popular fiction of the first decades of the 20th century in the work of authors like Zhang Henshui 張恨水 (1895-1967) and Bao Tianxiao 包天笑 (1876-1973). This way of writing differs markedly from that used by the writers who sought to modernize the Chinese written language as part of the New Culture Movement in the years before and after the Xinhai Revolution of 1911. After joining the nationwide demonstrations of May Fourth 1919, the writers of the New Culture Movement have become known as the "May Fourth Writers". They were responsible for the introduction of a new vernacular language,

---

1   For more on these films see Paul Bevan, "The Legends of Ma Suzhen and Ma Yongzhen: From Shanghai Silent Film to Hong Kong Martial Arts Cinema," book chapter in *Film History and Development of Screen Culture in and Beyond Greater China* (Forthcoming), and for more on Ma Yongzhen see Paul Bevan, "Ma Yongzhen: 'He Fought with his Fists in the Capitals, North and South'," in *Arts of Asia* (Summer 2023), pp. 48-54.

known as *baihua* 白話 (plain speech), rejecting the formal literary language that had previously been dominant. Despite the best efforts of these progressive writers, what they considered to be an "old-fashioned" style persisted widely in popular fiction. As a result, the writers of popular fiction were grouped together by their literary adversaries as exponents of so-called "Mandarin Ducks and Butterflies" fiction, and were considered to be highly conservative and even backward in their thinking.[2] In truth, rather than being a form of fiction that simply wallowed in its own world of love, romance, and adventure, this vast body of literature includes some quite sophisticated examples of storytelling, aimed at a varied readership eager to engage with reading material that was not of the didactic, or political sort, so forcefully promoted by the May Fourth writers. *Murder in the Maloo* belongs to this broad category of popular writing. For many in Shanghai in the early 20th century, including the authors of *Murder in the Maloo*, this type of fiction was part of the wider popular cultural discourse of the day, a phenomenon that was a whole way of life for many people. This could be seen in an array of cultural contexts: in the consumption of fiction and poetry in popular magazines and books; the presentation of the typically Chinese *Kunqu* and Peking Opera in teashops and theaters; the performance of the modern, spoken *wenmingxi* 文明戲 "civilized drama" in specially built modern theaters; in an engagement with the products of the burgeoning silent film industry, which often adopted the same themes as those in popular literature; and the performance of sung and spoken storytelling—live in

---

2   As noted by Xu Xueqing, "There never was a school of 20th century Chinese writers who called themselves the Mandarin Dick and Butterfly School, and no single writer has asserted its existence or acknowledged being a member." See Xu Xueqing, "The Mandarin Duck and Butterfly School", in Kirk A. Denton and Michel Hockx (eds.), *Literary Societies in Republican China* (Lanham, MD: Lexington Books, 2008), pp. 47-78.

the teashops and theaters of Shanghai, and second hand on the
radio and phonograph.

In *Murder in the Maloo*, the connection to the world of
storytelling can be clearly seen in the short interjections from
a narrator that appear throughout the text, and in the stylized
language used, for example, at the beginning of chapters, as
discussed on page 214. This points to the storytelling origins
of the authors themselves, Qi Fanniu and Zhu Dagong, both of
whom were active in Suzhou *pingtan* circles, as enthusiasts and
writers of performance scripts. In the original Chinese, these
interjections by an imaginary narrator, appear no different to the
rest of the text. However, for the sake of clarity, in this English-
language translation, these short passages are clearly indicated
by the use of italics. In these asides, the narrator often looks back
from the 1920s to the time when the story is set. A good example
of this being in Chapter Three, in which the narrator refers to an
area of Shanghai that was undergoing major roadworks in the
1920s.

> *Fair reader, the Shanghai of forty years ago was nothing like*
> *as lively as it is now. The area around the British Nanking*
> *Road did not yet bustle with excitement, and the land*
> *around North Nicheng Bridge had yet to be leveled out.*

Newspaper articles from October 1920 report on the leveling
out of land around the creek at North Nicheng Bridge, which
was carried out at the request of foreign tram companies.[3] It is

---

3   "Bei Nichenghe yi wanquan tianping" 北泥城河已完全填平 (The Leveling Out of
    North Nicheng Creek is Complete) in *Shibao* 時報 ("Eastern Times") (25 October 1920),
    p. 5, and "Bei Nicheng bang tianping gongjun" 北泥城浜填平工竣 (Works to Level Out
    the North Nicheng Creek are Complete), in *Minguo ribao* 民國日報 ("The Republican
    Daily News") (25 October 1920), p. 11.

clear that this was a significant news story for the writers and their readers at the time, and its inclusion in the narrative was designed to draw those same readers further into the action of the story. In *Murder in the Maloo*, we see two versions of the Shanghai metropolis divided by a period of forty years, but the distinction between the two, as described by the authors, is sometimes a little hazy. They tell a story of Shanghai in the Qing dynasty but sometimes, by accident or design, bring in aspects of the modern Shanghai in which they live.

The Book

The preface, with its complex and involved literary style, will no doubt prove hard going to all except the most seasoned Chinese literature enthusiasts. As a result, in order to avoid an unhelpfully slow start to the story before Chapter One even begins, the decision has been made to move the preface to the end of the book, so those who are interested can read it at their leisure.

The book is formed of twenty short chapters on various themes. In Chapter One, Qi Fanniu (who is said to have written the first half of the book) adheres to Chinese literary traditions by introducing the Ma family history, before moving on to the main substance of the story. To a certain extent this takes its lead from the preface, resulting in a first chapter that is thematically and stylistically somewhat different to the nineteen chapters that follow. By the second chapter, the writing style has loosened up considerably, and a gradual softening of language continues to pick up pace in those that follow, becoming increasingly more engaging as the story progresses. In this chapter, Ma Yongzhen is introduced as an expert horseman and a righteous hero striving for justice. With Ma's visit to a courtesan's house in Chapters Three and Four, aspects of Shanghai gaming and popular culture

TRANSLATED BY PAUL BEVAN

are presented, and this includes some of the first comedic content that comes to dominate later chapters. The story continues with Ma demonstrating his superhuman strength and his martial arts prowess, culminating in the mounting of the all-comers challenge arranged by his disciples to increase his prestige in the Shanghai underworld. At the end of this chapter, following his victory over the foreign challenger, Yellow Beard, Ma's downfall is predicted, and his nemesis, rival gang leader and fellow horse trader Scrofulous Bai, is introduced for the first time.

The second half of the book, said to be written by Zhu Dagong, presents an equally varied assortment of themed chapters. By Chapter Thirteen, the comedic element is consolidated, and this can be seen to draw heavily on the slapstick comedy of 1920s Hollywood film, thereby showing a direct correspondence between the book and the 1923 stage play, and how both influenced the film made by the Mingxing Company in 1927. In Chapter Fourteen there is an emphasis on the poetic, when Ma Yongzhen and Chai Jiuyun visit the Lungwha Temple together, at the time in spring when the peach blossom is in full bloom. Comedy continues to dominate throughout the second half of the book, and the action becomes ever more fast-moving. It culminates in Ma Yongzhen's tragic downfall, with a vicious attack by the Axe Head Gang, followed by a heart-rending account of his death in hospital, surrounded by his closest disciples.

It can be seen, then, that persisting with the rather slower-paced first chapter, does pay off in the end, and the result is a story that manages to be at times humorous, at times serious, sometimes tragic, sometimes poetic, but always thoroughly engaging.

This translation was never envisaged as an "academic" study, i.e. as a word-for-word translation to be studied, dissected and analysed in the classroom. Even so, it follows the original text closely at all times and aims to be a true and accurate rendition of the story in English. It is an example of popular fiction to be read for enjoyment but can also offer much to the student of Qing dynasty and Republican Era history, particularly if read in tandem with the essay on page 174.

CAST OF CHARACTERS

MAIN CHARACTERS ONLY, IN ALPHABETICAL ORDER

Ah Jin	Hua Baoqin's servant
Ah Hong	Hua Baoyu's servant
Bi Yuanshun (Stream Leaping Tiger)	Ma Yongzhen's disciple
Boss Wang	Proprietor of the Yileyuan restaurant
Chai Jiuyun	Ma Yongzhen's friend
Cheng Tianfu (Turbid River Dragon)	Ma Yongzhen's disciple
Cheng Zimin	Boss of the Axe Head Gang
Dog-Eared Gao	Local ruffian and thief
Dong Jiguang	A young nobleman and horse enthusiast
Eely Mudskipper	Scrofulous Bai's follower
Hua Baoqin	A courtesan who lives in Qunyu Fang
Hua Baoyu	A courtesan who lives in Puqing Li
Li Sibao (Knife-Wielding Demon)	Ma Yongzhen's disciple
Lin Deshen (Double-tailed Scorpion)	Ma Yongzhen's disciple
Little Ah Bao	Lu the Lackey's relative
Little Big Number Nine	Scrofulous Bai's stable boy

Long Feiyun	Horse trader of the older generation
Lu the Lackey	Scrofulous Bai's second in command
Lu Shouji	Ma Yongzhen's disciple
Ma Suzhen	Ma Yongzhen's sister
Ma Yongzhen	Our hero
Poxy Fang (Fang Sanzi)	Gangster and friend of Ma Yongzhen
Sanbao Headsplitter	Scrofulous Bai's henchman
Scabby Crabby	Scrofulous Bai's henchman
Scrofulous Bai	Ma Yongzhen's sworn enemy
Siguan Bloodspitter	Scrofulous Bai's henchman
Village Head Han (Headman Han)	Village Head
Wang Desheng (Single-horned Dragon)	Ma Yongzhen's disciple
Xie Yuanqing	Lu the Lackey's friend
Ye Musheng	A horse doctor
Yellow Beard	A foreign strongman
Yuan Zuzhi (Yuan Xiangpu)	Scholar and poet
Zhao Gongbi (Long-Armed Ape)	Ma Yongzhen's disciple
Zhao Lianyu	Chai Jiuyun's friend
Zhao Yixin	Long Feiyun's mentor

1

Long Feiyun single-handedly dominates the province of Shandong,
And Ma Yongzhen arrives for the first time in the district of Chapei.

In ancient books that tell of literary and martial pursuits, throughout successive dynasties there appear men of remarkable talent, and this has been the case since times long past. Those in the south have mainly engaged with the civil and literary; those in the north have been mostly involved in the martial arts. This country, its mountains and waters, have given rise to individuals of great talent, and this has been dictated by the environment. Zisi, grandson of Confucius, once said: "In the south the ambience is soft and gentle; in the north the ambience is hard and strong." As a result, those in the south are fond of literature and those in the north are fond of martial pursuits. This is a plan designed by heaven and earth, and is a pattern that cannot be changed.

Let us proceed to relate how since ancient times the states of Yan and Zhao have been known as places where heroes of profound thought have expressed themselves through tragic song. If a worthy man succeeds in his ambitions he may become a hero; if he does not succeed in his ambitions, then he emerges as a righteous warrior who roams the land. By the time of the first year of the reign of the Xianfeng Emperor, amongst the personnel stationed at Guanjiazhuang near Tianjin, there was a bodyguard named Long Feiyun. Through successive dynasties his family made their living by trading horses. Long Feiyun's father, Long Xiang, was possessed of the physical strength whereby he could defeat one thousand adversaries. With one hand he was able to drag a horse by its tail and pull it backwards over a distance of thirty *li*. The horse's hooves might bleed, but Long Xiang would not be even the slightest bit short of breath. He was tall of stature, standing more than ten *chi* in height, therefore, everyone knew him as "Long the Tall". Long the Tall had dealings in that stretch of land that lies between the fortifications of Zhangjiakou, Gubeikou, Tong Pass and Yumen Pass. When he bought and sold horses, he would never quote more than one price, and that was always fair. Whether making a profit or suffering a loss, he never revealed his feelings in the expression on his face to show happiness or anger. When doing deals with others, he was never even the slightest bit deficient. People owed him nothing and he owed nothing to them. At the markets and shops where he sold his livestock, he hung a golden plaque to demonstrate his worth and good reputation, and his prices were uniform and did not fluctuate. Young boy or elderly man, none did he deceive, and they were always given identical terms of sale. Because of this he was revered by all. Beyond the Great Wall, and north of the Shanhai Pass, all who traded in horses were delighted to have dealings with him.

Fifty years passed like one day, and during that time within an area of five hundred *li*, all came forward to admire Long the

Tall's conduct. He married one of the Jia clan who excelled in hand-to-hand combat and boxing, the daughter of a military commander. Her golden lily feet were no longer than four *cun* in length and on them she would wear iron-tipped shoes decorated with the heads of phoenix birds. Youngsters of twenty or thirty with whom she sparred, could not even come close to her.

She gave birth to one son, whom they named Long Feiyun, and from a young age he followed his parent's instruction in the martial arts. Whether in punching or kicking, wielding the staff or using the spear, he followed the example of his father and grandfather. There were none in the village who did not praise the talents of the Long clan's son — like a fine steed that could run one thousand *li*.

At seventy-six years of age Long the Tall fell victim to the plague. His wife, Madam Jia, also contracted the disease. Fortunately Feiyun remained safe and sound, but he had no older male relatives, nor any brothers, and was left all alone without companionship. When going about his business he did so by himself. He inherited one hundred *mu* of poor-grade land and a number of dilapidated buildings. By nature Long Feiyun was liberal and generous and he liked to make friends. When he saw the impoverishment and suffering of the people roundabout, he offered them a helping hand. And so it was that, before even three years were out, that hundred *mu* of poor-grade land and those dilapidated buildings had all been sold. Long Feiyun was unconcerned by this, but the villagers were worried and took pity on him. From that time on, he had no possessions to his name, and was left only with the physical skills and abilities he had acquired: the tools that would allow him in the future to honor his family name and glorify his ancestors. At this time he was only twenty-four years of age and had yet to take a wife, so he took up lodgings with a neighbor, one of his father's closest friends, Zhao Yixin. Zhao Yixin excelled at the Shaolin fighting staff. Long Feiyun sought Zhao out as his master and Zhao took him on as his disciple, imparting to him all he knew about this weapon and its methods.

Long Feiyun went about his business all alone, and often found things to be boring and lacking in interest. All around him, everyone was fed and clothed, but his own food was insufficient and his clothes had become threadbare. He raised his head to look at the skies and with both hands by his sides, pressing firmly against his thighs, he let out a long sigh.

"Oh heavens above!" he exclaimed, "I, Feiyun, son of Long Xiang, am tall and sturdy at seven *chi* in height. How can it possibly be that this is all there is to life!"

Just as he was about to heave another pathetic sigh, Zhao Yixin happened to walk through the door. Gently lifting his long beard to one side with his hand, he let out a hearty laugh.

"Oh, Feiyun you are worthy indeed. Strive your hardest and complain not of suffering. You are young and have great ambitions, what need is there for you to feel sad that you have not yet established yourself in a position that will allow you to live a prosperous life? The profession of the father shall be continued by the son. This makes perfect sense from both the emotional and rational points of view, and is simply a matter of principle. Furthermore, your father's name is admired and respected by all. My nephew, if you can follow his example, it will not be hard to continue in your father's business, and you will find it easy to restore your family's status. With a man of character such as yourself, so open and honest, there is no need for you to imitate Zhong Yi, the official of Chu, who, as prisoner of the state of Jin, shed tears with his compatriots, having made no plan.

Long Feiyun bowed to acknowledge this advice. The emotions of the young have always been easy to control.

"You may follow your father's business, while at the same time borrowing this time to go roaming, and get to know the noble heroes who live in this land. If you regret that your hands are empty, that you do not possess even one *cun* of wood, and are wondering how you are going to build your grand mansion, and at what time you will finally become successful, then put your sorrows behind you."

For a short time Long Feiyun's face revealed an expression of displeasure. But Zhao Yixin, that venerable old gentleman, had seen this coming. Lifting his beard to the side again and laughing heartily, he said, "My nephew, be not downcast. As for that trifling thing called money, this old fellow will take care of it. Do you know how many agreements you must reach before you will be able to ply your trade?"

Long Feiyun was delighted to find himself with money, and responded with the words: "My daily expenses are now taken care of, but according to your foolish nephew's meager understanding, when the inexperienced become involved in trade, even after much consideration, the taking of sure and solid steps is better than the taking of broad and bold strides. In order to shoulder the responsibility of being given six hundred silver coins and to carry things forward, one must invite good fortune and protection. To advance even one inch, one must handle things with care. But whatever I do, I will not turn my back on the great friendship and love shown to me by my kind and benevolent master."

Zhao Yixin nodded and laughed again. "As you are of a mind to do this, which day do you hope to leave?"

Long Feiyun hesitated for a moment and said not a word. After a while he stood up straight and proud, and told Zhao, "Since you have been so generous to me, I shall be leaving this very day, as soon as I have packed adequate provisions. Your nephew has heard the sayings of the ancients: when a worthy man enters the world, at first he must act like a virgin; when he is to leave home on a journey, he must move quickly like the rabbit; with plans decided and details settled, he must go forth with one ambition. If something is to be done, it should be carried out immediately and without delay: one should be swift and never tardy; one should go forwards and never retreat."

Zhao Yixin agreed that this was indeed the case and at once gave Long Feiyun six hundred silver coins. The young man prepared his luggage and said farewell to his friends, who numbered as many as five hundred. Those who were to leave with him for the first time, prepared a banquet at the Pavilion of Long Goodbyes, and, as was the custom, Long Feiyun was presented with a sprig from the willow tree as a token of good luck, and a cup of wine to see him on his way. Long Feiyun thanked everyone in turn, bid a respectful farewell to Zhao Yixin, and went quickly on his way. After this, Long Feiyun traded horses to the west of the mountains in Shanxi, and in Eastern and Western Shandong there were none who did not hold him in the highest regard.

Having got this far, you should be aware, fair reader that the history of Long Feiyun is only secondary to this tale. He is but a minor character in support of that man of great renown, he who is known to all, even to women and children, he who has "trodden on both shores of the Yellow River and has fought with his fists in the capitals north and south", Ma Yongzhen. It is Ma Yongzhen who is the protagonist of this story. Long Feiyun has merely been an invited guest with a supporting role. When the main character takes his place on stage, naturally the support act must depart. For the remainder of this book, I, your humble servant, needs must take courage, and use what energy I have to grind the ink-cake on the ink-stone to produce fine quality ink for my writing brush, and apply it in an elegant sufficiency to pages of fine Peach Blossom notepaper, to set down the story of Ma Yongzhen, from beginning to end; in its entirety; comprehensively and in great detail; item by item, part by part, for you, oh worthy reader, so that you may defeat the demon of lethargy, and dispel both boredom and gloom.

Let us continue to relate how Ma Yongzhen hailed from the town of Dengzhou in Shandong, and for generations his family had traded horses for a living. When his father was alive, he was a sworn brother of Long Feiyun. Long Feiyun brought horses from beyond the pass to Dengzhou and they were stabled at the residence of the Dengzhou Ma clan. All livestock would pass through the hands of Ma Yongzhen's brother, Ma Xiaoliang, who was always faithful, cheated no one, and was forever honest and sincere.

Ma Yongzhen possessed a natural gift of strength of limb that surpassed all others. With his arms he could draw five hundred siege crossbows. His physical appearance was also most extraordinary: his face was mottled, he had big bushy eyebrows, and his eyes glared with fury. Just to look at him was enough to terrify anyone. As soon as you clapped eyes on him, you knew he was a fighting man. Ma Xiaoliang admired the fact that Long Feiyun's martial arts skills were unmatched by others, and strove with all his power to seek him out as his master. Since Long Feiyun felt Ma Xiaoliang to be sincere, and was also fond of Ma Yongzhen's steadfast nature, he put his heart into teaching them both everything he knew.

Ma Yongzhen received Long's personal instruction. Every day he progressed one inch, and every month he advanced one foot, and eventually, just as the old saying from the Kingdom of Wu says—"The eighteen martial arts, each was he able to perform." The days and months flowed swiftly by and the years progressed smoothly without obstruction. Those who were mature and experienced naturally faded away, while younger heroes rose in reputation and stature. Of those in Jianghu— that underworld of traveling fighters, and wanderers of rivers and lakes—who revered Long Feiyun, for ten thousand miles around, there were none who did not know that by now Ma Yongzhen had surpassed his teacher in skill, demonstrating the truth of what was once said by the philosopher Xunzi, "Blue comes from the indigo plant but is bluer than the plant itself." The Ma clan's resources had multiplied and the clan had now become prosperous.

Ma Xiaoliang treated others with great generosity. Ma Yongzhen, on the other hand, took the opposite path. He was aggressive towards others and was narrow minded. If he discovered that someone had a fine thoroughbred in their possession he would do all within his power to acquire it for as low a price as he could. Otherwise he would extort them, make demands on them, impose on them, and be deliberately provocative, to the extent that he would hurl insults and get into fights, not considering this to be shocking behavior, but seeing it as perfectly normal. What is more, he would boast about his extraordinary skill in martial arts, and considered all others to be beneath him.

On his frequent travels, when passing through the regions of Yan, Zhao, Qin, Jin, Min, Zhe, Yu, and Gan[4] he encountered no one who could match his skill in bending the bow and shooting arrows, wielding the spear, and performing with the *jian* mace.

---

4   Yan (Hebei), Zhao (Southern Hebei), Qin (Shaanxi), Jin (Shanxi), Min (Fujian), Zhe (Zhejiang), Yu (Henan) Gan (Gansu).

Therefore, he acted recklessly and without scruple, and became unbearably arrogant, recognizing no one as his equal. Up to now, for the most part, his footprints had been planted in the north of the country alone. Those places to which he had not yet journeyed, were the "two lakes" of Hubei and Hunan, and Jiangnan: that place known as a peaceful land of literary culture, where ordinarily martial arts are not practiced. But, in truth, those from Jiangnan, including the first master of the fist in all under heaven, Gan Fengchi (who served the Kangxi and Yongzheng emperors), and the valiant general Hu Dahai (who helped Zhu Yuanzhang establish the Ming dynasty) and other gallants of former times, had surpassed those heroes of Hebei, and the ancient lands of You and Ji. In light of this, one should not dare to look down on Jiangnan, or the city of Suzhou as places that are merely placid and weak.

Ma Yongzhen had often hoped to see the Gusu Tower at Suzhou, and the Caixiang Path, made famous by poets of Tang and Song, and to visit where the sound had in distant times been heard, made by that remarkable beauty Xi Shi when she danced on the wooden boards of empty corridors wearing her delicate wooden clogs. He would have liked to pay his respects to ancient burial grounds, to see the old districts on the Ganjiang Road, that commercial way that runs through the center of Suzhou town, and to feast his eyes on what traces were left of extraordinary beauties and remarkable warriors of the region, and, by doing so, broaden his meager knowledge. What a pity it is not always so easy to do things as that. But as chance would have it, that year, the *wuyin* year, 1878, the fourth year of the reign of the Guangxu emperor, Dong Jiguang, the young master of a wealthy family in Huating, Songjiang—a noble youth of graceful bearing, living in troubled times—was fond of riding horses and practicing swordsmanship. Only, it happened that in the south there were no fine horses to be had. Enquiries were made all round and it was made known that he would not hesitate to spend as much as one thousand silver coins to secure a fine steed.

As soon as this son of nobility had voiced these words, they came to the ears of loafers and idlers, who were driven by self-interest, and saw there was money to be made in this. Young Master Dong's search for a fine horse meant there were large profits to pursue, so the task was taken on by many, but always without success. Then the news came to the attention of Ma Yongzhen. Though Ma could not quite be compared to Bo Le, that sagely equestrian connoisseur, he did possess a close affinity with fine horses that could run a thousand *li*, and was now preeminent in his field. As the Tang dynasty essayist Han Yu once said, after Bo Le traveled through the wilds of Hebei, no fine horses remained, as he had recognized their worth and taken them away. Ma was much the same. In the stables of the Ma residence at that time, there were fine horses that could gallop to the sun and call down the wind. When Ma Yongzhen heard there was a nobleman in Huating, Songjiang, who was looking for a thoroughbred — a horse that could match the eight steeds of King Mu of Zhou — he made plans to visit Jiangnan.

One day, as the sun was setting behind Ma and his followers, they raised their riding crops, and set out on their journey on the great road to Suzhou. They saw the blue mountains and green rivers, the shaded lands under the willow trees and the bright colors of the wild flowers. Birdsong, pure and mellifluous, could be heard all round, and the sounds of man were full of peace and joy. They passed through Hebei and Shaanxi, where the scenery was truly remarkable, though, as the ancient have told us, "The immortals north of the Wei River are nothing at all, when compared to even the chickens and hounds of Jiangnan."

I never used to believe this, but now looking at this springtime scene from the back of a horse, I have started to believe that in saying those words the ancients were really not mistaken.

Ma Yongzhen took hold of the silken bridle and guided the horse before him. During the day he and his men traveled between ancient staging posts and at night they rested in remote and desolate relay stations. Six young horse traders who had become Ma's disciples accompanied him. Master and disciples spurred on their horses with their riding crops. The road was long and winding, but in less than two weeks they had arrived at the Huating Way, close to the residence of Master Dong. Ma Yongzhen and his followers entered a monastery and with the permission of the monks, made it their temporary base. He gave the order to one of his proud disciples, Wang Desheng, to go to town in search of information concerning the whereabouts of the Dong mansion.

If you want to know if young master Dong Jiguang decided to buy a horse from Ma Yongzhen, please read the following chapter.

2

Buying a fine horse, a young nobleman expresses strong emotions,
And wresting back a small bird, a righteous warrior upholds justice.

Let us continue to relate how Ma Yongzhen, the horse trader from Shandong, heard on the grapevine that Young Master Dong Jiguang of Songjiang desired to buy a horse, and was not afraid to spend as much as one thousand silver coins to acquire a dragon horse that could run one thousand *li*. Ma Yongzhen received this news and gathered together six fine horses there and then. These splendid creatures had hooves that could chase the wind and pursue the lightning, and were colored in subtle tones such as master painters have used to shade the clouds and offset the moon. He took with him six disciples, and each of them rode one of those fine steeds. Passing roadside milestones that showed them the way, they traveled by day and rested by night. They sped from one place to the next on route to Jiangnan, making a shortcut at Nanking, where they crossed the Yangtze

River, then passing through Zhenjiang, Danyang, Changzhou, Wuxi, Suzhou, and Kunshan. On arrival in the county of Shanghai, the first thing Ma Yongzhen did was to visit an old friend, Shi Shenggao, a man possessed of remarkable abilities, who could dash up the side of a building to its eves, and sprint along its walls. Originally, Shi was from a family of Shandong bodyguards, but after losing his job as a guard, he made a living by selling his martial skills and medicinal potions in the world of Jianghu — that underworld of traveling fighters, and wanderers of rivers and lakes. Eventually, he settled in the Chapei district of Shanghai and often exchanged letters with Ma Yongzhen. Now Ma had come to pay his respects.

Coming across an intimate friend by chance, his joy need not be spoken of.

When the two friends met face-to-face Ma mentioned to Shi Shenggao that Young Master Dong of Huating, Songjiang, desired to buy a fine horse, and he had journeyed south because of this. Ma Yongzhen and his disciples spent much of the day at Shi Shenggao's residence, before saying their farewells, and hurrying on directly to Huating, northwest of Shanghai, where they made further inquiries as to the precise location of the Dong Mansion.

When they were fully appraised of this, Ma Yongzhen set off alone. On arrival at the mansion gates, he took out a red calling card on which he had written just one line of small neat letters: "Ma Yongzhen of Shandong bows his head in respect and desires an audience with your lordship." The guard at the gate took the calling card from Ma Yongzhen and on seeing his physical appearance was lost in admiration. He thought to himself, "Sure enough, the spirit and greatness of those from the north is formidable, and cannot be compared to the wretched and vulgar appearance of those of us in the south." The guard inquired a little about his background, and Ma Yongzhen respectfully informed him of the reason for his visit. The guard accepted the red calling card and asked the guest to wait a short while at the gatehouse. Thereupon, the guard walked through the gates into the mansion and Ma waited for him to reappear. He sat there for a while, and eventually began to feel really quite impatient, looking around him, first one way, then the other, up to the ceiling, and down to the floor. Finally, at last he saw the guard hurrying back out.

"The young master asks if you would be so kind as to join him in the study."

Ma Yongzhen followed the guard and entered the main hall. On one side of the hallway was a small study. With arm outstretched, the guard lifted the heavy curtain that covered its entrance, while announcing Ma's arrival. Young Master Dong immediately stood up to welcome him. Having ducked his head to enter through the curtain, Ma Yongzhen performed the sort of greeting that was practiced in the north: genuflecting, touching the floor with one hand, and wishing his host good health. After which, he stood to attention at the side. On seeing this, young master Dong clasped his hands in front of him, and returned Ma's greeting with a series of small bows, while inviting him to be seated, all performed with a broad smile on his face.

"Who am I to even think of sitting together with Young Master Dong?" Ma asked. "I really do not deserve it."

"How could it ever be the case that a friend visiting from afar should not be seated?" Young Master Dong asked rhetorically. "You must be tired after your journey. Please do not stand on ceremony."

They went back and forth with formal pleasantries, once,

twice, and three times, before Ma finally took a seat diagonally opposite Young Master Dong. A serving boy brought in tea and the two men proceeded to chat about everything to do with Jianghu. They then talked in some depth about the correct approach to rearing horses, and the secret methods of using horse physiognomy to judge a horse's worth, as had been practiced by Bo Le. To each question put to him, Ma Yongzhen gave his reply. Young Master Dong was full of admiration. He ordered Lai Fu, the page boy, to go to the kitchen and bring up wine and victuals. Presently, food was served, wine was poured, and they spoke of noble things.

"How many horses have you brought with you on your travels?" The Young Master inquired.

"I have brought six fine horses and I invite your honor to kindly look them over."

On hearing there were six horses, the young master was delighted. He thought to himself, "I want to purchase only one. He has as many as six, so I can choose one from amongst them. Can it be that my wish has finally come true? Even though the price is a little high, as long as everything else is satisfactory and agreeable to all, then why not see it through?"

The banquet was over and Yongzhen asked for instructions. "Young Master, when and where would you like to see the horses?"

Young Master Dong thought for a while. "How about tomorrow morning? If the weather is fine, it would be an excellent idea to take the horses for a run on the piece of open ground at the Drunken White Pavilion, down by the western city gate."

"This is the first time I've been to the south and I am unfamiliar with the lie of the land. I would be grateful if you would be so kind as to write the directions down for me, so my followers may know where by the city walls to take the horses."

The Young Master happily complied. He laid out a sheet of paper, and, holding his writing brush elegantly in his hand, quickly wrote a note and passed it over to Ma, the horse trader. Ma Yongzhen held his hand out to receive it, then placed it safely within the folds of his shirt. He said his polite farewells and arranged to meet the following afternoon at three o'clock on the piece of open ground by the Drunken White Pavilion. Ma walked out of the study and Young Master Dong accompanied him as far as the entrance hall. He left the Dong Mansion through the main gates to meet with his disciples in a small teashop nearby. About the search for somewhere to stay, and a safe place to keep the horses, and of the exercising of the horses, for the moment we shall say no more, and nothing shall be said either of what happened for the remains of the day.

The next day, Ma Yongzhen got out of bed at the crack of dawn and performed his ablutions. He ordered his disciples to wash and brush down the horses and to feed them their fill of bean feed. Then they were to take them out to be exercised. The disciples complied with what was asked of them. When it came to two o'clock in the afternoon, Ma Yongzhen saw his disciples off one-by-one astride their horses. He himself led out a black beauty with snow white hooves, a horse like 'Wuzhui', the fine steed ridden by the Hegemon King, Xiangyu, two thousand years before. It was saddled up securely and he mounted it. He struck the horse lightly on the rump with a blue silk riding crop with white tassels, decorated with inscribed floral patterns. With this, the horse knew exactly what its master desired. It snorted proudly, lowered its head and raised its tail, then, with its four legs set in motion, galloped forwards with a clatter of hooves. It was like dragons flying and phoenixes dancing, as if horse and rider were entering into a place where no mortal had ever been. The strength of this dragon horse was not inconsiderable.

Fortunately, Ma Yongzhen reared horses for a living and was able to force it into submission. If it had been any other person riding it, in little more than a few strides, they would have lost control of the horse, and would certainly have been thrown to the ground.

But enough of this idle chatter. This story is about Ma Yongzhen riding that fine horse like Xiangyu's steed, Wuzhui. In no time at all Ma arrived at the Drunken White Pavilion, where his six disciples were awaiting him. Ma Yongzhen dismounted and his followers took the silken reins from him and went off to exercise the horse. All were waiting in great expectation. On seeing so many fine horses arrive that day, the locals had come out to spectate, chatting idly amongst themselves. In town, the Young Master waited until the hour of three had struck, then, seated in a blue palanquin, he was conveyed by four carriers who chanted rhythmically as they made their way through the western gate, to the Drunken White Pavilion. Ma Yongzhen was the first to catch sight of them, and ordered his six disciples to stand to attention by the side. Thereupon, they took their places in line, standing erect and upright, in impeccable formation, with their arms hanging stiffly by their sides, bending over ever so slightly at the waist. Young Master Dong stepped out from the palanquin and Ma Yongzhen came forward and bowed his head by way of welcome. Master Dong returned the greeting, bowing his head and clasping his hands together before him. Under his breath, Ma Yongzhen gave instructions for his disciples to come forward in turn and each perform a bow. This was the custom in the north. Young Master Dong returned the bow with his hands grasped in front of him and ordered his own followers to come forward and greet the visitors. Then, one man with one horse, Ma's men came forward in turn, and took their horses for a run around the circuit, each showing off their remarkable equestrian skills. Master Dong sighed as he looked on, thinking to himself, "Sure enough, the men from northern climes are totally unlike those from the south." Borrowing an ancient phrase that the warlord Liu Bei once said to Sun Quan on spying a small boat navigating rough waters, "Southerners sail boats and northerners ride horses."

In saying these words, the ancients were really not mistaken.

Each man rode once round the designated area, then that fine horse, splendid like the hegemon's steed, was led out into the arena. Ma Yongzhen grasped his hands together by way of a salute, and jumped onto the horse as if he were flying into the saddle. He held his blue silk riding crop with white tassels, decorated with inlaid floral patterns in his noble hand and raised it high up in the air, waving it in the shadow of the setting sun. The man and his mount, there on the fragrant grass, resembled the mythical lion controlling the embroidered ball under its mighty right paw. When he saw this noble vision, Dong Jiguang couldn't help but yell and shout out loud. Those watching from the sides applauded loudly and Dong's five servants, and Ma's six disciples supported him with strident cries and cheers. Ma Yongzhen circled around the area twenty times more, then gently reined in his steed and dismounted. He walked over to young master Dong and addressed him, "It was nothing really, please forgive my poor performance. Master Dong, won't you try the horse out for yourself."

Dong Jiguang was a nobleman and had come merely to spectate. He was, as they say, "Only capable of viewing the flowers from the horse's back". How could he possibly be so bold as to actually mount the horse! With natural good manners he declined to ride. Ma then called on his disciples to take the horses round the circuit once again. Following their orders, the men jumped into their saddles and took the horses for another run. By the time they reined in their horses it was already approaching the time when the evening sun sets on the mythical Xian Mountain, and all around, darkness was setting in. Young Master Dong and Ma Yongzhen admired the fading scenery out in the wilds and talked about the history of the Drunken White Pavilion, that noble and ancient landmark. Then the Young Master invited all present to his mansion to eat, drink and be merry. Ma Yongzhen and the others, as dictated by custom, politely declined a number of times before finally agreeing to his kind invitation. Young Master Dong entered the palanquin. His carriers took their places and prepared to take him through the city gates, while Ma Yongzhen and his disciples mounted their horses and set off to follow on behind.

If you want to know what happened next, please read the following chapter.

3

Ma the strongman rides fine horses at the Shanghai Race Club,
And with Miss Hua, viewing flowers at the flower-viewing mansion.

Let us continue to relate how Young Master Dong Jiguang watched Ma Yongzhen's skills in horsemanship at the Drunken White Pavilion and felt deliriously happy and full of admiration. After the demonstration he invited everyone to his mansion for a banquet. Presently, master, disciples, and followers arrived at the Dong Mansion to drink wine. While the banquet was in progress, the subject of the price of the fine steed was raised. Ma Yongzhen proposed one thousand two hundred *taels* of silver. Young master Dong responded with a counter offer of one thousand *taels*, and they came to an agreement on the lower price there and then. All present drank their fill. Young master Dong happened to mention a fine Huamei bird, a Melodious Laughing Thrush, he had once kept as a pet, which had been stolen by a local ruffian, Dog-eared Gao. On hearing the story,

Ma Yongzhen bristled all over with anger. He asked where Dog-eared Gao lived, then rose to his feet to go and retrieve the bird. Dog-eared Gao was at home, just in the middle of eating dinner. He realized the situation did not look good for him, and as the saying goes, "A wise man knows better than to fight when luck is against him and defeat is right before his eyes," and realizing that tact would be his best defense, he had the birdcage brought in directly and handed it over to Ma Yongzhen. Ma took the cage and carried it back to Young Master Dong, who thanked him profusely. When the banquet was over, Young Master Dong personally saw Ma Yongzhen out through the main gates.

Ma had secured the price of one thousand *taels* of fine silver. The traveler now had much-needed funds. That night he rushed back with his disciples to his old friend's home, and the following morning went to look over a house he hoped to buy. It was in the vicinity of Sinza Road looking east towards Pudong. There were three main rooms plus two wings, and at the back was a spacious garden. He went to a furniture suppliers to find the furnishings he required, and provided stables and feed for the horses in the garden. His disciples would live in the wings. When all was in order, supper was prepared and everyone ate their fill. No more shall be said of what happened that day.

In coming south, Ma Yongzhen had hoped that he might be able to present his riding and martial skills to the public, and by doing so make a name for himself in Shanghai. Of the six horses he brought with him, that fine steed had already been sold for one thousand *taels* of silver, but he had five horses yet to sell. Even though he knew they would never achieve as much as one thousand *taels* each, at the very least they might achieve six or seven hundred. With that sum of money Ma would be able to embark on any project he desired. But, he was unfamiliar with people and places here, and no one he knew was in need of a dragon horse that could travel one thousand *li*. It came to Ma's attention that at Nicheng Bridge towards the northern part of Shanghai, there was a wide open space known as the Race Club, which was the place where foreigners raced their horses. The Chinese were not permitted to ride their horses there, but how was Ma Yongzhen to know the rules that had been established by foreigners in Shanghai?

Someone told him: "That this piece of open land is rented from the International Settlement. This is the same as when Chinese people rent houses from the Chinese. If you were the landlord would you really expect to be given access to live in those houses?"

As soon as this point was raised, Ma Yongzhen realized that it must indeed be the case, but, even though he understood this, he was still determined to race his horses there in order to establish his position in Shanghai. So he settled on the 1st of March to race his horses at the Race Club at Nicheng Bridge.

Fair reader, the Shanghai of forty years ago was nothing like as lively as it is now. The area around the British Nanking Road did not yet bustle with excitement and the area around North Nicheng Bridge had yet to be leveled out.

Time moved on apace and fliers and posters were posted all around, so by the time the big day arrived the event had already caused quite a stir amongst countless numbers of prospective spectators, all of whom wanted to experience things for themselves. On the day, there were men and women, young and old, those who arrived in rickshaws, those who took horse-drawn carriages and carts, as well as those who had walked in groups. This multitude of people, like a sea awash with humankind, or a mountain formed of human bodies, surrounded the perimeter of the racing track, and all were awaiting the arrival of Ma Yongzhen. When it was approaching two o'clock in the afternoon, Ma Yongzhen led his disciples, together with several Shandong fellow countrymen, to the Nicheng district. He looked around him and saw that the number of spectators who were coming to watch the display of horsemanship that day were many indeed. Ma Yongzheng felt extremely proud when he thought back to just a few days ago when he rode horses at the Drunken White Pavilion, and the people of Songjiang cheered him on. Now, he saw that Shanghai was ten thousand times bigger than the town of Songjiang, so there were bound to be one or two experts among the people there. Therefore, he instructed his disciples to be particularly vigilant and do their very best in their demonstrations, so as to avoid becoming a laughing stock to outsiders. Everyone replied by shouting their approval. The six disciples began to perform, adopting three different styles of riding. First they rode around the track individually; secondly, they rode in pairs, shoulder to shoulder; and lastly they rode around the arena in a group, six abreast, before finally dismounting. It was then that their master, Ma Yongzhen, entered the arena, shouting out orders. Each of the disciples gathered his courage and steadied his nerves, and remounting their horses began to display their skills, strutting around in pairs, like dragons jumping and tigers leaping. Spectators on all sides, lost themselves in wonder, clapping, stamping their feet, and cheering: "You are great!"…"He is great!"…"Everyone is great!"

By now, Ma Yongzhen's heart was full of joy. The people of Suzhou like to say – "Eighteen artists could not paint the scene," as the atmosphere was so hectic and everyone so overjoyed that it was simply impossible to make out all that was going on.

At about two o'clock, master and followers, seven men in all, having finished their demonstration were waiting to return to the residence, when out of the crowd walked a man of five *chi* tall. He had a round fair face, wore a patterned crepe silk gown, and was graceful of manner and elegant of bearing. He approached Ma Yongzhen, clasped his hands together in front of him, bowed, and addressed him with a broad smile that lit up his entire face.

"May I ask your honorable name?"

Ma Yongzhen responded to the man's greeting with a bow of his own. He told him his name and asked the stranger his.

"My family name is Zhao, and I am called Zhao Lianyu, I am from Huzhou in Zhejiang. In the past I was in the business of selling tong oil and sesame biscuits, but as a result of some good connections I was able to put that aside, and have become involved with the Green Gang, the biggest organization in Shanghai. Now, in addition to that, I serve as a bailiff under the leadership of Chai Jiuyun and am responsible for catching criminals and carrying out detective work. Over the past couple of years I've gained a little face within the International Settlement."

When they had finished their introductions, Zhao took Yongzhen's hand as a gesture of friendship, saying, "Today I would like you to join me, at the invitation of Chai Jiuyun, in visiting the establishment of Hua Baoqin to seek for flowers and ask of the willows," and proceeded to lead him to Hua Baoqin's establishment in Qunyu Fang, on Swatow Road, near Foochow Road, in Shanghai's courtesan district.

Hua Baoqin's boudoir was on the second floor, so, as Zhao Lianyu and Ma Yongzhen walked up the staircase, the male servant rang a small electric bell to alert those upstairs that guests had arrived. The maidservant, Ah Jin, peaked out through the curtain that sheltered the doorway, and on seeing Zhao Lianyu welcomed him with a look of sheer delight on her face. Zhao and Ma walked into the room and Chai Jiuyun came forward to greet them, while Ah Jin politely offered them pipes of tobacco.

> *In those days, in the brothels there were no cigarettes or cigars, and guests were welcomed with loose tobacco. Now, when saying these words, they certainly sound rather old fashioned, but, each era has its own customs and strictures, so one should not be swayed only by what one is accustomed to.*

Chai Jiuyun took his seat and Ah Jin brought over a stationery box so that more guests could be invited. He picked up the brush and wrote out ten red invitation slips. All the invited guests, needless to say, were people of influence. Just then, Baoqin came out to entertain them with a song.

> *As Chai Jiuyun had invited guests, Hua Baoqin knew that providing entertainment and singing for them made good business sense. Generally speaking, this was standard practice in brothels. If the guest came only to drink tea and talk to the girls, no matter how important a person they might be, the madam, the establishment, its girls, and male servants were all like cold water poured into an ice water jar — frigid and standoffish. If, on the other hand, the guests were there to drink wine and play* penghu, *whatever they said went, whatever they wanted was theirs, and the brothel workers would pat the horse's rump, and shower the guests with extravagant praise.*

35

Hua Baoqin, soft and slender, with an elegant demeanor like a sprig of plum blossom, gracefully entered the room, taking measured steps on her tiny golden lotus feet. On walking through the doorway she greeted Chai and Zhao and asked Ma Yongzhen his name. This was the first time Ma Yongzhen had been in the company of such elegant lilies of the valley. How could the lowly brothels of the north compare to such a place as this! He felt somewhat out of his depth. How was he to focus his mind on anything, under these circumstances! As the saying goes, "He was like a bodhisattva formed of mud on falling into a pot of boiling water," or to use another appropriate phrase, "When embroiled in affairs of the heart, even the most heroic of men lose their courage." In this way, from ancient times, countless thousands, nay tens of thousands of heroes and fine fellows, have bowed down before the pomegranate-colored skirts of women.

Before long, the invited guests began to arrive in close succession. Chai Jiuyun performed the introductions and one by one they told their names to Ma Yongzhen. Laughing delightfully, Ah Jin walked over to Chai's side, and gently placing her exquisitely powdered face close to his ear, she asked him, "Would you like to play a game of *penghu* first or drink some wine?"

Chai Jiuyun nodded his head to show he understood, then standing on top of the plush day bed, he called out to the assembled company, "Brothers, would you like to play *penghu* first and then drink wine, or drink wine followed by a few rounds of *penghu*?"

The majority decision was that they would like to play four rounds of *penghu,* then drink some wine, and follow that with four more rounds of *penghu*. Thereupon, they counted the numbers and it was confirmed there were nine invited guests, and together with Chai Jiuyun, Zhao Lianyu and Ma Yongzhen, that made twelve players.

"Who'd have thought it?" Baoqin said with a laugh. "As luck would have it, twelve people make up enough players for three tables."

"What luck indeed, what luck indeed," Chai agreed, and ordered the tables to be prepared: two were placed in the reception hall, and one in the pavilion. Everyone took their seats.

> *Only Uncle Ma was alone. For one thing, it was his first time in Shanghai, and for another, he was socially rather unsophisticated. The game of* penghu, *although it is played for stakes, is not like the poker and mahjong of today, in as much as with those games, even if you have never played before, at least you will be familiar with the rules. This game* penghu, *in contrast, uses many obscure terms, such as "Yellow River Formation," "Old Number One Under the Same Banner," "Ruthlessly Slaughter," and "Dead Consume, Alive Contend." It really is not all that easy to understand.*

Ma Yongzhen was not one of the initiated, and he felt that his only choice under the circumstances was to invite someone to play in his place. Chai Jiuyun immediately suggested Baoqin. Hua Baoqin, that high-class courtesan, loved to gamble as if her life depended on it. But she was not at all keen on *penghu* and much preferred to play the rather less taxing game of *wahua*. Now that Chai Juiyun was inviting her to stand in for Boss Ma, she wanted to change things around a little and proposed that her table play *wahua* instead. Those old frequenters of brothels were always willing to comply with the wishes of others.

Whichever game was played made no difference; whatever made the ladies happy was agreeable to them. So they settled on *wahua* and decided on the stakes.

If you want to know whether the lady won or lost the *wahua* game, please read the following chapter.

4

Under the green willow the stone ding *tripod is lifted,*
And at a ceremony on the Bund new disciples are initiated.

Let us continue to relate how Chai Jiuyun invited Ma Yongzhen to drink wine and play *penghu* in the boudoir of the high-class courtesan, Hua Baoqin. Ma Yongzhen didn't know how to gamble, so he invited Miss Hua to play in his place. The courtesan's skill was considerable. On this day her luck was good and the pieces were in her favour. After completing eight rounds of *wahua,* her winnings were calculated. Altogether, she had won thirty-three silver dollars, and more than sixty small silver coins. The entire sum was bestowed on her, and she stood up to thank Ma Yongzhen with a smile and a demure nod of the head. Neither of the *penghu* tables had finished their games. One table still had more than one round, and the other had two rounds yet to play. Chai Jiuyun then laughed and said, "Today it has been a rare treat that your distinguished person has been able to grace us with your presence. In my considered opinion, it would be most desirable to invite your worthy disciples to join us. I don't know if you have any thoughts on this, Brother Ma."

Ma Yongzhen thanked him repeatedly, but out of politeness declined the invitation. Chai Jiuyun insisted, so Ma Yongzhen could only give in to his wishes. Chai picked up a writing brush, ink-stone and ink-cake and wrote out the invitations. He asked for everybody's names and Ma Yongzhen told them to him, one by one. When Chai had finished writing, he called the male servant, "the turtle", over and instructed him to deliver the invitations to Ma's residence in Sinza Road. In a matter of minutes, the six disciples had arrived. They announced their names in turn and the servants at the brothel brought them tea and tobacco. The games of *penghu* were now over and everyone rose to ask the names of the six new arrivals.

> *This is a social custom and is just for show, according to convention. The information just enters the east ear and comes out of the west ear. They are questions that might as well not be asked, and answers that might as well not be given at all.*

Chai Jiuyun invited everyone to be seated and naturally gave way for Ma Yongzhen to sit in the seat of honor. This was the first time Ma Yongzhen had ever drunk wine in a high-class brothel like this. How could he know the established practice in places such as this? Ma Yongzhen thought to himself, "I am usually asked to take the seat of honor but I had always imagined that the seat of honor was the one that faces south. Now I see Chai Jiuyun's friends taking their places one by one in the seats facing south, while my disciples and I are being directed to be seated in the row opposite. I simply don't understand it. Could it be that this is the custom in Shanghai? I have no way of knowing. In the end, perhaps it's better to play along and show 'false courtesy.'" He thought about it and decided that would be best. Ma Yongzhen and his disciples with "false courtesy" took their seats with the others.

Hua Baoqin poured a cup of wine for all the guests in turn. Ah Jin offered tobacco to each of them, and Chai Jiuyun suggested that everyone should invite their favorite courtesans to join them. The ten guests who had been initially invited, were all old local Shanghai bosses, so of course they had their regular female companions. As for the outsiders, Ma and his followers, how could they possibly have their own women to call on? So, Chai Jiuyun acted as matchmaker and called for two women entertainers, known as "young masters" to accompany each of the seven guests. Presently they arrived in single file, entering one after the other. The regular companions took their seats behind their usual guests, while the "young masters" who had been called on by Chai Jiuyun, greeted him and relied on his instructions as to where they should be seated.

The musicians arrived and began to perform. The *huqin* fiddle player played the *huqin*, the *dizi* flute player played the *dizi* and there were others who played the lutes — the *pipa* and the *yueqin*. In no time at all "pearls and jades", beautiful women of outstanding talent, were present all around, having brought along with them a refined atmosphere heavy with the scent of flowers. Even those Twelve Beauties of Jinling from the noble families in *The Dream of the Red Chamber,* when they gathered together before the jade lantern screen to play that guessing game, were not as glorious and splendid as this. For Ma Yongzhen and his six disciples, it was as if they had entered an enchanted world and their souls had departed their bodies. Their vision was blurred, and their minds in utter confusion. No wonder people say, "Shanghai is a heavenly land of fairies and the Buddha." Today they really had arrived in the land of the Buddha and had met with fairies from the heavens above.

They certainly didn't want to think about returning to Shandong and eating the local fried bread there. Here, endless cups of wine were raised in honor, and course after course was served, each one the rarest of foods, with delicious flavors and remarkable bouquets. To delight the ear was the music of the silk and bamboo ensemble, a pure and elegant sound. After a while, the musicians left the stage and the courtesans departed, by which time the clock on the wall had already struck two. Then, the guests began to leave, one after the other. Ma Yongzhen asked Chai Jiuyun his address so that on another day he might return the invitation. He departed and his disciples followed on behind, walking together in one large group. Chai Jiuyun saw them off to the top of the staircase. Of him returning to the room and talking with Hua Baoqin we shall say no more.

The master and his followers set out on foot, but they did not know the way home, so they called for seven rickshaws to take them back to Sinza Road. Giving thanks to the kindness of Chai Jiuyun, strangers had come together by chance and had unexpectedly entered into deep friendships, while paying no heed to social status. Suffice it to say, as the saying goes – "Within the four seas, all men are brothers." For the moment nothing more shall be said of this.

When it came to the following day, after lunch Ma Yongzhen went out to take a stroll with his disciples. From Nicheng Bridge they walked west, taking a roundabout route to Foochow Road (known locally as Fourth Avenue), and were just passing the intersection with Hoopeh Road when they saw a weeping willow, drooping under the weight of countless silken catkins. Behind that verdant tree was a small pavilion, under the eaves of which hung a small horizontal plaque on which the words "Weeping Willow Terrace" were inscribed. Below this, was a single line of smaller calligraphy, which read: "Inscribed by the Old Master of Cang Mountain in spring, on the banks of the Huangpu River, Shanghai." This was the place where master Yuan Xiangpu, also known as Yuan Zuzhi—grandson on his mother's side of that renowned poet from the reign of the Qianlong emperor, Yuan Zicai, better known as Yuan Mei—composed poetry, wielded the paintbrush, quaffed good wine, savored fine tea, conversed with friends, and delighted in reading.

All manner of trees grow in the port of Shanghai, but only in this one place could a green willow such as this be found. With things physical, it is scarcity that renders them remarkable, and Weeping Willow Terrace was considered to be a pure and elegant place in the noisy and bustling world of Shanghai. Independent scholars, literati and writers, intellectuals and poets, and those bureaucrats who had been exiled to Shanghai, frequently came here to pay their respects to Master Yuan. Ma Yongzhen, on the other hand, was a worthy hero of martial arts circles. His speciality was to talk of the spear form, and the complex movements associated with the Shaolin staff, but when it came to the sayings of Confucius, or quoting from *The Book of Songs,* or trying his hand at the subtleties of poetic rhyme and meter, there would be much shaking of heads and holding of noses, as if the listener where afraid to smell the foul stench of farts. Having said this, even though he didn't know the marvelous mysteries of literature and poetry, he was able to admire elegant scenery as much as the next man.

Ma and his followers wandered about in admiration in the shadow of the Weeping Willow Terrace. It really was too much to take in all at once. There was a surfeit of spectacular things to behold so they were reluctant to depart that wondrous scene.

43

All at once, by a fence the color of cinnabar, they came across an enormous stone *ding* tripod incense burner lying on its side amongst the luxuriant and fragrant grass. Everyone imagined this *ding* must once have graced the halls of the palace of the gods. Of its three original legs only two remained, and one of those was half broken off, so it was lying on its side in the grass. Ma Yongzhen saw it and was overjoyed. Laughing heartily, he said to his followers: "We have been in Shanghai, if you count on your fingers, for two weeks already and have clearly been neglectful of our training. Why don't you all come over here and we'll see who can lift this *ding*, as a way of exercising our sinews and muscles."

When they were in Shandong, Ma's followers practiced with the Shaolin long staff every morning, and at night they polished their swords. Lately, they had found themselves with little to do, and were beginning to feel rather impatient. Literature and martial arts are much the same. For example, when one hasn't read a book for a while, as soon as one sees a remarkable edition of a fine old book, one cannot help but pick it up, leaf through, and read from it aloud. Likewise, martial men, when they see a weapon, must pick it up, test its weight and hold it in their hands, in order to determine their strength that day. The assembled disciples heard what their master said and were itching to get started. Not one of them did not cheer and joyfully applaud. After a moment they raised their hands in agreement. Putting aside their status and rank, and making no distinctions with regard to seniority, they came forward to lift the *ding* in whatever order they pleased. Amongst those six men, although the strength of each of them was out of the ordinary, there were those who had specific talents and those with particular strengths. There were those who could only lift the *ding* to chest height, and could lift it no higher. There were those who could lift it to their shoulders but had to fling it straight back down again; there were those who lifted it as high as their eyebrows and then suddenly had to let it drop. There were those who lifted it with both hands up above their heads, at which point their arms would begin to shake. Meanwhile, the number of passersby kept growing, and the area around Daxing li and Xinmin hutong, in the vicinity of Foochow Road, became overcrowded with curious spectators. It just so happened that at that time the landowner upstairs, Master Yuan Zuzhi, was entertaining honored guests by hosting a poetry contest, when he heard the sound of shouting and cheering coming from down below. Leaning over the railings he spied a crowd of stout fellows who looked as if they hailed from distant parts. They were taking it in turns to lift the *ding*, and testing their strength to see who could lift it highest. He thought to himself that this was really quite remarkable, and the martial prowess of those from the north was far superior to the literary achievements of those in the south. He observed those five stout fellows, taking it in turns to lift the *ding*, and competing to see which of them had the strength to lift it highest. Last to come forward was a man of about forty years of age. He was the tallest and sturdiest of them all. First he performed some boxing moves on the grass and practiced his kicks and sweeps, then he took off his shirt and jacket, while someone came forward to retrieve them for him. The man became more and more energetic in his display of martial prowess. Valiant, and full of vigor, his whole face showed to all that he was expending a considerable amount of energy. He reached out his right hand to grasp the looped handle of the *ding* then, extending his left hand, he seized the opportunity to drag it towards him. All eyes were transfixed on that stout fellow lifting the great *ding* high above his head, straightening his arms then bending them again at the elbow, lifting and lowering, several times in a row, just as he wished, as if there were nothing to it and he was expending no energy at all. Of the surrounding onlookers, not one was not cheering and shouting his praise, just as if he were a great star performer, like that famous player of female roles, Zhou Fenglin when he sang "Jumping the Wall," from the *Romance of the Western Chamber*, on the Kunqu Opera stage. But today it was as if that stout fellow had sung more marvelously than Zhou Fenglin ever had, and the cheering was even more formidable than it had ever been in the opera house. Even that group of sour-faced, wretched old scholars up in the Weeping Willow Terrace—those "poetry loons," "monsters of poetry," "slaves to poetry," and "poetry ghouls," who prefer to refer to themselves in more favorable terms, as "poetry immortals," "poetry Buddhas," "poetry lovers," and "poetry sages"—even they, on the other side of the railings, wiped their noses and lifted their long wispy beards to the side to shout out in approval. The man lifted the *ding* five times in a row without breaking a sweat, or becoming in the slightest bit short of breath, before gently placing it down in its original place and putting his shirt and jacket back on. This man was Ma Yongzhen, and all eyes were now fixed on him. He and his followers idled about for a while before going about their business, and the spectators followed them for a short time, before breaking off and heading home, but we shall speak no more of this.

Ma and his followers returned to the residence, and from that day on, the three words that make up the name, "Ma Yong Zhen" became known to everyone. From the time he lifted the stone *ding* his fame gradually spread from the few to the many. People began to learn of this event, and what is more, Chai Jiuyun's followers extolled Ma's virtues far and wide and began to have frequent dealings with him. Shanghai now had a Ma Yongzhen and he wanted to make a real name for himself there. Hoping to stand out from the crowd and to show himself to be a good fellow, both magnificent and extraordinary, he thought that the best way to achieve that would be to take on more followers and thus consolidate his power. He discussed this with his old disciples at a tea party at the Wusheng Pavilion teashop, and all agreed it was a fine idea. Ma devised a plan to spread the word. As it happened, Ma knew of a disparate group of naïve youngsters, whom he was hoping might become his disciples.

If you want to know what happens next, and whether a disciples initiation ceremony is held, please read the following chapter.

5

Over tea at the Wusheng Pavilion invitations are written,
And at Pahsienjiao notices for a tournament are posted.

Let us continue to relate how at that time Ma Yongzhen and his followers were holding a tea party at the Wusheng Pavilion teashop and were discussing holding an initiation ceremony to accept new disciples so that Ma could increase his prestige. It was decided that local bosses should be approached, and persuaded to stick up posters and distribute leaflets to spread the word.

"In the past few days we have been deeply indebted to Chai Jiuyun," said Ma Yongzhen, "but I have not repaid him for the kind generosity he showed us in inviting us to Hua Baoqin's establishment. I feel this is rather remiss of me. Recently, I have had no time to go to the city to pay my respects, and I feel most ashamed. I think today we should take the opportunity to visit Chai Jiuyun's residence and invite him to drink tea, and at the same time trouble him to point us in the direction of some eminent people of the area, so we can invite those he names, and contact them for information with a view to looking out for each other. The old saying sums up the situation well—'An evil dragon cannot grapple with a local snake'—a stranger, no matter how formidable, cannot compete with a ruffian with local knowledge. We are strangers here. This is their home ground and strangers are unable to compete with those on their own territory. What think you of this?"

"Our master's words are true indeed," Ma's devoted follower Wang Desheng replied.

"I would like you to take a letter to Chai Jiuyun to invite him to leave the confines of the Chinese City so we can get together to discuss this matter. Please go to Chai's place and ask him for a reply."

Wang Desheng agreed to do this, so he set out for the Chinese City to pay a visit to Chai Jiuyun's residence. At that time Chai Jiuyun's status as a senior policemen was unknown to them. But whenever his name was mentioned, people all around praised his abilities and spoke of him as a man of honor. Now that Ma Yongzhen desired to hold a ceremony to take on more disciples so that he could make a real impression in Shanghai, he would most certainly need the help of local men of substance. Wang Desheng carried out his master's orders, and taking the invitation in his hand he hailed a rickshaw to convey him to the Chinese City.

At that time Shanghai didn't have any *huangbaoche*, those luxurious rickshaws that have become so common in Shanghai today, and all the Japanese-style rickshaws that were then in the city had shaky wooden wheels that were shod with iron. Now Wang Desheng needed to hire one of these, so he bit the bullet in order to get to Chai Jiuyun's house as quickly as he could. He told the rickshaw puller, a man from the Jiangbei (one of the poorest provinces in the region)—who, in common with many

49

of his compatriots, had taken on the lowliest jobs available when he moved to the metropolis—that the faster he could get him to his destination the better, adding that if he made the trip in good time he would give him a few extra coins. On hearing that his passenger was willing to give extra copper cash, the man from Jiangbei set off immediately these words entered his ears.

> It was as if wooden bolts, above and below, had been secured across the massive wooden gates of one of the local gated communities – all else was forgotten and was locked out of his mind while he single-mindedly attended to pulling his rickshaw. He really was happier than words can describe. Those two little mud-spattered hairy legs ran like crazy, as if he were in flight, and the heels of his feet knocked against his buttocks with every step he took.

Before Wang Desheng knew it, they had arrived at the front gate of Chai Jiuyun's residence. He inquired within and as luck would have it he had caught Chai Jiuyun just before he was due to go to work at the *yamen* and was in the process of changing into his official garb.

Chai Jiuyun saw a man he vaguely recognized enter the vestibule, but he couldn't quite place him. Wang Desheng had already met Chai in Hua Baoqin's establishment, so, without standing on ceremony (as Wang knew Chai even if Chai didn't know Wang) Wang handed him the note. Chai Jiuyun invited him to take a seat, while he opened the letter to read it, and the female servant brought in tea and cigarettes. Only then did Chai recognize his visitor as one of Ma Yongzhen's followers. "No wonder his face seemed so familiar," he thought to himself.

"Today I am indebted to your master for sending this letter inviting me for tea and pure conversation, and to discuss matters of importance. Your humble servant would naturally hope to accept the invitation in all good faith, but there have been a number of cases of robbery in the province and they have been booked in to be heard in court at dusk. The particulars of these cases are very serious indeed, and they all have connections with northern provinces. Each case has been solved by my own detectives. Some of the details are very complex, so the County Magistrate will be at court to preside over them in person. Your humble servant must be by his side to prepare for the hearing and oversee the proceedings of the case. Therefore, I can only decline your master's gracious command. Please pass on my unworthy apologies and be sure to express my deep regret to him. I humbly request that your noble self tactfully reports this. On another occasion your humble servant shall certainly be delighted to leave the city and visit Brother Ma's noble residence. Please communicate my sincere apologies to your master."

When Chai Jiuyun finished speaking, Wang Desheng had wholeheartedly hoped to extend the gracious invitation to him for another day, and with a broad smile on his face began to speak, "Uncle Chai..." but before these words had even left his mouth, the sound of someone calling could be heard outside the window.

"Director Chai, Director Chai! The County Magistrate is waiting in the office and is in a filthy mood. Quickly! Quickly! He has called for you and has some important questions to ask."

Chai Jiuyun heard the governor was angry, so he could no longer pay attention to his guest. All he could do was perform a swift bow, and with a firm but friendly smile and some brief words of apology, leave with the messenger in all haste. Wang Desheng followed them out and called a rickshaw to take him back to the Wusheng Pavilion teashop, and inform Ma Yongzhen of the outcome. The master and his disciples had already agreed

51

to write invitations to drink wine at the Yanleyuan on Kwangtung Road, and for the followers to go their separate ways and deliver them. The master and disciples finished their tea party at the Wusheng Pavilion, paid the bill, descended the stairs together and returned to the Sinza residence.

Even before the disciples initiation ceremony was held, word had got round that this Ma person was a man of real ability, and so a group of naïve young men, including apprentices graduated from machine rooms, and copper works gaffers planned to join Ma Yongzhen's ceremony to be inducted as disciples. These young men were highly enthusiastic, so they decided to "search out the teacher" and "join the selection of the master".

According to the rules of gangland culture, to "search out the teacher" and "join the selection of the master" were alternative ways of saying, to seek out intermediaries and those who could endorse them, as they were required to submit letters of recommendation in order to attend the ceremony.

On the day of the ceremony, the atmosphere in the hall was unusually lively. Incense burned all around, and there was a magnificent display of candles. Today 101 disciples were to be initiated into the ranks. The master provided them with names, all of which were taken from the names of the thirty-six Heavenly Spirits and the seventy-two Earthly Demons, of *The Water Margin*. Beginning with the first two in the list of Heavenly Spirits: "Protector of Righteousness", the nickname of Song Jiang, leader of the outlaws, and the "Jade Qilin", the nickname of Hu Junyi. These names were given out in turn, and continued until all thirty-six were allocated, down to the final two in the list of seventy-two Earthly Demons: "Flea on a Drum" and "Golden

Haired Hound". When the new group of followers received their nicknames, they actually believed themselves to be the heroic characters from the novel, "Panther Head", "General of Double Spears", and "Nine Tattooed Dragon".

> *Young men like that, devoid of the most basic knowledge, to be lured into a trap such as this! Please let me know what good you think there is in this, it really is quite puzzling to me.*

That day, new disciples and old shook hands, and exchanged brotherly greetings. Then, one by one they went their separate ways. On this day, Ma Yongzhen accepted 101 disciples, and together with himself and his established followers, this brought his band of brothers to 108, the same number of outlaws as appear in *The Water Margin*.

Now he felt like a lion that had sprouted wings, as his prestige had increased several fold. Within Shanghai and without, ruffians in the foreign city, and as far as the regions of Pudong, Nanxiang, Bao Shan, and Nan Hui, had now all heard the three words that make up the name, "Ma Yong Zhen". Ma Yongzhen was possessed of natural talents and was full of determination. He was a man of remarkable skill. He had hoped to make a name for himself with his journey to the south, and now, all of a sudden, an unusual and splendid idea came to him. In his youth he had read a few books, and often heard talk of the tournament that took place at Pingbotai in *The Legend of Jintai*. Now he wanted to emulate the story of Jintai, that hero from Huguang, by organizing a martial arts tournament in Shanghai, so that all brave fellows from roundabout could contend with each other in martial skills. He told this to his disciples, most of whom were now young men who welcomed a challenge. How could they possibly not approve? From the older disciples' point of view, they saw it as an opportunity to expand their own prestige. The new disciples, on the other hand, knew that now that they had sworn allegiance to the big boss and were to mount a tournament to compete in martial arts, in the future they would be able to say that they themselves were followers of Ma Yongzhen, his "children", and this would be widely considered to be an awe-inspiring and impressive achievement.

> *Dear readers, this type of lowly scoundrel may have other things in mind. What could they actually gain from paying allegiance to a gang boss? Well, of course, they could get into as many fights as they like; have their say in the teashops in gangland disputes; become involved in extortion and swindling rackets. Nothing less than coming forward to help cause trouble. For someone who does business entirely according to the rules, what reason could they possibly have to pay allegiance to a gang boss? To be accepted as his child? If you think about this carefully, it is really laughable. They have their own accounts, they value friendship. But they can never escape the two syllables that make up that word "money". Face! Friendship! To talk about these things is simply to talk about a little money. When I hear the tone of voice of people such as these, it makes me simply furious. But let's have no more of this idle chatter and return to the matter in hand.*

Let us continue to relate how Ma Yongzhen made his decision, and the new and old disciples all approved. Some said the martial arts tournament should take place on the Bund. Some said it should take place in the French Concession. Some said it should take place in the International Settlement. A number of ideas were put forward but no firm decision was made. Ma Yongzhen was thoroughly confused, as he listened to the various arguments concerning which of these choices would be best. Amongst the new children in his fold was a man called Lu Shouji. This man was the eldest son of the constable of Baoshan County and currently served as a registered bailiff in the district of Shanghai. He was twenty-six or twenty-seven years of age and already had much experience. He knew that for his new big boss to put on a tournament was no small matter, and could never be considered child's play. Furthermore, Shanghai was one of the five Treaty Ports and could not be compared with any of the towns or cities in the interior. If something bad were to happen here the repercussions would be truly calamitous, so it would be best if an alternative plan were sought. He hurried over to Ma Yongzhen's residence to visit his master, and told him in detail what he thought might happen if foreigners were to become involved, adding that everything must be done correctly, and there was no room for error. He also suggested that to use the term "hold a tournament" did not seem like a good idea to him, as it might attract unwarranted attention from foreigners.

"Master, if you want to be compared with the great heroes of all under heaven, I, your child, approve and desire to assist you in this. But you must reconsider the use of the term 'hold a tournament'."

As soon as he heard this Ma realized his disciple was not wrong. But his instructions had already left his lips and his other disciples were aware of his plans. If he were to go back on his word now he would lose face.

"I accept the good intentions of your words," Ma replied to Lu Shouji. "Since you have come to offer me advice, bearing in mind all you have said, what do you think might be the best way to proceed?"

If you want to know what Lu Shouji said in reply, please read the following chapter.

6

A boasting foreigner contests his martial skills,
And an old woman sends a letter urging caution.

Let us continue to relate how at that time Ma Yongzhen's new disciple, Lu Shouji, was talking about Shanghai as a vast city amongst the five Treaty Ports of China, and suggesting that matters were dealt with there in different ways to how they were treated in other parts of the country. If a martial arts tournament were to be mounted in Shanghai, he feared foreigners might try to interfere. What he said was certainly shrewd and Ma Yongzhen himself considered there to be some truth in it, but he had already given his word on this. If he were to change his mind now he would lose the respect of his followers. Within his heart he felt most apprehensive and an expression of sadness was revealed on his face. The other disciples were full of joy, and were making preparations to finalize the location of the tournament. Now, seeing their master looking so despondent, everyone began to whisper among themselves. His disciples numbered more than one hundred, and it was only one of their number, Lu Shouji, who was urging Ma to cease preparations. How could Ma challenge the support of more than one hundred people? He was naturally proud and arrogant. He relied on the strength of his fist and long staff, and was afraid of nothing. But now that his disciples were becoming discontented he needed to make a final decision. He instructed his beloved disciples, who went by the nicknames of two of the 108 heroes of *The Water Margin*, "Turbid River Dragon" and "Stream Leaping Tiger" to make a search for a suitable site. Turbid River Dragon had the family name Cheng, and was called Cheng Tianfu; Stream Leaping Tiger had the family name Bi, and was called Bi Yuanshun. They came from families that slaughtered pigs and oxen for a living and now worked in the dairies of the Fan Wangdu district. Keen of eye and swift of hand, they accepted their master's instructions as if they were foot soldiers carrying out the orders of their general. They promptly set their limbs in motion and went in search of a suitable place. East to the Bund, west to Caojia Ferry, south to Route Pottier, and north to Soochow Creek, they searched the whole day but found nowhere suitable. Then they took their search to the area around the Jing'an Temple. This was where the famous Bubbling Well, known as "the number six spring in all under heaven" was located. Here, all was spacious and expansive. It was a place of tranquillity amid the hubbub of Shanghai, not too far from Nanking Road, with both the Zhang Garden and the Yu Garden close by. On that day, Turbid River Dragon, Cheng Tianfu, and Stream Leaping Tiger, Bi Yuanshun, those brothers-in-arms, had their eyes set on this area as a possible venue for the tournament. They had been walking the entire day, were weary and their legs were aching, so they stopped at a rural teashop by the Bubbling Well to savor a cup of tiger soup to revive their strength and satisfy their thirst. They chatted for a while and began to feel really rather contented, thinking ahead to the time when their master would enter the arena and finally be in the public eye. They drank the soup for a while, then paid the bill, after which, in some haste, with the setting sun behind them all the way, they made their way back via Jessfield Road and Avenue Road to Sinza Road, so that they could quickly report their findings to their master.

"A venue has been found," they told Ma Yongzhen. "It is in the area of the Jing'an Temple near the Bubbling Well. It is a place of tranquillity amid the hubbub, with exceptionally fine scenery and plenty of fresh air. It is a place designed by earth and constructed by heaven, and one would be hard pushed to find anywhere else like it."

Ma Yongzhen listened to what they said, while nodding his head and expressing his approval. Of them eating dinner that evening nothing shall be said.

When morning came, Ma performed his ablutions and ate steamed buns for breakfast, then, with Turbid River Dragon, Cheng Tianfu, and Stream Leaping Tiger, Bi Yuanshun, he called three rickshaws and sped over to the area of the Jing'an Temple. The Jing'an Temple was in a remote part of western Shanghai. Signs of human life were few, and it was both spacious and secluded. Originally it had been a small village but now it had a main road running through it, and those places of pleasure, the Zhang Garden and the Yu Garden were situated close by. In front of the main gate to the Jing'an Temple was the ancient site known as, "the number six spring in all under heaven" — called the "Bubbling Well" by foreigners, and, because of this, a few sightseers made their way there to admire it. Ma Yongzhen and his disciples looked around for a while, then went to a small teashop to drink tea and to seek out the Village Head.

A busybody in the teashop told them what they wanted to know: "This area around the Jing'an Temple originally was in the hands of Qian Ah Bao of Beixinjing not too far from here. When Qian Ah Bao died, he was replaced by the local butcher, Village Head Han. Headman Han is a real talker and welcomes visitors. Money, he puts to the back of his mind. If you want to visit him, he lives on the very edge of the village, not far from here."

Thereupon, having been given directions, Turbid River Dragon and Stream Leaping Tiger stood up, left the teashop and walked in an easterly direction towards the edge of the village. There they came across a grocers shop that sold oil and alcohol. Stream Leaping Tiger, Bi Yuanshun walked up the steps and with a broad smile on his face asked the shopkeeper for directions to the residence of Headman Han. The shop assistant informed him that he lived next door, just a little further to the east. Bi Yuanshun thanked him and walked next door with Cheng Tianfu. With great respect they entered the front gate together. From there they could see a portly, middle-aged man, who had a distinctive forehead that protruded out over the top of his eyes as much as two or three inches. He was sitting in the centre of the courtyard. On seeing him, Cheng Tianfu guessed that he must be Headman Han, so he advanced one step to greet him. Headman Han saw that these people were unknown to him and they spoke with a Shandong accent, so he invited them to be seated.

"What sort of people are these official-looking types," Han asked himself, "and what do they want coming to see me, the village head? They seem to have no specific reason for being in the area and have certainly not come to visit the Temple of the Three Treasures. They must have come on business." Thereupon, with a broad smile on his face, according to custom, he asked them their names and where they came from. The two men politely replied. Headman Han exclaimed that their visit was a rare honor indeed, and asked them their business. Bi Yuanshun looked at Cheng Tianfu and Tianfu already had the answer. "Today we have come to visit you, for no other reason than the boss of our humble organization, Master Ma Yongzhen, has expressed a wish to borrow a piece of land in your esteemed district, desiring to set up a fighting ring to be used to practice and compete in martial arts with the heroes of your honorable district. The area by the side of the Bubbling Well has been chosen, so we have come to your esteemed residence to discuss this with you, and seek your kind permission to make use of it. From this day on, we shall forever be in your debt."

As he finished, Bi Yuanshun looked again at Cheng Tianfu. Tianfu understood the ways of the ruffian, so he fished out two Mackellar Bank five dollar notes, and, under the cover of their voluminous shirt sleeves (in the usual way such transactions were carried out at the time) he pressed them into the Headman Han's hands. Headman Han spent some time pretending to refuse, but in reality with money in his hand he was like a yellow dog on seeing a pork bone—how could it possibly be that he would not eat it up?

While they told him of Ma Yongzhen's fame as a horse trader, he thought to himself: "If they want to play on that piece of vacant ground (as they have already given that small consideration of ten dollars), then by all means they should be allowed to play there. What harm could there possibly be in that? To comply with their request and to grant them this favor, would be no more taxing than pushing a boat out into a swift running river."

Thereupon, he beat his chest once with his open palm, and agreed to do all he could to help. Everything was arranged.

Think about that everyone, this is the power of money, is it not horrifying!

Bi Yuanshun and Cheng Tianfu stood up to go and Headman Han saw them out, asking them which day they had in mind for the tournament. Bi Yuanshun assured him that when they had settled on a date, they would come again to confirm, and pay him their respects. Headman Han expressed his approval and he and the two disciples parted ways. The disciples returned to the small teashop to inform their master that the venue had been agreed on, and Ma Yongzhen was delighted with the result. He paid the bill and they talked and laughed as they walked to the residence, admiring the scenery along the way.

After dinner, Ma's new disciples, named "Double-tailed Scorpion", Lin Deshen; "Double-headed Serpent", Ji Qianwei; "Sacred Handed Scholar", Wen Xiangsheng; and "Dryland Alligator", Jin Shoushan, gathered in the main room of the residence with their master. Ma Yongzhen took out a volume of the *Fujian Almanac* from a bureau drawer, and opening it at the appropriate page, selected the 13th day of the 5th month (the birthday of Guandi, the God of war) as a propitious day on which to hold the tournament. Then, last of all, he troubled Sacred Handed Scholar, Wen Xiangsheng to write an inscription for a horizontal calligraphic plaque, the size of a wicker basket, with the words "Martial Arts Arena", and in addition, he instructed him to write a pair of rhyming couplets that would hang vertically down the sides, reading as follows: "He has trodden on both shores of the Yellow River and has fought with his fists in the capitals north and south." Ma Yongzhen dictated these lines and Sacred Handed Scholar wrote them down as a *duilian* rhyming couplet. None of the disciples, Jin Shoushan, Ji Qianwei, Lin Deshen, Bi Yuanshun, or Cheng Tianfu, had seen anything like it before, and looked on with their tongues hanging out, unable to roll them back in.

When the first of the month arrived they were given orders to confirm the date of the tournament with Headman Han, and to take the rhyming couplet and horizontal plaque inscription to the carpenters to be copied and carved in wood. Together they were designed in the style of a colorful *pailou* archway and the finished structure was erected on the piece of grassy land by the Bubbling Well.

Word spread by the tens and then by the hundreds. In this small Shanghai Bund, and the ten-mile foreign city, there was not one person who did not know about the tournament, not one person who was unaware. But who was the horse trader Ma Yongzhen of Shandong going to complete with? There was no choice but to wait until the thirteenth to find out. Everyone wanted to watch him fight and experience the mighty spectacle.

On the thirteenth, before it had even reached ten o'clock, visitors had already trampled the green grass around the Bubbling Well into a slippery mire. A host of peddlers arrived with their stalls, taking the opportunity to carry out some business. When Ma saw that midday was approaching, with a long silken jacket draped over his broad shoulders, he mounted a fine yellow steed with a silver embroidered saddle. More than twenty fine horses followed along behind him and mounted on each was a handsome young man done up in all his finery.

> *Gallant and brave, not one of these young men did not possess a noble spirit that stands out from the common herd, with a lively air about them that transcends the average crowd.*

Behind the horses was a group of seventy or eighty young men marching in ranks. In the eyes of onlookers, there was no doubt that these were the students of the master. Ma Yongzhen entered the arena, dismounted from the silver saddle and stood directly in the center. He bowed deeply to the audience on all four sides, and then addressed them with a series of polite civilities, using words and phrases commonly spoken by those of the Jianghu underworld. Then he called on his followers to demonstrate their abilities with fists and spears. By now this had already caught the attention of a blond French fighter, who entered the arena and announced his wish to contend with Ma Yongzhen. As soon as he saw that this man was a foreigner — remembering Lu Shouji's warning — Ma Yongzhen dared not agree to anything, as he was truly afraid that he might make a grave miscalculation and arouse the unwelcome attention of foreigners.

If you want to know if they compete or not, please read the following chapter.

7

Yellow Beard is thrice thrown to the ground,
And Scrofulous Bai gathers volunteers at Yidongtian.

Let us continue to relate how Ma Yongzhen mounted a martial arts tournament at "the number six spring in all under heaven" where he performed to the assembled crowds. The audience numbered in the thousands, and even the tens of thousands. Shanghai has always been a place where people gather together from all points of the compass, with Chinese and foreigners living side by side. One of these foreigners was a French strongman. Because his facial hair was a bright shade of yellow he was known by the name, "Yellow Beard". This Yellow Beard was more than eight *chi* tall, his hands were the size of those large palm-leaf fans widely used in Shanghai in the hottest months of summer, and he was so big and strong that he could carry a pair of oxen under his arms. He had been in Shanghai for seven or eight years and had never met his match, among foreigners or Chinese alike. Now he saw that Ma Yongzhen had arranged this tournament and was inviting people to compete. He made his way through the crowd, and looking directly at Ma Yongzhen with his sparkling green eyes, removed his hat and clasped his hands together in a half-Chinese, half-Western form of greeting. Ma Yongzhen couldn't understand what he was saying, but amongst his new disciples there was a man called Zhao Gongbi, who went by the *Water Margin* name of "Long Armed Ape". It turns out that he had been born into a family who tailored Western clothes, so he was able to speak pidgin and could get by in English. Zhao Gongbi and Yellow Beard exchanged a few words and Zhao relayed what was said, making clear the reason for him coming forward. From this, Ma understood that his intention was to challenge him to a friendly bout. Zhao Gongbi continued to act as interpreter between the two parties and translated their conversation, which turned out to be not much more than an exchange of pleasantries and self-introductions. The two sides were like a marriage of the deaf and dumb, both just nodding their heads and flashing knowing smiles, clasping their hands together in greeting, and doffing their hats. As a result of Zhao's explanations it was understood that this foreigner simply wanted to test his strength against Ma and was not looking to fight in anger.

The two men stood firm on the grass, then they began to pace around, their feet hovering just above the ground, circling three or four times, before coming to a halt. Then, gathering their strength, both men raised their right hands, and, grasping that of their opponent, they began what was in effect a sort of wrestling using the arms alone. By this time crowds of spectators were surrounding them on all sides, and several thousand eyes were focused on just these two men. Now, when looking at them walking in circles as if wading in water, squeezing their hands together, in this simple contest, the crowd could not help cheering loudly and clapping their hands to spur them on. Yellow Beard squeezed Ma Yongzhen's hand in a downward motion, and used all the strength he could muster to keep it down. Ma Yongzhen's hand was now turned over but he remained unflustered, and thought nothing of it. When Ma lifted his hand a little, to test his opponent's strength, he thought to himself that the foreigner really did have something about him, and should certainly not be underestimated. Yellow Beard did all he could to push Ma Yongzhen's hand down further, hoping to push him to the floor, but how could he have known that Ma would take the opportunity to borrow his opponent's strength when it was at its peak, and push upwards, to flip his hand right over! Yellow Beard's hand was now beneath Ma's, so he seized the opportunity to try and turn over Ma's hand again. But, how could Yellow Beard endure Ma Yongzhen's superhuman strength! His hand was turned over, his wrist was hurting terribly and he could not struggle free. He promptly lost his footing, and as soon as Ma Yongzhen let go of his hand, Yellow Beard tumbled over onto the ground. Try as he might he could not get up, and spectators on all sides were clapping their hands and shouting in approval. Yellow Beard was thoroughly embarrassed and turned a deep shade of red under his blond beard, while his bright-green eyes darted about like two luminous dragonflies. He set his eyes on Ma Yongzhen and let out a hearty laugh in order to hide his nerves. Yellow Beard had taken a tumble, he was embarrassed and was becoming increasingly resentful. Although he was in awe of Ma's martial skill, he was far from happy, so he came forward to fight again. Ma Yongzhen remained calm and unflustered. He already had the upper hand and was in a winning position, so he had the courage to fight with renewed vigor. As before, they exchanged some polite formulaic niceties and again these were translated by Zhao Gongbi. Though Uncle Beard had a smile on his face, and said a few polite words of admiration by way of formality, he was actually quite furious. He now stretched out his hand, the size of a palm-leaf fan, and as round as a large bulb of garlic, in order to grasp hold of Ma Yongzhen's hand again. Before coming forward, Ma Yongzhen clasped his hands together in front of him and bowed to Yellow Beard. They then set about pacing around the arena again, once, twice, in a circle, hand in hand. The crowds were now bigger than ever, the more they gathered together the more cramped everything became. The circle of people was becoming smaller and more compact, so much so that eventually it might become impossible to hold the contest at all. Ma's disciples were afraid that if this escalated into a real fight, it would be hindered by this overcrowding, and members of the audience might even get hurt. One of the disciples was a tall stout fellow, whose nickname was "Golden Wings Brushing Against Clouds". He came out into the center of the arena, and, according to the practice of those who sell herbal remedies and martial skills in the world of Jianghu, he addressed the spectators on all sides, clasping his hands together in front of him and bowing, while smiling from ear to ear.

"Everyone listen to what I have to say," he began. "Today, Master Ma and the foreigner are testing their fighting skills. Please make room for them so that things don't become too cramped, otherwise, I'm afraid someone might come to grief. Please show your respect in this to avoid any risk of injury. Otherwise, do not say that you didn't bring it on yourselves; don't say I didn't warn you."

Having given this polite warning, he bowed again, clasping his hands in front of him, and left the arena to rejoin the crowd. At this time Yellow Beard's hand was on top of Ma Yongzhen's and he was using all the strength he could muster to try to push

Ma down, and hoping to bend him over. By this time, Yellow
Beard was not as strong as he had been just a few minutes before,
as he had already suffered a fall, but with all his might, and for
all he was worth, he still tried to bend Ma's arm all the way
down. But Ma Yongzhen was not an easy opponent to defeat and
he used all his strength to resist, while at the same time hoping
to flip him over as he had done before. But this time it was more
difficult to topple him. Yellow Beard clenched his teeth and his
face went a bright shade of red. He raised his body to its full
height and used all his strength to follow Ma's palm with his
own, hoping to make him fall to his knees in pain. But how was
he to know that this Ma man's speciality was to borrow strength
from his opponent and direct it straight back towards him? Ma
took advantage of Yellow Beard's sudden rush of force, and
striking while the iron was hot, first lowered himself down, then
immediately rose up again to his full height. Although Yellow
Beard's power was formidable, how could he possibly resist Ma
Yongzhen's superhuman strength and offer any defence to this
at all! Just as when one stone is used to strike another, the bigger
its size the more it will shatter. Now, everything happened so
quickly. As Ma lifted himself up to his full height, Yellow Beard
was brought along with him, his tall, massive body was thrown
off balance, and he became unsteady on his feet. Ma Yongzhen
raised his left hand and struck Yellow Beard firmly on the
shoulder, while at the same time allowing his right hand to
suddenly relax. Yellow Beard staggered back ten paces, just as if
oil had been smeared on the soles of his feet, and he could not help
himself from flipping over like an acrobat in the Peking Opera,
ending up with his legs pointing straight to the heavens, and his
back glued firmly to the ground. People all around cheered with
one voice, shouting their approval. Ma Yongzhen's face glowed,
while Yellow Beard's was completely drained of color. Yellow

Beard had fallen on the grass and he was now so stiff that he was finding it difficult to right himself. Everyone laughed heartily, and Ma Yongzhen stood up straight in the arena, as proud as could be. Yellow Beard was both embarrassed and angry, but with great difficulty he finally managed to right himself. Now, paying no attention to his meager ability in the martial arts, or to how weak he had become, he charged forward for all his life was worth, hoping to finally demonstrate who was buck and who was doe. Ma Yongzhen thought it rather funny that this foreigner simply couldn't understand that it was he who was in charge here, so he came forward again to cause some suffering.

Don't blame him for that. If an army threatens attack, the defending general must stop it; if a raging fire approaches, water must extinguish it.

At this point, Yellow Beard felt that he must at all costs swallow Ma up in one final mouthful. He crawled up from where he'd been lying on the grass, raising up his fierce jade-green eyes, waxy yellow beard, red swollen face, and sweaty black hairy back, and made a ferocious dash for Ma Yongzhen. Without as much as a by your leave, without even waiting for Zhao Gongbi to translate the formal niceties, he raised his fist and aimed it directly at Ma Yongzhen's chest. Then, using the martial arts attack known as "Black Tiger Steals the Heart" he tried to land a punch. Keen of eye and swift of hand, what sort of person would Ma Yongzhen be if he hadn't seen this coming. Without waiting for Yellow Beard's fist to land, he raised his own right hand, and with the move "The Iron Eagle Pounces on the Tiger," deflected Yellow Beard's punch. While deflecting the punch he raised his fist and performed, "The Hungry Wolf Swallows the Lamb." Then Ma lifted up his left hand and followed with the move "The Bee Enters its Nest" to welcome Yellow Beard's face head on. Yellow Beard pulled back his left fist and hit out with his right, hoping to plant a punch on Ma Yongzhen's arm. With legs bent and with perfect balance, Ma Yongzhen took one step back, then utilized *peng* "ward off" — the first of the thirteen methods — to deflect Yellow Beard's fist. This *peng*, quite unexpectedly, looked like nothing more than the sort of thing a child might use against an adult, but nevertheless Yellow Beard sprang off to a distance of more than ten feet. Now, unsteady on his feet, he ran uncontrollably backwards, patter, patter, patter, patter…staggering back to a distance of another ten feet, then, having completely lost control of his legs, his whole body crashed to the ground. The spectators on both sides were cheering and applauding, dancing on the spot, clutching their bellies and laughing uncontrollably.

By now it was already past six o'clock, and the time set aside for the tournament had been exceeded by half an hour. The disciples began to tidy up the arena. Yellow Beard had already suffered enough after his third fall. The people of Suzhou have a saying, "once, twice, but not exceeding three times", in this case, implying that if three times were exceeded, things would most likely take a turn for the worse. Now he had been toppled for the third time, Yellow Beard dragged himself up off the ground as fast as he could, and scurried off in the direction of Bubbling Well Road. At the same time, many thousands of spectators were departing in continuous succession, going their separate ways, north, south, east, and west. High up in the sky the crows were cawing, dancing around in circles and flying in the light of the setting sun. The group of disciples mounted their horses and squeezed through the crowds, shouting out for them to make way for Ma Yongzhen, while they escorted him from the tournament arena. In the Tingsong Pavilion, a small rural teashop by the side of the Bubbling Well, they washed their hands and drank some tea. Some people who had not yet gone home formed a crowd at the front of the teashop gates and were idly chatting away. Some were saying how heroic the Chinese people are. Some were saying that if foreigners are insulted they always take revenge. Others picked up on this and were saying that because Yellow Beard had suffered no serious injury it would be unlikely to come to anything. Everybody had their own opinions on the matter. Ma Yongzhen drank tea for a while, paid the bill, then, with his disciples following close behind, rode slowly along the road, taking a roundabout route past the front of the gates of both the Zhang Garden and the Yu Garden, then on towards Jessfield Road, and Carter Road, where they made a detour, passing the Sampan Factory Bridge at Markham Road, before finally arriving at Sinza Road. For the whole length of the ride, those who had watched Ma's fight with Yellow Beard at the Bubbling Well, now saw him passing in front of their homes, so, naturally they huddled together in groups of threes and fours, pointing at Ma, and expounding on the extraordinary abilities of the people of Shandong. Ma Yongzhen observed this as he rode along. Even though he didn't catch all of what was said, he certainly heard more than half of it, and considered it all to be just over-exaggeration and unwarranted praise, so he was not altogether happy about it. Little did Ma know, just now, while the fight had been in progress, watching on from within the crowd was a local ruffian who went by the name of Scrofulous Bai. Scrofulous Bai got increasingly angry as he watched Ma Yongzhen's display, seeing it as nothing but unruly and wild behavior. He went back to gather his followers together to hold a tea party at the Yidongtian teashop, with a view to one day facing down Ma Yongzhen.

If you want to know what happens next, please read the

following chapter.

8

Eight fine steeds suffer serious injury,
And a message is sent to enlist volunteers.

Let us continue to relate how ever since Scrofulous Bai saw Ma
Yongzhen and Yellow Beard compete by the Jing'an Temple —
when Yellow Beard was toppled three times, showing Ma's
strength could not be surpassed, and demonstrating in the eyes
of Scrofulous Bai, how Ma was running wild on the Shanghai
Bund — he found it really hard to bear. He felt thoroughly put out,
but was at a loss what to do about it. He gathered some friends
together to make a decision on whether Ma should be merely
pacified or taken out once and for all. After they had decided
what to do, Scrofulous Bai went to the Yidongtian teashop on
Pakhoi Road. Yidongtian, from top to bottom was a place where
gangs of police informants, horse traders, and ruffians met for
tea parties, and it was at these "tea parties" that the gangsters
conducted their business. This was where gangsters gathered to

hatch their plans, and not a place for educated merchants and business men to hold their meetings. Scrofulous Bai was also a horse trader and at any one time had between twenty and thirty good horses in his stables. He served as an agent for the foreigner's Race Club and also carried out business with horse and carriage companies. Everyday Scrofulous Bai held a tea party at the Yidongtian teashop. This morning he was ascending the staircase with a look of utter fury on his face. A lowly horse groom who went by the nickname of Lu the Lackey saw him arrive and stood up to greet him. Scrofulous Bai walked over and took a seat at his table. Of the remaining customers there, seven in ten knew Scrofulous Bai. Lu the Lackey called for some snacks and a bowl of shredded eel noodles. Scrofulous Bai ordered the same and they were promptly sent over to them. As they were eating, Scrofulous Bai said to Lu the Lackey, "You are no doubt aware that the day before yesterday that Ma Yongzhen fellow held a contest of fighting skills by the Bubbling Well with that foreigner Yellow Beard."

"I didn't go to watch it myself," Lu the Lackey replied, "but I have heard others speak of it: of Yellow Beard being toppled three times, of Ma's overbearing manner and of the carved poetic sign that read, 'With his fists he has fought on both sides of the Yellow River and his feet have trod in the capitals north and south"; and of the large number of disciples he has taken on; his unrivaled skill in horsemanship; of the strength of his arms that can lift weights as heavy as two thousand catties. Apparently, he is capable of defeating seventy or eighty contenders, all at one time. But can any of this truly be believed?"

Scrofulous Bai guffawed loudly. "The awesome strength of this man is certainly not in doubt," he said. "But his reckless and wild behavior is another matter entirely. He looks down on us Shanghainese as being only half civilized, and has become recklessly out of control. He respects nobody and our brethren have lost face because of him. We must do our best to move forward and draw up a cunning plan to show that we ourselves are possessed of comparable skills. If everyone just carries on doing their own thing and allows Ma to be as unscrupulous as he is now, in the future we will be able to do nothing about it. I wonder what you think about that?"

Lu the Lackey was a sycophant, a real expert at sucking up to people, boasting, and telling untruths, while at the same time relying on his friends to feed him from day to day. If you were to say east wind, he would say east wind; if you were to say west wind, he would say west wind. Furthermore, Scrofulous Bai held a position of seniority amongst the ruffians of Shanghai, while Lu the Lackey was still only able to take little boy's steps. How could he possibly not suck up to his elder and superior this morning! He waited for Scrofulous Bai to finish speaking. From the tone of his voice it appeared that he was asking his opinion, so Lu the Lackey became even more convivial and talkative. He took a sip of tea, and, with his gravelly voice, continued to agree with everything that was said to him.

"Quite right! Quite right! How can there possibly be enough room for two bosses in Shanghai. Can we really suffer the shocking behavior of this man from Shandong! It really is outrageous! As your grandmother's family would have said, "Everyone should think of a way to teach him a lesson and force him into submission. Oh, how wonderful that would be!"

The first brilliant plan was Scrofulous Bai's own. He suddenly thought of a horse he had at home. "Foreigners have offered to pay more than one thousand, three hundred *taels* of silver for it," he told Lu the Lackey, "but I have been unwilling to sell. This is an unusually fine horse that comes from the plains beyond the Great Wall. It is fortunate that Ma Yongzhen is a horse trader, who buys and sells livestock for a living. Now, I am relying on you Brother Lu, to act as go-between. Let's pretend this horse belongs to a member of the gentry and this man is moving back to his ancestral home. But to take the horse with him would be impossible, as the terrain of the country, with its high mountains and deep rivers, would make travel impractical. He wants to dispose of the horse at a good price. In Shanghai no one recognizes a good horse when they see it, and people are never willing to pay a good price for one. So we must pretend we have been asked to make discreet inquiries and approach Ma Yongzhen, as he alone is possessed of a keen eye and might be willing to pay a good price. So let's see if he is willing to offer shelter to this horse. It would be much like when a splendid bird chooses a tree in which to nest; or a worthy minister chooses a master for whom to work. A precious sword should be presented to a martyr; quality rouge should be presented to a woman of beauty."

Lu the Lackey listened to what Scrofulous Bai said and slapping his chest with the palm of his hand, jumped up from his seat. "Worthy old man," he exclaimed. "Please do not blame me, a member of the younger generation, for being so brazen this morning, but I am certainly not exaggerating when I say I will be successful in dealing with this matter. I'll make that Ma man fall into our trap and scurry headlong into our cage. Have no fear of those donkeys and dogs who work for him."

Scrofulous Bai always knew the importance of mediation, and realized that to actually carry things through one must be shrewd and swift. However, those four words "play it by ear" were still acceptable to him, and now he felt strongly that he must act according to the circumstances. So, he entrusted Lu the Lackey with visiting Ma Yongzhen at home.

Lu the Lackey accepted Scrofulous Bai's instructions as if he were receiving an important military command. He pulled on his leather boots, ran down the stairs of the Yidongtian teashop, called for an iron-tired rickshaw and clattered along to Sinza Road in search of Ma Yongzhen. As luck would have it, Ma was in the middle of eating lunch and had not yet left the house. Lu the Lackey just couldn't help behaving like the clown in Chinese opera. As soon as he saw Ma Yongzhen he made known his name and began to chatter away at great length, using all sorts of flattering words in an effort to butter him up. Now, Ma Yongzhen was just a simple man from Shandong. He did have much knowledge, and had experienced many things in his life. Only flattery had he not experienced. And so, on seeing that Ma was susceptible to flattery, Lu the Lackey piled it on even more thickly, and continued according to his plan—using strong medicine to combat the disease. No sooner had he told Ma about the horse, than everything was settled. They arranged that the next day he would view some of Scrofulous Bai's horses and take them for a ride on some open ground near Sungshan Road in the French Concession. Of what happened for the remains of the day, no more shall be said.

When it came to the following morning, Lu the Lackey thought of all the money he was going to earn as a go-between, and was quite overjoyed. Just before three in the afternoon, as he had done before, he went over to Sinza to pick up Ma Yongzhen with all good manners and exaggerated politeness. Ma Yongzhen took along his disciples, Double-tailed Scorpion, Lin Deshen and Single-horned Dragon, Wang Desheng. The four men crossed the North Nicheng Bridge and hailed a horse and carriage. With a crack of the whip the horse's four hooves were set in motion and the four wheels of the carriage rumbled loudly as they raced on ahead, almost as if they had taken off into mid-air. They soon arrived at Pahsienjiao in the French Concession, and made their way to a piece of grassy open ground by Sungshan Road. Ma Yongzhen and the others got out of the carriage, were introduced to Scrofulous Bai by Lu the Lackey, and exchanged the customary pleasantries. Scrofulous Bai instructed his servants to lead out the eight horses he had brought along. Ma Yongzhen looked them over one by one and praised them all as outstanding. He was then invited to try them out and a price was discussed. Ma Yongzhen instructed Double-tailed Scorpion, Lin Deshen to fetch the silken riding crop. He did so, then took charge of preparing the saddle. As was customary, Ma Yongzhen apologized to Scrofulous Bai, Lu the Lackey and all the other attendants, before clasping his hands together in front of him by way of a bow, and jumping into the saddle. Double-tailed Scorpion stepped forward one pace and presented the silken riding crop to his master. Ma Yongzhen took the crop in his right hand and with his left he held the silken reins. The horse immediately realized that he was carrying an expert horseman. It lowered its head, raised its tail and snorted loudly. It had hooves that had trodden the snow and straddled the waves. Ma wielded the riding crop and pulled on the reins, and that fine steed, that precious horse that could fly to the moon and play amongst the stars, sped off over the open ground like a whisp of smoke, the sound of those nimble hooves like the clink of small bells ringing gently with every step it took. Ma sped forward, came back and did the same again, making five or six circuits of the piece of open ground. Then he praised the quality of the horse and dismounted. Scrofulous Bai invited him to try another, so, as before, he took it for six or seven laps. He then rode three or four more horses in turn.

But enough of this tedious prattle. When the eight fine horses had been ridden in turn, Ma Yongzhen walked over to Scrofulous Bai.

"All eight of these horses are fine specimens that could be

ridden proudly into battle," he enthused. "Sure enough, they live up to their reputations. As for a price, tomorrow please honor me with your presence at my humble abode and present me with a bill so that we can arrive at a fair price."

When he finished speaking, he noticed that time was marching on, so he bowed to the crowds that had assembled to watch him and bid everyone farewell. As before, he took along with him his beloved disciples Lin Deshen and Wang Desheng. Taking the same carriage they had arrived in, they hurried back to the Sinza residence. Before long they arrived home and paid the driver. Of what Ma did with his two disciples we shall say no more. The story will now turn to what happened after Lu the Lackey took Ma Yongzhen to try out the eight fine horses.

Scrofulous Bai and Lu the Lackey ate dinner and drank together in a small local restaurant. They were waiting in anticipation for the next day to arrive, when they were hoping to receive news from Ma Yongzhen in Sinza. After dinner they said their goodbyes and went their separate ways. When it came to the following morning, they met again at the Yidongtian teashop, where it was agreed that in a short while they would go together to Sinza Road. Lu the Lackey suggested that Scrofulous Bai write a bill for the horses in advance, so they would have something to begin negotiations with when it came to talking to Ma Yongzhen. Scrofulous Bai asked the waiter to bring some writing things. The waiter did as he was bade, and came back with an old worn ink-stone, a tired, ragged brush, a piece of moldy ink-cake, and a small sheet of torn paper, and placed them on the table. Just at that moment, all of a sudden, two people came rushing up the stairs.

"Daddy! Daddy! Come home quickly," they called out at the top of their lungs. Those new arrivals were none other than Scrofulous Bai's children. They told Scrofulous Bai that every one of those eight fine horses was now vomiting and foaming at the mouth. Scrofulous Bai heard this as if a bolt of lightning had struck on a fine day, and Lu the Lackey jumped high up into the air in fright. Neither of them was able to utter a word as they made their way down the central staircase.

If you want to know if those eight horses live or die, please read the following chapter.

9

Scrofulous Bai contacts Yellow Beard,
And the Single-horned Dragon assists the Double-tailed Scorpion.

Let us continue to relate how Scrofulous Bai and Lu the Lackey were in the Yidongtian teashop drinking tea, fully planning to go to Ma Yongzhen's Sinza Road residence that afternoon, and were discussing the result of the sale of the horses, when, quite unexpectedly, Scrofulous Bai's son and daughter came to tell him how his eight fine horses had suddenly been taken ill. When Scrofulous Bai received the news, his face was like thunder, and he rushed home immediately with Lu the Lackey in tow. In the thatched stables on the piece of open ground at the back of the house, he carefully examined each of the horses in turn, from head to tail, and discovered that they had identical complaints: watery, bloodshot, cloudy eyes; foul smelling sputum oozing from their mouths; front legs subject to involuntary spasms. Each one of them looked to be in terrible pain. On seeing the situation,

Scrofulous Bai felt thoroughly dejected. Realizing that the horses had suffered some sort of internal injury, he knew that he must call for the horse doctor to prescribe medicine and treat the condition without delay. He was terrified that the horses might not make a full recovery. If even one or two of them were to die that would already be a terrible thing. One horse, was worth four or five hundred Mexican silver dollars, so eight of them together might be estimated at around four thousand dollars. This was certainly no laughing matter.

"What do you think," he asked Lu the Lackey. "How should we go about dealing with this problem?"

Lu the Lackey frowned and said not a word. Scrofulous Bai couldn't think what else to do, so he quickly sent his servants to invite the horse doctor to examine the animals and prescribe the appropriate medicine. He would wait until the medicine had been prescribed before deciding on what to do next.

He decided that later on he would go and find Ma Yongzhen, to tell him that the horses had fallen ill after he rode them, and he must pay compensation. That goes without saying. If this is not taken care of, there is no question that it will lead to far greater losses in the future. This had put him in a difficult position, and he held Lu the Lackey partly responsible, though it was not entirely his fault. Under such circumstances it is best to wait and see what the horse doctor has to say. After all, for the right diagnosis one should always rely on a doctor. Even though things seemed dire, Scrofulous Bai still held on to a glimmer of hope.

Those eight horses not only fell ill without warning, but their illness had very suddenly taken a turn for the worse. Just the day before yesterday they were such magnificent animals, so strong and full of life. But, after Ma Yongzhen rode them yesterday, they turned out like this. Can it be possible that Ma hadn't acted dishonestly and deceitfully! Scrofulous Bai imagined what he was going to say to Ma Yongzhen, "You hurt my fine horses. You are a horse trader and you too rely on horses to feed and clothe yourself. I am also a horse trader and rely on them to support my mother, father, wife, and children. I buy and sell, and work within such narrow profit margins, margins that are no bigger than a fly's head. We are of the same profession. We have never met before now, and have never had a dealings with one another. As the saying goes, "In days gone by, we have had nothing to complain of; there has never been any hatred between you and I, Ma Yongzhen! Why did you deal this treacherous and dastardly blow, and harm me for no reason at all? I simply cannot understand it."

The more he thought about it the more resentful he became. The more he thought about it the more furious he became. The three spirit-fields inside his body, according to the principles of Chinese medicine, the upper, middle, and lower fields, were jumping around in fury, and it was as if steam was spouting from all seven of his facial orifices.

In no time at all the horse doctor, Master Ye Musheng arrived. Scrofulous Bai welcomed him with all reverence and ceremony, and asked him why he thought his horses had fallen ill. Master Ye nodded his head and a knowing smile could be seen to spread across his face. They stood up and walked to the back garden to see the horses together, Scrofulous Bai in front, Master Ye following, and Lu the Lackey bringing up the rear. They arrived at the stables, entered the stalls and spoke to the stable boy, Little Big Number Nine from Jiangbei, who told them every little detail that had happened to the eight horses, from yesterday up to the present time. Master Ye took a close look at the animals.

"The way horse doctors and human doctors examine their patients is very different." Little Big Number Nine began to speak to one of the horses. "The way they look at them, the way they feel them, and the medicines they prescribe are all different. Human doctors need to check a patient's pulse; look at the coating of their tongue; enquire about the cause of the disease, all sorts of procedures. A horse doctor looks first at the animal's appearance; then at the condition of its coat and the clarity of its eyes, then he will take a careful look at its ears, its head, its tail and all four hooves in turn."

Master Ye examined the eight horses one by one. Then the three men, Master Ye, Scrofulous Bai and Lu the Lackey, returned to the reception hall where they sat down to listen to Master Ye's verdict.

"As far as I can determine, these horses have all suffered damage to their internal organs, hence the watering of the eyes and the twitching of the legs. I'm afraid it's doubtful they will make a quick recovery. Luckily, we have caught this early and it is unlikely they will suffer any lasting damage, but because they have experienced internal injuries it will take some time for them to recover. Even after several days of improvement, the silkiness and sheen of their coats and manes will continue to fade, and the spirit and vigor they showed in the past, will take a long time to return."

When Master Ye finished speaking, he ground some ink on the ink-stone, spread out a sheet of paper, picked up his writing brush, and wrote out a prescription, which listed much the same sort of medicines that would be given to humans. The eight horses had all come down with the same illness and there were two types of prescription for each of them. Scrofulous Bai immediately sent a servant to the local herbalists to have the prescriptions filled, and on their return promptly administered the boiled concoctions to the horses. Scrofulous Bai saw Master Ye out, then returned to discuss with Lu Lackey just how thoroughly despicable he thought that Ma Yongzhen man really was.

"If he wanted to buy them then he should have gone ahead and bought them, but why did he take my fine horses, all my worldly goods, and ride them so they ended up in such a terrible state as this? Why is that sort of person even put on this earth? It should not be allowed to happen!"

Lu the Lackey's background was as a horse groom and petty hooligan, so his intentions always tended towards the narrow-minded and contemptible. Knitting his eyebrows as he pondered the problem, a plan began to take shape in his mind. He thought it over for a while, working on the idea, then suddenly got to his feet.

"That Ma Yongzhen must be slaughtered without mercy." Gesticulating wildly, he was unable to restrain himself and began to curse and swear, blaming and scolding. "I have thought of a way to deal with him and wonder if it might just work. Let's talk it through with everybody. If it's going to work then let's do it, if it's not going to work then let's do something else."

"What brilliant idea have you had?" Scrofulous Bai asked. "As long as it sorts that Ma man out, I'm sure it will be worthwhile. I, Scrofulous Bai have an irreconcilable hatred for that man, and it has come to the point where either it is he who must be killed or I who must die."

"That Ma man's physical strength is certainly nothing to be scoffed at," Lu the Lackey interrupted. "Without question we are in no position to match him. I recall two days ago when Ma Yongzhen set up the challenge by the Bubbling Well at Jing'an Temple and fought with the foreigner Yellow Beard. Yellow Beard was toppled three times in a row. If this grievance is not settled now it will escalate and spiral out of control. Why don't we search out Yellow Beard! We can put a stop to it with his help by making

86

things difficult for that Ma man. If in the end Ma is capable of showing some respect, we must ask that he compensates us for our losses. That will be the beginning in trying to sort this problem out. If he is unwilling to show us respect, then we will have to get serious, and that will mean fisticuffs. This is known as using diplomacy before resorting to physical violence. What is your considered opinion on this, boss?"

Scrofulous Bai very much approved. "Have you ever met that foreigner, Yellow Beard?" He asked.

"I don't know him and am unable to speak foreign languages," Lu the Lackey replied, "but my brother-in-arms works as a 'boy' in a foreign lawyer's office and is able to speak English quite well. He is called Xie and his full name is Xie Yuanqing. He knows Yellow Beard very well. If we want to get in touch with Yellow Beard we should seek out Xie Yuanqing and he will be able to arrange a meeting for us."

Scrofulous Bai was delighted to hear this and entrusted Lu the Lackey with the task of going to see Xie Yuanqing and talking the matter through with him. Lu the Lackey asked Scrofulous Bai for three silver dollars Mex, then, setting his limbs in motion, he left through the front door and hailed a rickshaw to take him to Rue du Consulat in search of Xie Yuanqing.

The matters of the world, if they do not happen by chance, do not get written down for us to read.

By an extraordinary stroke of luck, Xie Yuanqing was actually with Yellow Beard. They were chatting away, arm in arm, and were walking in the direction from which Lu the Lackey was arriving. Sitting in the rickshaw Lu the Lackey could see them right in front of his eyes.

"I say! Brother Xie!"

Xie Yuanqing was puzzled. He heard someone call his name, so he raised his head, only to discover it was none other than his brother-in-arms, Lu the Lackey. It turns out that the two had always been very close, so when they came across each other in the street like this they would always stop and chat. Lu the Lackey got out of the rickshaw, paid the fare and walked over to Xie and Yellow Beard. He performed a foreign greeting, doffing his hat and shaking their hands, and promptly addressed Xie Yuanqing.

"Brother Xie, this morning I have an important matter I'd like to discuss with you, and, by a strange coincidence, with this gentleman too. I have a small matter I would like to trouble him with."

Hearing that he had something to ask of him made perfect sense to Xie, but to hear that it involved the foreigner Yellow Beard too, made him most puzzled, and he was impatient to hear more about it.

Lu the Lackey looked cautiously about him in all directions. "This isn't the place to talk," he said. "Let's go to a restaurant and we can discuss it to our satisfaction over a cup of coffee."

Xie Yuanqing spoke to Yellow Beard in a foreign tongue: "A-B-C...D-E...F-G-H-I...J-K", and the foreigner nodded his head by way of a response. The three men walked slowly to a magnificent foreign restaurant called Yizhixiang, where they went up to the second floor and ordered some foreign food. Lu the Lackey told Xie about when Ma Yongzhen rode the horses and of Yellow Beard being toppled in the fight.

"Scrofulous Bai is more furious than words can describe. He came up with the idea to seek assistance in earnest from Yellow Beard and for him to come forward and get involved. If that Ma man will not take our advice, then we will invite him to taste a little suffering."

Xie Yuanqing relayed what he said to Yellow Beard, word for word. The foreigner listened. His face was turning redder by the second, he raised his feet off the floor and his eyes stared straight ahead. Then, with his fists tightly clenched he beat upon his knees, and from his mouth flowed a series of incomprehensible words: "Ligulu gugu lujili…"

Who knows what on earth he was saying. I certainly don't!

"The foreigner very much approves," Xie Yuanqing told Lu the Lackey. "Please relay this to Brother Bai, decide on a date, and Yellow Beard will certainly comply with his instructions and do everything he can to help. He will do his very best to help you, and he will do all he can to help himself. "

Lu the Lackey heard this and was delighted. The three men ate a few dishes then called for the bill. Xie Yuanqing did not want Lu the Lackey to be out of pocket, and in truth Lu the Lackey did only have two or three paltry silver coins to his name. His funds were insufficient so he suggested they split the bill. But they were brothers-in-arms, so, finally came to a friendly agreement, by which Xie would spend his money now, and Lu the Lackey would repay the debt another day.

The three men walked down the stairs and went their separate ways. Lu the Lacky took a rickshaw as before, and returned to the French Concession where he told Scrofulous Bai all that had passed between them. Scrofulous Bai was delighted, and agreed that a day should be found for them to go and seek out Ma Yongzhen.

If you want to know what happens next, please read the following chapter.

10

In a local teashop the first fight takes place,
And in the lawcourts a personal grievance is heard.

Let us continue to relate how Scrofulous Bai entrusted Lu the Lackey with the task of inviting Yellow Beard to join them and was planning to take his own personal revenge on Ma Yongzhen. Yellow Beard clapped his hands in approval. As Scrofulous Bai now had Yellow Beard as a shield to protect him, all of a sudden he became courageous and bold. He looked at the horses in his stables and since taking the medicine prescribed by Master Ye they were gradually returning to normal. Their eyes no longer watered and they were no longer sweating abnormally. He guessed that if they continued with the medicine for a little while longer they would soon be right as rain. But the vengeful feelings he felt in his heart did not abate, and day and night he could not forget. He pondered the saying, "a silk thread cannot a thick rope make, and a single tree cannot a dense forest form" —

if men are too few, it will not be possible for things to be carried through, and he realized he would run into difficulties if he tried to take revenge all alone, knowing clearly that he was no match for Ma. If he wanted to parade in victory with banners and drums; if he desired to send troops against the guilty, and for the guilty to admit their crimes, he would have to see this plan through. He thought about it over and over again, scheming and calculating, and came to the decision that he must keep a secret weapon hidden up his sleeve. In that way, Ma would be unable to formulate a defense, and would be prevented from making preparations in advance. If he wanted to make Ma suffer so that he would be unable to establish himself in Shanghai, a cunning plan, Scrofulous Bai decided, would be to have a word with Lu the Lackey's relative, Little Ah Bao. Little Ah Bao had drifted along in Shanghai for many years and understood all the dirty tricks and dodgy tactics of the underworld gangster. So, when Ah Bao heard what Scrofulous Bai told him, he confirmed he thought it was a good idea and was particularly approving of the fact that Scrofulous Bai had taken measures to – "Know his enemy and know himself" – as the military strategist Sunzi once said. And so it was decided. There is a saying: "It is easy to dodge a spear in the open, but hard to guard against a hidden weapon." In this case, they agreed it would be expedient to use the strategy of the hidden weapon. Yellow Beard should be informed that a suitable day must be found when they could make their move, and Lu the Lackey must be entrusted with the task of finding out where Ma spent his time. It was also agreed that Scrofulous Bai should invite his group of old friends and followers to come along and help. So, Scabby Crabby, Eely Mudskipper, Siguan Bloodspitter, Sanbao Headsplitter, that despicable band of ruffians, all received instructions to prepare themselves for a fight. It was like the fist commanding the arm: brave upstanding, and full of spirit, like the awe-inspiring authority of a great general directing his troops on the battlefield. Scrofulous Bai sent people out to find out where Ma Yongzhen habitually drank his tea. As luck would have it, on that day Ma Yongzhen had taken his disciples Double-tailed Scorpion, Lin Deshen, and Single-horned Dragon, Wang Desheng, to a small teashop in Yangjingbang, the area between the Chinese city and the French Concession. By chance, Little Big Number Nine, Scrofulous Bai's stableboy, spotted Ma in the teashop and immediately set his feet in motion and ran along to the Yidongtian teashop to tell Scrofulous Bai. Just then Scrofulous Bai and Lu the Lackey were having a heart-to-heart over a cup of tea. As soon as they heard what Little Big Number Nine had to say, Scrofulous Bai instructed Lu the Lackey to go and find Yellow Beard and tell him to make his way to the teashop in Yangjingbang.

Lu the Lackey voiced his agreement, put on his boots, and ran down the staircase as if he had sprouted wings. He hailed a rickshaw, and broad stride by broad stride they traveled west in search of Yellow Beard. All the time Lu the Lackey was urging the unfortunate rickshaw puller to run faster. That poor man from Jiangbei was so frantic that he couldn't catch his breath, while he continually shouted and yelped in fear, as he did his best to dodge all obstacles that obstructed their way. In the end they finally tracked down Yellow Beard.

As soon as Yellow Beard saw Lu the Lackey he understood the situation, and using a form of speech that muddled together the Chinese and English languages, he asked:

"Mar…Yung…Zen…coming?"

At last Lu the Lackey showed he had some wits about him, and on hearing him say the name Ma Yongzhen, nodded his head in agreement. Yellow Beard left his home together with Lu the Lackey. They joined four other passengers on a public carriage that happened to be passing by (a "pheasant carriage" as they were known), and, with a great sense of purpose, set off towards the small teashop in Yangjingbang. Fortunately, the Jing'an Temple and Yangjiabang districts were not far from each other. The wheels rumbled slowly, the horse's hooves clattered steadily, but in no time at all they had arrived at their destination. Yellow Beard and Lu the Lackey got out of the carriage, paid the modest fare and took a furtive look around. Ma Yongzhen was drinking tea together with two of his disciples but Scrofulous Bai's men were not yet there. Lu the Lackey thought to himself that if he and Yellow Beard were to confront them there and then, it would not be good for them at all.

"Help has not yet arrived and with just the two of us we would most certainly never be able to defeat the master and his two disciples," he thought to himself. "It would be wisest for me to wait here and think up a plan."

As soon as he had made up his mind what to do, he led Yellow Beard to the Longquanlou to drink tea. As they were walking up the central staircase the waiter saw Lu the Lackey in the company of a foreigner. Not knowing that a plan was afoot, he came over to greet them. "Mr Lu, have you come with a foreigner for your tea party today?"

Lu the Lackey just nodded his head and sat down with the foreigner. The waiter brought over a pot of tea. "Bring another pot," Lu the Lackey told him. The waiter responded with a nod and brought over a second pot as he had been instructed to. Lu the Lacky fished out some change and sent the waiter downstairs to buy a cigar, which, when it arrived, he handed over to Yellow Beard. With exaggerated politeness, he struck a match, lit the cigar for him, and invited him to remain seated.

"I will go and look for Scrofulous Bai," he said. In reply, Yellow Beard said a few incomprehensible words in a foreign tongue, which left Lu the Lackey completely stumped. He paused, then just nodded his head a few times and rushed down the stairs as if he were in flight.

When the two of them spoke together, neither understood the other, and even I couldn't understand what they were saying.

Let us continue to relate how Lu the Lackey rushed out of Longquanlou to go to the Yidongtian teashop on Pakhoi Road, but when he was only halfway there he caught sight of Scrofulous Bai, Scabby Crabby, Eely Mudskipper, Siguan Bloodspitter, and Sanbao Headsplitter — that band of brothers — all walking in the direction of Yangjingbang. Lu the Lackey caught up with them.

"Yellow Beard is in Longquanlou drinking tea," he told Scrofulous Bai. "You go on ahead to the teashop and he and I will follow close behind."

"Very well," Scrofulous Bai replied. "We'll go there now and you and Yellow Beard can meet us there. Remember, there is no room for error!"

Lu the Lackey showed he understood, quickly greeted everyone else in turn, then setting his feet in motion, ran off once again in the direction of the Longquanlou.

Moving on from the Longquanlou, for the moment we shall speak no more of Lu the Lackey and Scrofulous Bai and their plan to deal with Ma Yongzhen, but let us continue to relate how Ma Yongzhen and his two disciples had come that day to the small teashop to wait for friends. Just as they were getting tired of waiting, they caught sight of Scrofulous Bai and his gang, all dressed up for a fight. They couldn't think of a reason why they should be there, so they stood up immediately in expectation. Double-tailed Scorpion noticed that they were all local Shanghai men. How could he not know the way things were done in this city, so he quickly warned his master: "Be careful, they are here to cause trouble."

Before he could finish speaking, Scrofulous Bai walked in at the head of the crowd and addressed Ma Yongzhen, "Brother Ma, you also trade horses for a living. You rely on horses to put food on the table, and you rely on horses to clothe yourself. We are of the same profession and by rights should help each other out. So why did you injure my eight horses when you took them for a ride? Each one of them has become quite useless to me. Do you consider yourself to be a worthy fellow? Apart from you alone, other people do not count, do they? To make sure you do not look down on others again in the future, we have come here today to urge you to pay your bill, and wipe the slate clean so as to bring all matters to a close. You and I are both of the same profession and should be polite and well-mannered to one another. But, if you do not agree, we will have to put to the test which of us really is top dog, and take the discussion further."

Ma Yongzhen listened to what Scrofulous Bai said and could not help flying off into a rage. His martial skills were formidable and he was totally unafraid. He looked at the assembled crowd and didn't think much of them. So he raised himself up to his full height. "Did you not go to make inquiries before approaching me?" He asked Scrofulous Bai. "I, Ma Yongzhen, have never been bullied by anyone. You should take a look at yourself. If your aim is to swindle me, there will be consequences. It would be like provoking the star-god Tai Sui, or swatting a fly on a tiger's head. Don't even think about it. You suppose because you are many in number, you can make me back down."

Scrofulous Bai heard what Ma Yongzhen said and was absolutely furious, while at the same time thinking that this was not going to be that easy after all.

He raised his fist and yelled, "I, Scrofulous Bai am not afraid to get involved!" Taking that as a signal, the whole gang, Scabby Crabby, Eely Mudskipper, Siguan Bloodspitter, Sanbao Headsplitter rushed forth together like a roaring wave and surrounded Ma Yongzhen. Ma's followers, Double-tailed Scorpion, Lin Deshen, and Single-horned Dragon, Wang Desheng, also joined the fray. All that could be seen were people hitting each other over the head, and the sounds of punching and slapping could be heard all round. There were quite a number of people watching from the street, but no one dared come forward to make peace. Just at the moment when everything was getting particularly lively, Lu the Lackey and Yellow Beard walked through the door. "What's this!" The bystanders asked themselves. "Have foreigners also come to fight? This really is most unusual." And even more people joined the crowd of onlookers as a result. The two gangs fought for a while, resulting in both sides coming out badly. Scrofulous Bai's henchman Siguan Bloodspitter was given a good beating by Ma Yongzhen and really did end up spitting blood. Sanbao Headsplitter, also lived up to his name and got a nasty gash on his head. As things progressed, even Yellow Beard was pushed to the ground. On Ma Yongzhen's side, his disciples were also hurt. No one on either side had injuries that were life threatening but that poor innocent little teashop, which had got dragged into it along the way, was in a sorry state. Tables were without tabletops, stools were missing their legs, and cups and teapots were strewn all around, to say nothing of the stoves and kettles scattered here and there. Every single thing was out of place and nothing was left unbroken. Some customers who wanted to keep themselves to themselves chose the wise option — to "flee to gain advantage" — something they had learned from the Thirty-six Stratagems. They had not received a refund for the money they had spent, so they went outside to watch the excitement from there. This was indeed an incident that left many at a disadvantage. But how was it all going to end? Yellow Beard had suffered himself, so was he really going to let it lie! He shouted to Scrofulous Bai not to let Ma Yongzhen escape, and jumped into a rickshaw, which took him all the way south to the French Concession to report the incident at the police station on Rue Du Consulat, known to the locals as the "Big Chiming Clock" because of the large clock on the central tower above the entrance. He told the police chief and his subordinates about the incident, then led the bailiffs and detectives to the small teashop in Yangjingbang to arrest Ma Yongzhen. That Ma Yongzhen, though, was a worthy fellow. He had good intentions and fully believed that justice was on his side. What was there for him to be afraid of? So he went back with the police to sort the matter out. The detectives took the four injured men to the hospital in an ambulance and it was decided that they would give evidence in court the following day. The owner of the little teashop wrote a bill for damages and handed it over to the bailiffs so that compensation might be sought. When the bystanders saw the case was done and dusted, they gradually went their separate ways.

How Ma Yongzhen fares at court, and of Scrofulous Bai's second fight, of reconciliation meetings over tea and victuals, and discussions concerning a plot to kill Ma; of the three times Bai took revenge, and how Ma Yongzhen finally met with harm; how Ma's arm was severed, and how he lost his life because of it; the grand funeral; and how Ma Yongzhen's sister, Ma Suzhen took revenge for her brother, and slaughtered her enemies in broad daylight—all these remarkable and extraordinary events, cannot be recorded here in any detail, due to limitations set by the length of the book. We must wait for Master Zhu Dagong of Yushan to write the sequel to this volume, as I, fair reader, your humble servant, Qi Fanniu, must bid you farewell.

11

Talking of friendship Ma Yongzhen invites honoured guests,
And hoping for a peaceful resolution Chai Jiuyun urges reconciliation.

It has been said since ancient times that the soft can overcome the hard and the weak can conquer the strong. This is certainly not incorrect, and has everything to do with the way man conducts himself in society. In the end, with a little effort and some patience, there should never be a reason for one to be at a disadvantage. Though it must never be the case that when spat in the face one should allow the spittle to dry of itself, at the very least one must be a little tolerant. Confucius said: "a little impatience can ruin truly great plans," and that is what is meant by this. In the end, force and power can never be relied on. The saying, "However strong you are there will always be someone stronger," shows that both parties will always come out badly in the end. Is it really worth the trouble? But enough of this idle chatter, let us return to the matter in hand.

In the first volume, Mr Qi Fanniu told us about the fight in the teashop between Ma Yongzhen and Scrofulous Bai, which resulted in everyone being arrested and taken down to the police station. Gentle reader, please do not grumble that Mr Qi Fanniu has been in some way remiss, by leaving you in suspense. It is simply due to a question of length that the first volume had to end where it did. This author is aware that you, oh, gentle reader, are anxious to read about what happens next. Therefore, I have taken the liberty of continuing to write the story, blow by blow. This tale is a matter of fact of which all should be aware. However, this author's skill with writing brush and ink cannot be said to be of the highest level, and for this, gentle reader, I beg your forgiveness.

Let us proceed to relate how Scrofulous Bai and Ma Yongzhen were fighting in the teashop and everyone and everything was left in a sorry state. There were those who were spitting blood and those whose heads had been split open, as well as those with broken legs. The whole place was one great big mess. In the end, Yellow Beard reported the incident to the police. Everyone was taken into custody, and they were due to go to court the following day to hear the judgment of the magistrate, having suffered the indignity of being locked up overnight. Despite all of this, those who were hurt were not too badly injured. Though Siguan Bloodspitter spat up several mouthfuls of blood, after a while nobody even noticed he was injured. Sanbao Headsplitter had a gash to the head, but after it was bandaged up it gave him no trouble at all. As for Ma Yongzhen's two senior disciples: Single-horned Dragon dislocated his arm, but after it was set back in place he was fine; and Double-tailed Scorpion's carapace had taken a good drubbing and as a result he suffered considerable swelling, but this was not too big a problem; when Yellow Beard returned to his residence, someone noticed he was missing a few tufts of his beard, which they presumed had been lost in the fight, but he had not been aware of this himself and it is likely that this has its origins in some sort of joke. We shall say no more of what happened that day.

When the following day arrived, the chief of police attended court in person and read aloud the declarations relating to the fight. The magistrate, an Englishman, was known for his integrity and honesty, and listened to what both parties had to say. Thereafter, the verdict was translated and read aloud:

"Both sides are partly to blame and should by rights be punished according to the severest penalties. But, because this is their first offence, instead, the sentencing will be lenient. Both parties are to find a guarantor, after which they will be released. In future such a disturbance must not be allowed to happen again."

In the end it was declared that Ma Yongzhen and Scrofulous Bai should each pay a ten dollar fine, as what they had done violated the laws of the International Settlement. The case was to be closed when the fine was paid.

When the followers of Ma Yongzhen and Scrofulous Bai heard about the incident, they came to be present at the hearing and to wait for the verdict to be announced. Some planted themselves at the main entrance, while others drank tea in nearby teashops. There were twice as many people there on that day as there had ever been at any previous gathering of its kind. Immediately any news was heard, it was relayed from one person to another, just as if they were a colony of ants. By the time they heard the verdict, they had made all preparations for paying for the release and settling the fine. After just a short while, the money was sent into the courthouse and those inside were released. All present divided off to guard their own people, and took their own routes to leave. Just as Ma Yongzhen and his party, Single-horned

Dragon, Double-tailed Scorpion and his other close followers, were departing through the main entrance of the courthouse, Ma noticed someone coming towards him, calling to him from afar.

"Brother Ma! Brother Ma, I haven't seen you for days!"

Ma Yongzhen heard someone calling out to him, and when he raised his head to look, he saw that it was none other than his good friend Chai Jiuyun.

"Brother Chai, what a nice surprise, how did you get the time off work?" He asked him.

"I don't really have any free time, but today I've taken leave of absence because I heard that you, my good friend, had been involved in a fight and were taken down to the police station. I was terribly concerned that you might have suffered hardship, so I've come to see how you are."

"Thank you for your concern," Ma Yongzhen replied. "I am most touched." He took a furtive look around. "This is not a good place to talk. Let's go and find somewhere to drink a cup of tea and we can talk about it there."

Chai Jiuyun agreed and the two men set off together with Ma's disciples to find a teashop on Foochow Road. On arrival, they went up the central staircase and chose a table. The waiter came over. "Would you like to drink tea, or perhaps you'd like to eat something?" he asked them.

It turns out that most of the teashops at that time served light meals. Whether this was actually the case or not, I simply do not know.

"Have you eaten?" Chai Jiuyun asked Ma Yongzhen.

"Indeed I have not," was Ma's reply. "And you?"

"Me neither," Chai Jiuyun told him, so the waiter was instructed to bring four bowls of beef noodles and two teapots, one of black tea and the other of plain hot water. The waiter nodded to show he understood and shouted the food order downstairs, then brought over the tea and some hot towels. He also provided them with water tobacco pipes, and before long the guests were puffing on their pipes, eating noodles, and chatting away.

"Brother Ma, how did the confrontation begin?"

"It was all down to Scrofulous Bai, something to do with me riding his horses. And then he tried to extort me." Ma told Chai everything in detail, as he understood it.

Chai Jiuyun ventured a series of replies. "According to the sayings—'It is better to quash bad feeling than to keep it alive.' 'When eating dinner away from home, it is desirable to have the company of friends.' 'A single tree will never form a dense forest and shall forever be unsuccessful all alone'."

They finished off their noodles as they talked and the waiter brought over more hot towels for them to wipe their faces. Ma Yongzhen was in the process of pouring a cup of tea for Chai Jiuyun, and was just about to say something, when he noticed a man walking up the staircase. He was a little more than thirty years of age and stood at five *chi* in height. His face was rather plump and he had a fair, clean complexion, except that across the bridge of his nose, there was a collection of small pockmarks, and it was these that gave him his nickname, "Poxy Fang". Poxy Fang wore a *changpao* long gown of Prussian-blue crepe silk, over which he had on a soy-sauce-coloured Nanjing silk, *majia* jacket. He wore a skull cap with a tassel of bright red silk and walked up the stairs with an impressive air. On seeing Chai Jiuyun, he walked straight over to greet him.

"Brother Chai! I see you are holding a tea party."

Chai Jiuyun stood up and replied: "Brother Fang, you are here so early in the morning! And have also come for tea, I presume." As he said this he poured an extra cup and presented it to him, while politely gesturing for him to be seated. Poxy Fang sat down as instructed and the waiter brought over his own pot of tea. It turns out that this man was a regular customer at the teashop and often held tea parties there himself, so he was known to everyone, and might be considered to hold a certain amount of prestige there.

But enough of this idle chatter. Let us continue to relate how the man went to take a seat, and clasping his hands together in front of him, bowed respectfully to Ma Yongzhen. Then he performed a greeting according to the gangland etiquette of Shanghai, while speaking a few words of underworld argot.

> So what is meant by these two terms "gangland etiquette" and "underworld argot"? It turns out that in the gangland culture of the time they had their own protocol and used a secret jargon. Unfortunately, fair reader, this author does not understand the inner workings of Jianghu – that underworld of traveling fighters, and wanderers of rivers and lakes – so is unable to write this jargon down for you to see. All I can do is leave it blank. I beg the reader's forgiveness for this. Even Ma Yongzhen dared not say those words out loud.

"Ma Yongzhen, at your service, may I know your honorable name?"

"Oh, so you are Ma Yongzhen," the man replied with some surprise. "I have long heard mention of your name. I am Fang Sanzi, your humble servant. I hail from Yangzhou, but for some years now have muddled along in Shanghai – for my sins."

"There is no need to be so modest," Ma replied.

"Brother Fang, don't be so formal," Chai Jiuyun interrupted.

"This is Ma Yongzhen. He is one of us, and should not be treated as an outsider."

"Although we are now meeting for the first time." Ma Yongzhen said. "After a while, Brother Fang, you will come to know that I am not an unreasonable person."

"Quite right," Fang replied, "when a worthy fellow attends to things, of course, he does so in a frank and straightforward manner. There will most certainly not be anything shady about his conduct and he will not be afraid of his own head and tail."

Ma was very taken with what Fang said, and responded to everything with a nod of the head and a series of "yesses".

"Brother Fang," said Chai Jiuyun, "since you are in the same line of business as Scrofulous Bai and work with him so closely, might it be possible for you to urge him a little with regard to a certain matter. After all, as the saying goes — 'It is better to quash bad feeling than to keep it alive.' Everyone should be at peace. As the old saying tells us, 'Stout upright fellows cherish and respect stout upright fellows.' There is no need for both parties to come off badly; that will always result in everybody getting hurt."

"Of course, of course, I am of the same opinion," replied Fang. "Everyone should be at peace."

"In that case might I ask that you go and have a word with Scrofulous Bai," Chai beseeched him. "Tonight I shall act as host and would like to invite him as my honoured guest to a feast at the Yileyuan restaurant, where I shall urge him and Brother Ma to drink a cup of conciliatory wine, while at the same time inviting all our brothers to appraise the situation."

"I'll go to Scrofulous Bai and expect that he will not decline your invitation. At this time of day he'll be holding a tea party at the Yidongtian teashop."

"On this occasion I would like to act as host," Ma Yongzhen interrupted. "Brother Chai, the day before yesterday, I sent my disciple to extend an invitation to you, but unfortunately you were busy at work and were unable to attend. It is indeed a rare opportunity that today, by lucky chance, yours truly is now in a position to spend a little money in your honor.

"Please don't speak like that!" Chai Jiuyun replied. "We are all of one family, why would you want to create divisions between us!"

"Very well, so that's settled," said Ma Yongzhen. "Let us ask Brother Fang to go and see what he can do."

Poxy Fang agreed.

"We shall be waiting in the Yileyuan restaurant," Chai Jiuyun added.

Fang nodded his head to show he understood, took a sip of tea, stood up, and walked off towards the staircase. Chai Jiuyun quickly followed him and whispered something in his ear. Fang nodded his head and appeared to give his approval, then he flew off down the staircase and out of the teashop.

Chai Jiuyun hurried back to where Ma Yongzhen and the others were sitting. "Let's go to Yileyuan and wait for them there."

He paid the bill and went with Ma Yongzhen and his disciples down the staircase, and directly on to the Yileyuan restaurant. On entering, a waiter came over to greet them and the four men took their seats. Cups, spoons, chopsticks, and plates were placed before them on the table.

"Please wait a moment," Chai Jiuyun told the waiter. "We are awaiting the arrival of some guests. Let's wait for them before we start." The waiter responded with a polite nod, then brought over a plate of sunflower seeds for them to nibble on, and poured four cups of tea for the guests, before going about his business. The four men talked jovially amongst themselves. They waited for more than half an hour but still Fang and Scrofulous Bai had not arrived.

"Brother Chai, it looks like that Scrofulous Bai man is not coming after all," Ma suggested.

"Perhaps he had something planned and that is the reason for his absence," Chai replied. "Let's write him an invitation to prod him a little."

"There's no need for any prodding," said Ma. "If he comes, that's fine, if he doesn't come, that's also fine."

"Don't speak like that. I have entrusted Brother Fang with relaying the invitation and that is already a not inconsiderable effort."

Having said this, Chai called on the waiter to bring him the wherewithal to draft some invitations. The waiter brought over a writing box and Chai picked up the brush to write two invitations, one for Scrofulous Bai and the other for Poxy Fang. At the same time he wrote the following words on the back of each: "The guests have already taken their seats and are awaiting your esteemed presence. Please do not delay."

When he finished writing, he called the waiter over to take the invitations to the Yidongtian teashop and wait for a reply. The waiter nodded and did as he was bade.

"Now that is done," Chai Jiuyun said, "we must wait a little while. I know Scrofulous Bai will turn up."

"Let's see," Ma replied, not entirely convinced.

If you want to know if Scrofulous Bai accepts the invitation, please read the following chapter.

12

Ma Yongzhen causes havoc in Yileyuan,
And Scrofulous Bai loses face on Fourth Avenue.

Let us continue to relate how Ma Yongzhen and Chai Jiuyun were waiting for Scrofulous Bai in the Yileyuan restaurant. Chai Jiuyun was hoping to act as go-between to make peace between Ma Yongzhen and Scrofulous Bai, so as to avoid things becoming disadvantageous to all. Ma Yongzhen agreed to this and offered to host a meal at the Yileyuan, and they were now waiting impatiently for their guests. Just at that moment, through the upstairs window, they saw two iron-tired rickshaws pull up outside, and two men jump down from them and boldly and vigorously walk in through the front door. The waiter came forward to welcome the men and invited them to be seated. They shook their heads and brought out bright red invitation cards to show him. As soon as the waiter saw these he invited the men to follow him and guided them into a private room upstairs where the hosts were already waiting. Chai Jiuyun was the first to see them enter; he stopped what he was saying, and promptly stood up.

"Brother Bai, I am honored by your presence. You have at last been able to accept my invitation."

"There is really no need for you to go to such expense," Scrofulous Bai replied, searching for something to say.

"Please do not stand on ceremony," Chai Jiuyun said. "This is a rare occasion indeed and Brother Fang kindly offered his assistance to arrange it. We are, after all, all of one family. Why would one say anything that does not acknowledge the truth of this!"

"Of course, of course. It was no trouble at all," Poxy Fang responded.

Ma Yongzhen politely half rose from his chair to welcome them. Everyone took their seats and the waiter brought some additional cups and chopsticks.

"Today I have brought brother Ma to act as host," Chai Jiuyun said, "and have instructed the waiter to prepare a sumptuous ten-dollar banquet."

"You really shouldn't have gone to such expense," Scrofulous Bai said again. "Just a few dishes would have done, there was no need to have ordered such an extravagant spread."

"Today we are all drinking together as a celebration of peace," Chai Jiuyun replied. "So, by rights, we should enjoy a lavish meal."

"Then how about if we eat a six-dollar banquet," Fang suggested. "That means we will still be enjoying a celebratory drink, and it is a celebratory drink that is most fitting for the occasion. There is no need to go to any unnecessary expense."

Just at this moment the waiter brought in the wine together with four appetizers.

"We have ordered a ten-dollar banquet, but why don't we select one that costs six dollars instead," said Fang, reiterating his suggestion.

"What is the difference between the ten- and six-dollar banquets?" Chai asked the waiter.

"With the ten-dollar banquet you get a whole chicken and a whole duck, four different seafood dishes, and four side dishes."

"What about the six-dollar banquet?"

"For that you get half a chicken and half a duck, two seafood dishes, and two side dishes."

Chai Jiuyun gave no reply but Fang quickly piped up. "Make it a six-dollar banquet then."

The waiter agreed with a polite nod and went off to prepare the food for a six-dollar banquet.

Chai Jiuyun picked up the wine pot and poured drinks all round. When the food arrived, the six men paid attention only to eating the chicken, duck, fish, and meat, devouring it greedily, without lowering their chopsticks. After a while, Chai Jiuyun broached the subject: "Brother Bai, I urge you to make peace. Do not make a mountain out of a mole hill. It is always prudent to be peace loving. Brother Ma, you are in a place far from home, so you must at least be a little tolerant of things. Please do not be overly bold or take too many liberties."

"Those of us who are away from home and are guests in a foreign land know that we must compromise a little, unlike this…" Before Ma could finish his sentence Scrofulous Bai interrupted, his mouth going wherever his mind led him: "How can it be that I've bullied you? You think about it for yourself. I instructed Lu the Lackey to sell you eight fine horses, well…if you didn't want them you should have just said so. You shouldn't have ridden them to the point where they became exhausted. Brother Chai, you act as referee here. Who owes who? As the saying goes, a bachelor should not say impolite things, otherwise he will not get what he wants. If it is I, Scrofulous Bai, who is in debt, despite everything, then please decide on my punishment. Brothers-in-arms are never hasty in saying negative things about one another. It is that Ma man who is at fault, but whatever is to be done shall depend on your goodwill, Brother Chai. I have come today and shall listen to your mediation, but you must also listen to reason. I am not one to use forceful language, so whatever you have to say I'll go along with it. But you must not be prejudiced in what you say."

"Neither has what I've said strayed from the truth," Poxy Fang said. "This is all in the past now, there is no need to go collecting snails in clear water — as the saying goes — to stir things up that have already been dealt with."

"Brother Bai, why don't we let this matter rest?" Chai Jiuyun suggested. "We are all of one family. Please give me some face, forget all about it and speak of it no more. Why don't we just drink wine and everyone will be happy. Let's say no more about it."

In response, Scrofulous Bai drank three cups of wine, one after the other. Then, feeling a little worse for wear, he got to his feet. Scrofulous Bai's capacity for alcohol was limited. "Let's drink then!" He said. Thereupon, he threw back his head and downed three more cups in turn. When the wine reached his stomach, the situation deteriorated very rapidly. The gods of the five inner organs had already gathered together and forbade the demons of wine to approach any further, but they were just at that minute attacking, one after another, and the situation remained unresolved. Suddenly, several other wine demons joined the attack. How could the gods of the inner organs tolerate this! They joined forces to retaliate, creating havoc in Scrofulous Bai's belly so that he saw no respite at all and his stomach felt truly terrible.

Meanwhile, his face was turning redder all the time. Having drunk several cups of wine, Scrofulous Bai lost all scruples and started to address them again, now at the top of his voice.

"Brother Chai, today you have invited me for a drink, but unless that Ma man compensates me for the price of those eight horses, you must tell him to get down on his knees and knock his head on the floor in front of me three times."

...Everything came to a sudden stop...

"Let's...let's not talk this way," Fang said, trying to save the situation.

"Rubbish!" Scrofulous Bai shouted. "If I'm not allowed to talk about this, you are allowing that Ma Man to refute everything. If you are ganging up to bully me some more, that doesn't bother me at all."

He just wouldn't stop talking, and what he did say became more and more incomprehensible. Ma Yongzhen listened to everything he said and was far from pleased. A sudden burst of fury arose in his belly.

"Spawn of a turtle!" He yelled, banging his fist on the table.

That blow did not seem to be particularly heavy, but it sent everything on the table flying in the air, wine cups, plates, and spoons. Ma stood up and bellowed at Scrofulous Bai: "I have bullied you? You bag of pus. You dare to say that I have bullied you!"

As he said this, he made a grab for him across the table. Chai Jiuyun and Poxy Fang saw this coming and stood up to urge him to desist.

"Brother Ma, let him go and we can talk about it," Chai said.

"Brother Ma, there is no need to be like this," Poxy Fang added. "Brother Bai has just had too much to drink."

"That despicable knave!" Ma Yongzhen interrupted. "Is he even human? What he drank just now wasn't wine at all, it was piss from his own piss pot."

When he heard Ma Yongzhen suggest he had drunk his own urine, Scrofulous Bai began to bellow at the top of his voice: "What I drank is the finest Shao-Hsing Huadiao yellow wine. It's you who is a piss guzzler!" As he said this he grabbed a full cup of wine from the table and aimed it, wine and all, at Ma's head. Ma Yongzhen was keen of eye and swift of hand. He caught the cup in mid-air and flung it straight back. It flew directly with great accuracy straight at Scrofulous Bai's head. But he too was swift of eye, and he ducked out of the way to avoid being hit.

"You would dare hit me!" Scrofulous Bai screamed in response to Ma throwing the cup. He had deflected the cup, that entirely innocent cup, which ended up smashed to pieces in place of a person. Ma Yongzhen heard Scrofulous Bai's slanderous suggestion that *he* had tried to hit *him* and was overcome with fury.

"You bag of pus," he bellowed. "If you think I hit you just now, then watch how I really hit you. How are you going to protect yourself now?"

As he said this he jumped up, and facing Scrofulous Bai head on, raised his arm and aimed a punch at him. At which point, Scrofulous Bai drunkenly spurred him on. He too went to land a punch, but was unsteady on his feet. He slipped backwards, fell head over heels, and lay flat on his back looking straight up at the ceiling.

It turns out that the contest between Ma Yongzhen and Scrofulous Bai was an uneven match. Naturally, as Scrofulous Bai had drunk several cups of that yellow wine, he was unable to defend himself against Ma Yongzhen's

*superhuman strength, and just lay on the ground, shouting
and bellowing away.*

Ma Yongzhen rushed over and straddled Scrofulous Bai's
body, raining down punches on him until he was squealing
like a pig in a slaughterhouse. Chai Jiuyun and Poxy Fang did
their best to ease the situation, but Scrofulous Bai had already
been beaten to a sorry state, to the point that he was now almost
unrecognizable. Double-tailed Scorpion and Single-horned
Dragon both did their best to placate their master and sat him
down by the side. Fang and Chai helped Scrofulous Bai up from
the floor and urged him to be seated. They called the waiter over
to bring some napkins and hot towels, then wiped Scrofulous
Bai's face, poured a cup of tea and implored him to calm down
and rest for a while. He was seated in a chair, but was still panting
heavily. Catching his breath he mumbled: "You lot have ganged
up to plot against me. Chai Jiuyun, weren't you supposed to be
some sort of mediator and were here to pacify everything? It
turns out that you have a bellyful of wickedness. You made me
drink too much and got that Ma man to beat me up." He was
saying all this to himself. Chai Jiuyun knew he had had too much
to drink, and it was just the wine talking, so he paid no heed and
allowed him to continue spouting nonsense.

"Brother Bai, enough of this drunken talk," said Poxy Fang.
"Everyone has behaved in good faith, and were just offering you
advice, taking it upon themselves to try to mediate peace. You
have been drinking. It was you who drank that yellow wine all
by yourself, and you who said those drunken words."

"You! You're ignoring your friends and colluding with
outsiders," Scrofulous Bai shouted at Poxy Fang, "and have
helped those interlopers to do all those terrible things to me.
Today, I, Scrofulous Bai, would rather not go on living, and will

fight to the death with you all. You have bullied me into this state and I have lost all face, and won't be able to meet anyone in person ever again, so I may as well die right here, right now."

When he had finished ranting, he got up off the floor, and, like an old vulture flapping its outstretched wings, went straight for Ma Yongzhen. Ma simply stepped aside and a loud crash could be heard in the empty space that was left behind.

If you want to know what happened next, please read the following chapter.

13

Scrofulous Bai gets drunk and makes a scene,
And Poxy Fang smokes opium and talks of personal things.

Let us proceed to relate how Ma Yongzhen saw Scrofulous Bai lunge forward and quickly ducked out of the way, and how Boss Bai collided with thin air and came crashing to the floor, turning an already-ruined banquet completely upside down. Cups, plates, spoons, and bowls were strewn all over the floor, and the whole room was in a complete mess.

The sound of everything falling to the floor, though, was ever so pleasing to the ear.

Leftover food and assorted liquids were spilled all over the place and Poxy Fang's new Prussian-blue, crepe silk *changpao* was now spattered all over with grease spots. Fang was furious. He pulled Scrofulous Bai up off the floor and spoke to the room:

"How can a person be so reckless!"

Scrofulous Bai had been pulled up off the floor but he was unsteady on his feet. His body was like a weeping willow swaying in the wind and he was in real danger of toppling over.

"Brother Fang, you're bullying me too," moaned Scrofulous Bai. "No wonder that Ma man has hit..." Before he could finish what he was saying, Scrofulous Bai had grabbed hold of the front of Poxy Fang's brand new gown to steady himself, and pulled down on the neckband with such force that it ripped all the way down the front. Fang was fuming. He was already upset about the grease spots, but now that his gown had been ripped in two, he became absolutely livid. With nothing left to grab onto Scrofulous Bai fell to the floor again, flopping forward as he hit the ground. Outside the private dining room, the waiter heard the sound of smashing crockery and men arguing, and hurried in to see what was happening. He saw that the whole place was strewn with shattered crockery and someone was lying on the floor. Someone else was standing over him shouting furiously, and his gown was ripped right down the middle into two quite separate pieces. The waiter looked on and didn't know what to do, so he backed out of the room and went to tell the owner, Boss Wang. As soon as Boss Wang heard news of the fight, he hurried over to take a look. He saw that the man who had been lying on the floor had been helped to his feet, but was still cursing nonstop at the top of his voice, while another man standing next to him was trying his best to pacify him.

He took a look around and addressed Chai Jiuyun: "May I ask your name, sir?" What sort of man was Chai Jiuyun if he didn't know that the real reason for Boss Wang entering the room was to obtain compensation for the broken crockery?

"Your humble servant, Chai Jiuyun, at your service," he promptly replied. "All breakages shall of course be paid for." As soon as Boss Wang heard these words he realized this was a man of substance, who must hold some influence in Shanghai society, so he calmed down considerably, and when he understood Chai was even willing to pay compensation, he said, with a smile like the spring breeze lighting up his face: "Mr Chai, it is not that I have come to ask for compensation. The waiters told me a fight had broken out, so I came straight over to try and calm things down. No doubt someone has had a little too much to drink. Don't trouble yourself about those broken things," he added as he looked about him in all directions. Then he noticed Ma Yongzhen was also present and walked over to talk to him.

"Boss Ma, you are here, too, please excuse my lack of manners."

"I am here indeed. Please draw up a bill for the breakages and I shall pay you compensation."

"Understood, understood." Boss Wang replied. Then he called the waiter over and told him to clear up everything off the floor and bring hot towels for everyone to freshen up. With this he backed out of the room and went off to draw up a bill, which moments later he brought back in himself. News of the fight had spread, and in no time at all everyone around got to know about it. Amongst them was a man called Li Sibao, who was one of the hundred and one men who had been inducted as Ma Yongzhen's new disciples. His nickname "Knife-Wielding Demon" was that of the character Cao Zheng in *The Water Margin*. As soon as he heard that Ma Yongzhen was involved in the fight, he quickly dropped what he was doing and rushed over to the restaurant. When he saw that Ma Yongzhen was indeed present, he saluted him, using the secret gangland salute he had so recently learned.

"How is it that you are here, too?" Ma asked, as soon as he saw this.

"I work as a comprador close by," Li Sibao replied and turned to greet his brothers-in-arms, Double-tailed Scorpion and Single-horned Dragon. Boss Wang came over and handed a detailed bill to Ma Yongzhen. Ma took it in his hand and read it through. Together with the six-dollar banquet, it came to roughly eleven dollars.

"All in all it comes to eleven dollars, is that correct?" He asked Boss Wang, and it was confirmed to be the case. Ma Yongzhen promptly fished out a crisp ten-dollar, Mackellar Bank note and handed it to Boss Wang. "Is it all right if I make up the balance later?"

"Please do whatever is most convenient," Boss Wang replied.

"I don't have it today but I shall let you have it tomorrow, if that's alright."

Before he even had time to answer, Li Sibao came over and addressed the owner:

"Boss Wang, please return the ten dollars to Master Ma. I'll give you eleven dollars myself."

Chai Jiuyun also overheard that Ma was about to pay and walked over.

"Whoever heard of such a thing? How could I expect Brother Ma to be out of pocket!"

Thereupon he took the money from Boss Wang's hand and passed it back to Ma Yongzhen. Then he fished out two five-dollar notes from within his sleeve, where he kept his money, and gave them to Boss Wang. Li Sibao saw that someone else was settling the bill and decided to say no more about it.

Meanwhile, the effects of the drink had worn off considerably and Scrofulous Bai was beginning to realize that he had created a rather embarrassing situation, so he sneaked off without saying a word to anyone. After a while, everyone stopped what they were doing, and on seeing that Scrofulous Bai was no longer there, concluded that he had departed in embarrassment.

Thereupon, all the guests left the restaurant and sped off in a westerly direction.

"Why don't we go to an opium house and smoke a modest pipe or two," Poxy Fang suggested to Chai Jiuyun. "Then we can talk about what just happened."

"So you like to smoke then?"

"Although my habit is not much to speak of, when I'm in a good mood I often take a puff.

"I also like to smoke a little for fun," Chai said. "But it is just as well I rarely smoke, for, as soon as I partake of it, it makes me very tired indeed."

The two of them were chatting away as Ma and his disciples walked behind them, and they were so engrossed in conversation that they were surprised when they arrived in front of the opium house. All five men then entered through the front door. As soon as the opium servant saw Poxy Fang he stood up to greet him. Fang returned the greeting and asked him if any couches were available. The servant replied that there were, and led them into an adjacent room. He lit an opium lamp, prepared a pot of tea, brought out a water pipe, and selected two small boxes of fine quality *chandu*. Poxy Fang then indicated to Chai Jiuyun that he should lie down on the couch.

"I have no craving at the moment," said Chai. "Why don't you lie down and smoke first?"

Fang did not stand on ceremony and took the place of honor.

"Brother Ma, would you like to take a place on the couch next to me?" Chai Jiuyun asked Ma Yongzhen.

"I have never liked to partake," Ma replied. "When I smell opium smoke, it makes me feel rather queasy. It would be best if I sit at a little distance away. Brother Chai, why don't you have some?"

Thereupon, Chai Jiuyun lay down on Fang's right and waited

for him to cook the opium over the glass lamp.

"Today Scrofulous Bai was a real disgrace," Poxy Fang said. "Even falling over and taking a beating from Brother Ma. That is nothing but a sin against his own person."

"He drank far too much today and made such a terrible scene," agreed Chai Jiuyun.

"Yes, when you drink wine you should at least have some sense of decorum," Fang exclaimed. "Just now he made such a pig's ear of everything."

"Though he behaved badly, and brought the beating on himself, since he came at our invitation I do feel a little sorry that he went home in that state all alone."

"How can a person like that speak of friendship?" Poxy Fang asked. "If he knew what friendship was he would never have ended up like that." As he said this he prepared the opium pipe and handed it to Chai Jiuyun.

"Please do take some yourself," Chai politely declined. "I am quite all right for the moment. You satisfy your craving first."

Fang took a draw on the pipe as he cooked it over the flame of the opium lamp, and when he had fully satisfied himself, he took a sip of tea. He stretched out on the couch and rested for a while, then spoke—now in a slow and drawn out way, "Brother Chai, you are aware that having suffered this loss, there is no way Scrofulous Bai will let things lie. He'll most certainly want to retaliate and come looking for us. There is no way of knowing what he'll do next. Thankfully, I am not of a timid disposition."

"In the end, I cannot refute what you say," replied Chai. "Even his own brothers-in-arms don't know what he has up his sleeve."

Poxy Fang lay on his right side, cooking more opium as he held the pipe in his right hand above the glass chimney of the metal lamp. He shook his head, to show his disapproval of Scrofulous Bai's conduct, without lifting it from the porcelain pillow on which it was resting. Still lying down, he stretched out his left hand to grasp the pipe and placed it down on the tray in front of him, after which he replenished it with opium, and again invited Chai Jiuyun to smoke. This time Chai accepted the invitation and he took three long drags on the pipe in quick succession. Then, when he had finished off everything in the pipe, he took a sip of tea.

"Brother Chai, how do you find the taste of this opium?"

I'm not a regular smoker so I can't really tell if it's good or bad just by smoking it, but I feel it is quite flavorsome, and there is nothing at all gaseous about it."

"The opium in this place should be considered amongst the best in the city," continued Fang. "It is much the same as that sold at Nanchengxin on Kiangse Road, Shanghai's finest opium house. They are one of my customers, and are always especially attentive in achieving the desired result."

"No wonder after savoring this opium there is a fragrant aftertaste that lingers in the mouth," enthused Chai Jiuyun.

"We tend to find that *chandu* opium from Madras produces a fine quality ash, which can be gathered up and used again."

"How often do you come here?" Chai asked, changing the subject.

"I come here every day, rain or shine."

The two of them lay on the couches talking freely and were starting to feel really quite relaxed. Ma Yongzhen, on the other hand, was getting rather impatient, and suddenly got to his feet.

If you want to know what happened next, please read the following chapter.

14

Strolling round Lunghwa, on the dyke horses are ridden,
And climbing the pagoda, in the suburbs falcons are flown.

Let us continue to relate how Poxy Fang and Chai Jiuyun were
chatting together in the opium house. Just as they were reaching
a state of total satisfaction, smoking opium and sipping tea, and
driving their cares away, Ma Yongzhen, who had been sitting off
to the side, began to show a little impatience.

"I must be going now," he said, suddenly getting to his feet.
"I'm afraid I am unable to keep you company any longer and
offer you my sincerest apologies."

Chai and Fang both sat up. They told him they would be
staying, and apologized for not seeing him to the door.

"Please feel free to do as you wish for now," said Chai Jiuyun,
"but the day after tomorrow is the third day of the third month,
the Double Third Festival. Anyone who's anyone in Shanghai will
be going to Lunghwa to take a stroll amongst the peach blossom.

There will be an endless stream of horses and carriages, and the festive atmosphere will be brimming over with expectation and excitement. What do you think, Brother Ma, about being refined and elegant of mind, and going there together to view the peach blossom on that day?"

"That sounds like a fine idea to me, I should say so! I am but a visitor here and still feel rather lonely. As Zhou Bangyan wrote in his poem: at this time of year, while far from home, I should regret allowing time to pass in vain. The light in spring is fine and bright, just perfect to go roaming amongst the peach blossom. I will certainly accompany you there."

"That's settled then. The day after tomorrow I shall go to your residence and we'll proceed to Lunghwa together from there."

Ma Yongzhen said a few words of agreement, bowed his head, clasping his hands together in front of him, and bade farewell to Chai and Fang. Then, with bold broad strides, he walked out of the opium house.

A single brush cannot write two lines at once; one mouth cannot tell of two things at the same time. I shall set aside one matter to talk of another.

Let us continue to relate how Ma Yongzhen bade farewell to Chai and Fang. He came out of the opium house, taking his two disciples with him, and went straight to his residence on Sinza Road.

If there is something to be said, it should be described in detail; if there is nothing to be said then the description should be kept short.

It was the third day of the third month, the time of the Double

Third Festival. The weather was clear and bright and the sun was pleasantly warm. Not even the smallest particle of dust could be seen floating in the air. It was a time of mild and tranquil weather, perfect for the joys of sightseeing and horseback riding.

That day Ma Yongzhen woke up early. Before noon he had already performed his ablutions and was waiting for Chai Jiuyun to come to his house. When Chai arrived, Ma Yongzhen welcomed him with much excitement and invited him to be seated.

"The weather today is magnificent, and many people are already out and about viewing the peach blossom. I suggest it would be a good idea if we two were to set off sooner rather than later," said Chai.

"Brother Chai, have you eaten lunch?"

"Why yes, the clock has already struck two and I ate lunch before leaving home."

"Very well, I agree that we should leave right away."

"Let's go there by carriage," Chai suggested.

"Carriages are too slow. I think riding there on horseback would be more invigorating. Brother Chai, do you like riding?"

"Brother Ma, as you want to go there on horseback, I shall certainly accompany you, but my horsemanship cannot be compared to yours. You are a famous rider and everyone in Shanghai knows about that time you took the Race Club by storm."

"Brother Chai don't make fun of me," he said with false modesty. "That incident is not even worth mentioning." Ma Yongzhen instructed his servants to bring out two horses and the two men made themselves comfortable in their saddles and set out to ride all the way to Lunghwa. The sound of the hooves on the road clop, clop, clop, contrasted with that on the green fragrant grass that carpeted the ground like a soft mattress, as they followed along the long dyke to Lunghwa. Here grew peach and willow trees, the contrasting shades of red and green, most satisfying to the eye.

> *The petals of the peach blossom and the catkins on the willow trees bring about feelings of sorrowful regret, like those one experiences in a foreign land far from home, or like those of a young lady cosseted in an attic room, looking down on the world from a window high above, experiencing melancholy at the arrival of spring. On seeing the green willows of the season by the side of the road, the poetry of Wang Changling is brought to mind, causing one to experience a heightened sense of nostalgia and remembrance.*

Ma Yongzhen and Chai Jiuyun rode their horses along the long dyke by the river, observing the splendid scenery as they passed by. Meanwhile, the carriages and horses of the pleasure seekers filled the roads. All around there could be seen silken riding crops and hats, and beautiful ornamental carriages like those described in the poetry of Ouyang Xiu, a bustling and joyous atmosphere that it is hard to put into words. Soon, Chai and Ma arrived at Lunghwa and encountered crowds of men and women, as numerous as the threads in a piece of woven cloth, or as fish swimming together in a shimmering shoal. Ma Yongzhen selected an empty piece of land at which to dismount. Chai Jiuyun joined him there and they tethered their horses to a willow tree, allowing the animals to graze on the lush green grass that grew there. The two men patted off the dust from their clothes as they walked over together to the Lunghwa Temple. All manner of things were on sale at the peddlers' stalls that had been set up by the main gate of the temple. There were edibles to be consumed and many other things for practical daily use.

Throngs of people had arrived, and Lay Buddhists, male adepts and female devotees, entered the temple in an endless stream. Some carried yellow cloth incense bags over their shoulders and in their hands were long chains of silver ingots made of paper, threaded together to be burnt as offerings to the ancestors. They squeezed through the crowd and the paper ingots came along with them. Ma Yongzhen pushed his way into the throng of people that had gathered at the massive double gates and entered the temple complex.

A gang of wastrel youths was loafing around, shallow and slippery young men. When they saw women they deliberately moved forward to surround them and indulged their desires by touching their bodies on the sly. The women were helpless in the big crowd, and could do nothing but scream out loud. On seeing that sort of thing, how could Ma Yongzhen tolerate it? He pushed his way through the crowd and pulled those young ruffians out. How could they resist Ma Yongzhen's superhuman strength? They were soon expelled, flying this way and that, and eventually managed to stumble away from the crowd. Those young ruffians thought about making it hard for Ma Yongzhen, but amongst them were a couple of horse grooms who recognized him, and they signaled to the others to warn them off, saying that this was the man who had beaten up Yellow Beard. Realizing they were no match for Ma, the young delinquents scattered in all directions, like stars in the sky at night.

Just then, Chai Jiuyun, who had fallen behind, noticed Ma Yongzhen in the crowd, so he squeezed in, turning sideways to push his way through, as he called out to him. Ma Yongzhen heard someone call his name, so he looked around and finally realized who it was.

"Brother Chai, where did you get to just now?" he asked.

"I went round the back to take a pee and saw some falconers

with their birds of prey. I watched them for a while, then came here to look for you, but you are so quick on your feet and had already made your way into the crowd. No one can be blamed for calling you by your nickname, 'four-footed Ma'."

"I noticed that you were nowhere to be seen," Ma replied, "so I went by myself through the main temple gate to take a look. There I saw a gang of young ruffians surrounding women devotees who had come to burn incense, and they were doing exactly as they pleased with them, laughing lasciviously, and even touching their bodies. When I saw them daring to do that sort of thing in the broad light of day, right before my eyes, how could I possibly allow it to continue?"

"Young ruffians, sure enough, will always be young ruffians, but why would you go and interfere with them?"

"If I wasn't going to chastise them, what would I be doing in middle of this crowd?"

"Brother Ma, it turns out you have been saving damsels in distress."

Ma Yongzhen didn't even have time to reply, before he noticed that the women he'd saved a moment ago heard Chai Jiuyun's words, and blushing to the roots of their hair, they lowered heads, and hurried off into the temple.

"Brother Chai, let's go in and enjoy ourselves for a while too." Chai Jiuyun agreed and they entered Lunghwa Temple together. They visited the splendid Mahavira Hall and found that it actually wasn't all that different to the temples they had seen in the past. Nevertheless, they looked around them with great respect, then went to the pagoda to amuse themselves there.

From high up on the pagoda they looked out over Shanghai, that lonely city, all laid out before their eyes, just as if it had shrunk to a size where it could all be placed on a table top. In the distance, on the Huangpu River, sailing ships could be faintly made out, like pieces of white cloud floating past atop the waves. Ma Yongzhen watched for a while, thinking to himself that the scenery really was quite marvellous. Then he walked up another level. Leaning over the perilous railings he looked out as far as the eye could see.

"Brother Chai, come up here," he called out to Chai below. "You can see the whole city from up here. It's like looking at the stars dotted around in the sky, or chess pieces laid out on a board." He hadn't quite finished speaking when Chai Jiuyun hastily replied: "I can't come up. The soles of my feet are far too painful, and what's more, the upper floors are really quite dangerous. They haven't been repaired for years, and the condition of the balconies is very troubling."

"Brother Chai, you are being overcautious, although the pagoda is indeed run down, it certainly wouldn't fall if you, just one person, were to come up one more level."

"There's not much fun to be had upstairs. Let's go down again and find somewhere else to enjoy our stroll," Chai insisted, trying to hide his fear of heights.

Ma Yongzhen heard Chai Jiuyun's suggestion that they go elsewhere to take their stroll, so he descended one floor, as happy as could be.

"Come on then, let's go," he said cheerfully to Chai Jiuyun as he passed.

"Not so fast!" Chai said, as he pulled Ma over. "Come and look at what's happening over there. It looks like great fun." Ma Yongzhen went forward to the railings, looked into the distance but couldn't see a thing.

"What are you looking at? I can't see anything at all."

"Look over there, there are falconers flying their birds," Chai Jiuyun said, pointing into the distance. "Can you see that?" Ma Yongzhen looked in the direction to which he was pointing, and sure enough he could see a number of people flying their pet falcons. There were large falcons and smaller falcons; there were those falconers whose birds had come first — they were laughing heartily, and there were others whose falcons had come last — they were looking dejected. Ma Yongzhen saw this and couldn't help being overjoyed by the scene. He began to clap his hands and cheer, attracting the attention of bystanders. Ma Yongzhen didn't see anything untoward about this and continued to clap his hands and laugh.

"Brother Ma, let's go downstairs and take a closer look. It will certainly be more relaxing than watching it from high up in the pagoda."

"You can see everything quite clearly from here, and looking at things from above, of course, is particularly agreeable." The two men debated this for a while, and by the time they had finished they saw that the falconers were no longer flying their birds and the spectators had all moved on.

"As they're not flying their falcons anymore," said Ma, "let's leave the pagoda and continue our stroll elsewhere." Chai Jiuyun agreed, and the two men descended the pagoda, one level at a time, down to the lowest level, where no light penetrated at all and it was as black as night. Ma Yongzhen walked round this lowest level in the dark and called out loud to test the echo.

If you want to know what happened next, please read the following chapter.

15

Wine imbibed, Ma Yongzhen takes tea with courtesans,
And Chai Jiuyun laughs out loud in a high-class brothel.

Let us continue to relate how Ma Yongzhen and Chai Jiuyun descended the Lunghwa Pagoda down to its lowest level. It was so dark that Ma Yongzhen couldn't even see the five fingers of his hand when he lifted it up in front of him.

"Oh my heavens! It's so dark down here!" he exclaimed.

"Don't make such a fuss, the lowest level of a pagoda is always like this," Chai Jiuyun playfully chastised him.

They fumbled around in the dark for a while and eventually managed to find their way out through the main door. Then they went round the back of the tower to the place they had seen the falcons, but all that remained were a few wastrels tidying things up. They noticed a man holding four falcons. Others had more than they could possibly carry alone so they had hired others to help move them. By now the spectators had all departed when they saw there were no more falcons being flown.

"Brother Ma, let's go home, too! Look at the sun setting over the tops of the trees, sinking slowly, as if it were about to vanish behind the legendary Yanzi Mountains. The revelers are dispersing and returning to their homes. Each of them holding sprigs of peach blossom in their hands, delighted and overjoyed, showing to all that they have been strolling amongst the peach trees at Lunghwa."

"All right, let's go home then!" Ma Yongzhen conceded.

They retrieved the horses from under the willow tree. Ma Yongzhen mounted his horse, straightened out the reins, and struck the horse lightly on its rump with his riding crop. The horse bent its front legs, straightened its back legs, raised its tail up in the air, and with a loud and determined snort, set off in the direction of the setting sun, the sound of its hooves changing as it skipped over the short grass and smooth sand. Chai Jiuyun followed on behind. Ma Yongzhen, rode swiftly at a gallop, without pausing for rest, and before long he arrived at his Sinza residence. He dismounted and his followers came to take the horse away and unsaddle it in the stables. After a while Chai Jiuyun also arrived.

"Why the delay?" Ma asked.

"I bumped into someone I know at Nicheng Bridge. As we passed each other he called out to me, so I got down from my horse and chatted with him for a while. That's the only reason I was late getting here."

"Let's go in and rest for a while." Ma suggested, and Chai Jiuyun followed him indoors. Though the house was small, it was always kept clean and tidy. Upstairs was Ma Yongzhen's bedroom and his disciples slept in the wings. At the front was the reception room with a kitchen at the back, and there was a paddock and stables in the open ground behind the house. Chai

Jiuyun made himself comfortable and the disciples brought in tea, and poured two bowls of hot water for them to wash their faces.

"Today it is a rare treat indeed to be honored with your presence," Ma Yongzhen said when they had refreshed themselves. "Brother Chai, please join me for a meal."

"There is no need for such formalities, let's go out to eat," Chai replied. Noticing the clock had already struck seven Ma Yongzhen agreed, and taking Chai Jiuyun by the hand, he led him out of the door.

They called for two rickshaws to take them to Foochow Road. On arrival at the entrance to the Da Qingguan restaurant, they paid their fare, went inside, walked up the central staircase and found somewhere to sit. The waiter came over to greet them and Ma Yongzhen invited Chai Jiuyun to order the food.

"Just bring a few dishes as you wish, there is no need to discuss it," Chai Jiuyun told the waiter.

"A few fresh dishes will be fine," Ma Yongzhen agreed.

The waiter nodded in approval and shouted their order downstairs. After a short while he brought over the food and drink to them and they proceeded to pour wine and chat away with gusto.

After a while, Ma was starting to feel a little restless. "Drinking this 'mute wine' is no fun at all," he said. "Let's play a drinking game. That should liven things up a bit."

So the two men began their game, shouting out numbers and comparing how many fingers they were each holding up. They continued to play until neither was able to drink another drop.

"Brother Chai, tell me, who did you come across at Nicheng Bridge?"

"You know him too. Scrofulous Bai's second in command, Lu the Lackey."

"What did Lu the Lackey want with you?"

"Haven't you heard?" asked Chai.

"What about? Lu the Lackey and I are on opposing sides. He is Scrofulous Bai's man, and he and I have nothing to do with each other."

"That's right, Lu the Lackey is not on your side. He told me that Scrofulous Bai has called on the Axe Head Gang, and they will be coming to look for you."

"What! Scrofulous Bai plans to put out a hit on me? That's ridiculous. It would be like trying to crack a stone with an egg. What is this Axe Head Gang anyway? However formidable they may think they are, I, Ma Yongzhen, will never be afraid of them. This is just Lu the Lackey telling fibs. He is trying to put the frighteners on. It's like, as the saying goes — 'a dragon-fly shaking a stone pillar'. He's simply overestimating his abilities. Don't give it another thought."

"Even though what Lu the Lackey says can never be trusted, this time we should at least pay it some heed. Scrofulous Bai has suffered a serious humiliation and will not be willing to let it lie. He will cast aside all concerns and gather together the Axe Head Gang to fight to the death with you, if I'm not very much mistaken. There is a well-known saying — 'It is hard for one man to defeat four people; they are many and their hand is strong.' Your abilities as an individual are great indeed, but you will not be able to defeat them, as they are many in number. I think, my friend, you need to be very careful indeed."

"Brother Chai, I am indebted to you, and thank you for your concern. How could I not give my thanks to you! But I am not boasting, and please do not laugh at me when I say that in the end there is absolutely no possibility that they would be able to defeat me. Ordinarily, it would take ten or twenty men to even come close to beating me."

"Brother Ma, your martial skills are legendary and you are indeed very brave. But if they choose to play dirty and mount a secret attack, you really must be on your guard. There is a saying—'it is easy to dodge a spear in the open, but hard to guard against a hidden weapon'."

"Quite right, secret attacks and hidden weapons must indeed be guarded against," thought Ma to himself.

The two men ate their fill, drank much wine and ended up feeling rather tipsy. They called the waiter to bring two bowls of rice to finish off the meal, and once they had polished those off, they paid up and went downstairs. Outside, darkness had descended, and the streets were ablaze with lanterns. Everywhere was bustling with excitement as people crowded the streets, their colorful clothing resembling fine-patterned brocade as they rushed to and fro like shuttles in a loom.

"Brother Ma, how about we take a stroll in that direction."

"Let's go to watch an opera! What do you think?"

"What has been advertised on the billboards today?"

"I'm not sure either, said Ma Yongzhen. "In truth, watching opera is nothing but a little ephemeral excitement. It is over in no time."

"But this is no fun at all, either," Chai Jiuyun said. "How about we go to a bawdy house and drink some tea?"

It turns out Ma Yongzhen didn't care one way or the other, but strolling around without a definite goal didn't appeal to him either, so he agreed to go.

"Let's visit Hua Baoyu's establishment in Puqing Li, off Stone Street, and have some fun," Chai Jiuyun suggested.

"Very well then! Why don't we go there on foot?"

The two men set out for their destination and in no time at all they arrived at Puqing Li, off Stone Street (that is Fuhkien Road to you and me). They entered Hua Baoyu's place and the male servant, the "turtle", announced their arrival. Chai and Ma walked up the staircase, and found the maidservant Ah Hong had already come out to greet them.

"Boss Chai, ya aint bin 'ere fer ages. Please come in n' put yer feet up."

Chai Jiuyun nodded his head and entered the room with Ma Yongzhen. On entering, Ma looked around at the furnishings. There was a day bed made of *hongmu* wood, inlaid with enamel, which was hung with a light green, fine silk, mosquito net. It had a canopy and borders of crimson satin and the entrance to the bed was hung up with silver hooks. On the bed itself were two neatly folded crepe silk quilts. A vase of flowers, a chiming mantel clock, and things of that nature, sat atop the *hongmu* dressing table, which stood against the wall, and along the adjacent wall, under the windows, several tea tables and elegant folding chairs were placed. Among these was a *hongmu* wood *penghu* games table. Everything was scattered around and laid out in exquisite taste. Chai Jiuyun and Ma Yongzhen sat down and Ah Hong brought over some tea and tobacco.

"Would ya Adam and Eve it! She ain't 'iden, I swear. Miss 'as gorn ert singin' and aint come back yet. Boss Chai, I'm weerly sowwy." Ah Hong changed the subject, asking, "and what's va Monica of vis 'ere noble genttwmen?"

Ma Yongzhen was given no chance to reply before Chai Jiuyun jumped in. "He is Ma Yongzhen of Shandong, the same who thrice toppled the foreigner Yellow Beard."

"Ah! So you're Boss Ma, vat stout yeoman. No wonder you're such a fine figure of a man. Take a butchers at ya muscles, so firm and strong."

Ma Yongzhen heard Ah Hong speak with the mellifluous flow of the local language, but understood not even half of what she said.

"What did she just say?" Ma asked Chai Jiuyun.

"She said you're fine figure of a man and she wants to marry you."

"Is that true...really?"

"Of course it's true. Would I lie to you?"

Ma Yongzhen was delighted to hear this. "Will you act as matchmaker?" he asked excitedly.

"If I act as matchmaker, how are you going to repay me?"

"I'll invite you to my wedding."

Chai Jiuyun heard this and laughed out loud. The maidservant was standing at the side leaning against the table. A Shanghai girl through and through, she couldn't understand Ma's northern accent either, so chuckling nervously, she asked Chai Jiuyun: "Boss Chai, what is Boss Ma sayin'? Why ya larffin so lardly? What funny fing were ya tellin' 'im just now? Do us a favor, tew' me and make me larf 'n all!"

On hearing Ah Hong say this, Chai Jiuyun laughed even louder. Clapping his hands together, he just couldn't stop himself. Ma Yongzhen and Chai Jiuyun carrying on in this way made her even more curious.

"Boss Chai, what's so funny?" she asked again. "What's va egg yoke ya just told 'im?"

Chai Jiuyun repeated the question to Ma Yongzhen and thought it even funnier than before.

If you want to know what happens next, please read the following chapter.

16

Scrofulous Bai deliberates on how to get rid of Ma Yongzhen,
And Lu the Lackey engages the services of the Axe Head Gang.

Let us continue to relate how on hearing what was said Chai
Jiuyun began to loudly guffaw, clapping his hands and stamping
his feet. Ma Yongzhen was utterly perplexed. As the saying
goes — "he could not touch the head of the ten-foot monk" — it
was all a complete mystery to him. He stared vacantly at the
scene, looking a little downcast. The expression on his face was
such that if one were to invite Tang Ying, to copy it, even that great
master painter would be unable to capture its subtleties. This
made the maidservant even more puzzled. She saw one person
laughing their head off, while another was utterly bewildered.
Is this not laughable in itself! So, Ah Hong began to chuckle in
response. Ma Yongzhen realized that they were both laughing
at him and became so embarrassed his earlobes turned a bright
shade of red. The hilarity continued for a while, but stopped

abruptly when Hua Baoyu walked through the door, having returned from her singing engagement. Seeing Chai Jiuyun and the maidservant with tears in their eyes, she asked with some concern: "Boss Chai, Ah Hong, who's been bullying you?"

"We are both adults, not children of three or two-and-a-half years old," Chai Jiuyun said jokily. "Who would dare bully us?"

"Don't be afraid to admit it," Hua Baoyu said. "The proof that you were crying is still apparent with the tears in your eyes that are not yet dry."

On hearing mention of tears, Chai Jiuyun took a look in the mirror and realized what she meant.

"Those tears are from laughing, not from crying," he explained to her.

"What could have possibly made you laugh so much that you ended up in this state?"

Chai Jiuyun told her what had just been said and the maidservant blushed right to the roots of her hair. Hua Baoyu also laughed.

"Is this gentleman Boss Ma?" she asked,

"I see you have returned," Ma said rather awkwardly by way of an answer.

When Hua Baoyu heard this, she and the others began to laugh again, but Ma Yongzhen really couldn't understand what was so funny.

"Brother Chai," he addressed his friend anxiously, "why are you all laughing at me like this?"

Chai Jiuyun explained in detail. Ma Yongzhen listened and couldn't help but blush again. When he looked in the mirror he saw his face was as red as a pig's lungs. He decided that it was no fun sitting there anymore, and suggested to Chai Jiuyun that they should leave. Chai Jiuyun stood up, and Hua Baoyu and the maidservant, as was usual, accompanied them to the top of the stairs, where they exchanged a few friendly words of goodbye. The two men went down the stairs and left Hua Baoyu's establishment. After exiting Puqing Li and arriving on, Stone Street they said their farewells to each other, and called for two rickshaws to take them to their respective residences.

Let us continue to relate how on that day when Scrofulous Bai got drunk and was utterly humiliated, making a fool of himself at the Yileyuan restaurant, he returned home alone in a rickshaw feeling thoroughly depressed. He slept for the whole day. Then, the following morning, Lu the Lackey came over to visit him.

"Yesterday was the third day of the third month and you didn't go out! What were you doing at home all by yourself?" He asked Scrofulous Bai.

"I was sleeping," was the perfunctory reply.

"Were you feeling under the weather? Are you still unwell?" Lu the Lackey continued his questioning.

"I wasn't ill. I was just angry," he said curtly.

"What were you angry about? Who did you fall out with?"

"You insolent fiend, are you trying to make fun of me?"

Lu the Lackey laughed nervously. "Would I dare make fun of you, boss? I was just asking. Don't be cross. Quick, tell me what it was that made you so angry."

Scrofulous Bai told him about what happened when he drank too much yellow wine at the Yileyuan restaurant and how he fought with Ma Yongzhen.

"You have been too careless," Lu the Lackey concluded. "That Chai Jiuyun is in the same gang as Ma Yongzhen. When he invited you for a drink he was not doing so in good faith, and he deliberately used Ma Yongzhen to make you disgrace yourself. Now you alone are angry, while they are laughing their heads off, stamping their feet and clapping their hands in glee."

What Lu the Lackey said made him even more enraged, and

his face turned a steely shade of gray.

"It is all down to that bastard Fang," Scrofulous Bai continued, with real hatred in his voice. "He was in on the act too, when he came over to invite me, and as he was mediating during the quarrel. He said all those nice things; I thought he was my brother-in-arms; I trusted him entirely and followed him to that place. Who would have thought he would sell me down the river like that!"

"What has the world come to?" Lu the Lackey said, egging him on. "Is there even such a thing as friendship anymore? Have the sanctity of the words 'brother-in-arms' been entirely forgotten? If there is money involved, he just can't be trusted, that bastard with his thieving eyes. On spying shiny silver coins, he would go as far as to sell his own boss, not to mention his brothers and friends. He has violated the rules of the brotherhood. By rights, he should beg forgiveness and submit to the forfeit of 'three knives and six holes' stabbing himself with a sharp blade in the prescribed way. But this is just for show now. Would anyone these days actually put that into practice?"

"Anyway, let's not talk of things in the past," Scrofulous Bai said with a note of finality. "That's all done and dusted. Now I must think of a way to take that Ma man out, once and for all, and finally give vent to the hatred I feel within my heart."

"Now would be the time to invite the Axe Head Gang from over by the Zhengjia Wood Bridge in Yangjiabang," suggested Lu the Lackey. "When they fight they use foreign-made axes, and, without a care whether they live or die, ruthlessly attack their victims by chopping at them and hacking wildly. So now, whenever the name of the Axe Head Gang is mentioned, a sort of blind terror is felt all round."

When Scrofulous Bai heard this he was over the moon and pleaded with Lu the Lackey to look into contacting them and setting the wheels in motion.

"That shouldn't be too difficult," replied Lu the Lackey. "I can certainly go to speak with them now. That will keep you safe. But, in the end, they are bound to want to meet you face to face. Otherwise, if something untoward were to happen, who would they report to?"

"Since when were you so cowardly, and unwilling to shoulder responsibility?" Scrofulous Bai asked.

"It is not that I am unwilling to shoulder responsibility," Lu the Lackey replied. "I just think it would be best if you were to take charge of this one. I can't take the lead on this all by myself."

"Just go and see them today, and arrange a time for them to come to my house and talk things through tomorrow."

"Are you going out today or not?"

"I haven't made up my mind yet. In all likelihood I won't go out at all."

"But you really should go to Yidongtian. You've never missed a day there, not once in all your life. I'll go out with you today."

"Going out is all very well but where should we go?" Scrofulous Bai asked.

"What! You miss going out for just one day and you can't think of anywhere to go. Can it be Yidongtian has somehow fallen out of favor?"

"It's too early to go to Yidongtian," replied Scrofulous Bai. "Let's eat lunch there later on today."

"I'll be on my way now, and we can talk about things over lunch at Yidongtian."

"Are you going to meet the Axe Head Gang, then?"

"Yes, but the leader of the gang is an old opium fiend who doesn't get up till three in the afternoon, so it's far too early to go there now."

"Tell me, does that opium fiend go by the name of Cheng?"

Scrofulous Bai asked inquisitively. This was confirmed by Lu the Lackey. "And he's the all-knowing big boss of the Zhengjia Wood Bridge district. Is that right? That is the 'Cheng Zimin' we are talking about, isn't it?" Again, Lu the Lackey concurred.

"In that case I know him, but when did he become leader of the Axe Head Gang?"

"I understand he was elected by popular vote," Lu replied.

"How does an old drug hound like him get involved with an assassination gang? If a strong gust of wind were to blow from the northwest it would knock him right over. If I were to push that scrawny addict with just my little finger, he would fly across the room and land ten feet away."

"I have heard that that opium fiend doesn't actually go out and fight himself, but dispatches others to do his dirty work for him." Was Lu the Lackey's reply.

"That is the way he manages to feed and clothe himself, I suppose."

The two men continued to chat away, and before they knew it, the clock was chiming twelve noon, so they went to eat lunch at Yidongtian. When they were seated, the waiter poured them tea as usual. Once Scrofulous Bai had made himself comfortable, a group of young grooms and hooligans in his employ, came over and playfully fooled around with him. When it came to three o'clock, Lu the Lackey went off to Zhengjia Wood Bridge to look for the poppy fiend, Cheng. As luck would have it, Zhengjia Wood Bridge was only a flying arrow's distance from Pakhoi Road, and there was no need to take a rickshaw to get there, so he walked there at his own pace. Lu the Lackey was almost there, when on arriving at Hebangkou, he saw someone coming straight towards him carrying a small teapot in his hand. That man bent over at the waist when he walked, and had a prominent bow in his back, and as soon as Lu the Lackey saw him in the distance he knew it was Cheng Zimin. He quickened his pace and went to catch him up. His hunch was right, it was indeed Cheng Zimin.

"Brother Cheng, where are you off to?" He called out. "I've just been to your house to look for you, and they said you'd just gone out on business."

Cheng Zimin heard someone addressing him and came to a standstill.

"My brother, may I ask your name," Cheng asked, rubbing his eyes. "What can I do for you?"

"Brother Cheng," Lu the Lackey smiled. "You must be busy if you don't even recognize me."

"I haven't seen you for such a long time, so I can't immediately recall who you are." Cheng replied, still a little unsure.

"I am known by the name, Lu the Lackey."

"Ah yes! Of course," Cheng Zimin laughed. "Brother Lu! What can I do for you?"

"As the saying goes — 'one doesn't visit the Hall of Three Treasures without a purpose', so of course there's a reason for my coming to see you today. There is a small matter I'd like to discuss with you."

"This is no place to talk, let's go to the opium house to continue our chat," he said, looking cautiously around.

So the two men walked together in the direction of the opium house.

If you want to know what they talked about, please read the following chapter.

17

Lu the Lackey eggs on Cheng Zimin,
And Scrofulous Bai plans to murder Ma Yongzhen.

Let us continue to relate how Lu the Lackey and Cheng Zimin went to the opium house. When the servant saw Cheng Zimin arrive he bade him good morning. For the sake of politeness, Cheng Zimin asked if he had eaten, and with the courtesy required of him, the servant replied that he had. Cheng Zimin talked as he walked, and when he reached the couch he sat down. The assistant came over and lit the opium lamp, and Cheng laid down on the couch and asked him to prepare a few pipes for him.

Cheng Zimin took several drags to satisfy his craving and suddenly everything appeared calm and radiant, in contrast to just a moment before when he had felt so absentminded. He called the servant over and instructed him to go out and buy him a bowl of noodles, and at the same time spoke to Lu the Lackey:

"Brother Lu, you say you have a matter to discuss with me. Please go ahead and tell me what it is."

Lu the Lackey told him about the matter concerning Scrofulous Bai and Ma Yongzhen.

"I have heard people speak of this Ma Yongzhen," said Cheng Zimin. "At Weeping Willow Terrace he lifted the stone *ding*, then he toppled Yellow Beard three times, and held a ceremony to induct new disciples. I have wanted to cross paths with him for a while now. It is because of him that the brotherhood has lost face in the International Settlement and French Concession."

Lu the Lackey fully understood what Cheng Zimin was saying. What type of person was he if he wasn't able to rely on his wits to live from day to day, and his own version of "tact" was his one and only strategy? Now, hearing what Cheng Zimin said, he followed the lead that had been given to him.

"Brother Cheng you are right. We have dominated old Shanghai for these twenty or thirty years, and have gained considerable prestige. How can it be that Ma Yongzhen scurries down from Shandong, lives here for less than half a year, and starts to throw his weight around, while behaving absolutely atrociously? If he were to live here for more than a decade, just imagine! No doubt he'd want to be king of Shanghai. The standing of that Ma man increases all the time but we are losing face by the day."

Cheng Zimin nodded in agreement as he ate his noodles.

"If Scrofulous Bai loses face it means that you too lose face," Lu the Lackey suggested craftily. "The fact that Ma man recently bullied Scrofulous Bai may at first appear to have no rhyme or reason behind it. In the future, though, it will be difficult to avoid him bullying others. If it goes on like this, when all ruffians on the Shanghai Bund have been insulted by him, our paper tiger will be ripped apart and in the end we'll be scorned by outsiders, and will no longer be in a position to ply our trade."

When Lu the Lackey had said his piece, Cheng Zimin became quite furious. He sat back on the couch and in a rage smoked several pipes of opium in a row. He thought about this for a while and realized that this matter did indeed concern him very much. If he and his business were to be thrown into confusion by that Ma man, all the ruffians of Shanghai would lose face, and what he had to say at "tea parties" would mean nothing at all. So he put the pipe down on the tray by his side, took a sip of tea, and shut his eyes to ponder the matter. Meanwhile, Lu the Lackey was thinking to himself that so far he had proven really rather successful in persuading Cheng, and if he were to provoke him just that little bit further, he would be ready, and the plan will have been a resounding success. With a flick of the wrist he unfurled his fan, and, using it to shield his lips, he leaned closer to Cheng's couch, while in lowered tones he whispered, "Brother Cheng, I have heard something else on the streets that concerns what that Ma man has been saying, but please don't be angry at what I tell you."

"Come along, tell me quickly. Enough of this humming and hawing. Why all this hiding your head and revealing you tail? Anyway, what you want to tell me was not said by you, so why should I be angry with you! I hear infuriating things from morning to night; I don't know how many times a day I'm made to feel angry."

"I know you are a patient man," Lu the Lackey continued. "If you were not a patient man how would you be able to take on responsibility for so many important matters?"

"Just say what you have to say. Don't beat about the bush," Cheng Zimin insisted.

"That Ma man is spreading rumors all around. He has even had the cheek to say, apparently in the most sarcastic of tones,

'What is that Axe Head Gang? Who is that Cheng Zimin? If one day they were to fall into my hands I'd soon teach them a lesson, and really give them something to think about'."

"Are these words really true?"

"Of course they're true. Would I lie to you! It is common knowledge now."

Cheng Zimin slammed down his pipe in a rage. "That Ma man really is despicable," he shouted. "How dare he insult me in this way! It's just as if he were trying to bait the star-god, Tai Sui. Let's turn this all back in his direction and see what he's really made of."

"Do you need to prepare for this," Lu the Lackey asked deviously, "or would it be better if you were to make the first move?"

"If one is to make a move, of course it is best to do so first, rather than waiting for the other party to act, and taking revenge after the event. Would that not put us at a disadvantage?"

"A surprise attack is naturally the way to do it," Lu the Lackey agreed. "To strike and take advantage of his ill-preparedness, and take a 'chance'." This final word he said in his best Shanghai pidgin.

"Adequate preparations must first be made and only then should we make a move," suggested Cheng Zimin. "That way we will certainly not come to grief. Furthermore, that Ma man is a formidable opponent, so it is best not to look on him too lightly."

Lu the Lackey said "yes" to everything he suggested. Verbally he agreed with him, but within his heart he was just delighted to discover that Cheng Zimin had actually fallen for his ruse, and his plan was certainly turning out to be a success…that is, if he doesn't go back on his word. When he looked at the time it was already after six o'clock. At this time in spring when the days are getting longer, the setting sun is hovering over the western mountains. If this were winter, when the days are short, by this time it would be time to light the lamps.

"Let's talk more about this tomorrow. I must go back to discuss it with Brother Bai."

"Very well! This matter should most certainly be discussed with Brother Bai. After all, he is the boss, and I am only the hired help."

Everyone is doing their utmost so that the brotherhood doesn't lose face." Lu the Lackey said as he stood up, promising to see him again tomorrow. Cheng Zimin nodded his head without raising it from the pillow, said goodbye, and agreed to meet him the following day. Lu the Lackey hurried directly over to the Yidongtian teashop on Pakhoi Road. As he went up the staircase he saw that all was still and there was not even a single gang member to be seen. So he asked the waiter if Scrofulous Bai had already left.

"That is correct," the waiter replied. "Boss Bai said if you want to see him now, you should go to his house."

Lu the Lackey showed that he understood. He went back down the staircase and called for a rickshaw to take him directly to the French Concession. When he arrived at Scrofulous Bai's house he got down from the rickshaw, paid the fare and raised his hand to knock on the door. Inside, the servant inquired who it was and opened up when it was clear he was no stranger. Lu the Lackey walked into the reception room and saw that Scrofulous Bai was just in the middle of eating dinner.

"You have been gone so long!" Scrofulous Bai said to him rather impatiently. Lu the Lackey told him everything that had happened in the opium house, after which Scrofulous Bai invited him to join him for dinner. Lu the Lackey's tummy was rumbling, so, without standing on ceremony, he sat down to eat.

"Would you like a drink?"

Lu the Lackey refused without saying a word, and proceeded to stuff two bowls of rice into his mouth, one after the other.

"Eat a little slower. You're not robbing anyone now!"

"I always eat a little quicker when I'm hungry."

"Since Cheng Zimin has agreed to the plan, we must make preparations."

"Naturally! Even though Cheng Zimin has agreed to help," Lu the Lackey suggested, "the matter in hand has everything to do with you saving face. This is your battle."

"Yes! Quite right. As always, I would be grateful if you would please go and engage Scabby Crabby, Eely Mudskipper, Siguan Bloodspitter, and Sanbao Headsplitter."

"Of course we should invite them, but last time they went to so much trouble for nothing. This time, of course, they may not be so willing."

"The imperial court does not send forth hungry soldiers," Scrofulous Bai answered briskly. "Of course this time we must spend a little money on them."

"If that's the case, I'll invite them for a meal tomorrow, and we can tell them all about it round the dinner table, face to face. There is no way they will not agree to it."

"While you're about it, you should invite Cheng Zimin as well."

"If we are to invite Cheng Zimin it will have to be at night. He doesn't get out of bed until three or four in the afternoon, and even then has to satisfy his opium craving. How about meeting at eight or nine o'clock?"

"Nine o'clock is too late," said Scrofulous Bai.

"Of course nine o'clock is late, but if we want Cheng Zimin to come, it will have to be at eight or nine.

"May I trouble you to deal with this tomorrow?"

"Of course I'll deal with it, but please don't mention that word 'trouble'. I assure you it is no trouble at all. Your business is my business. There are no distinctions to be made between us."

"We can't allow that Ma man to escape," said Scrofulous Bai. "He holds too much power in his hands now."

"It will be best to hit him at a time when he's on his own, so we can demonstrate our might. To strike first will be the strongest move. In that way we can catch him unawares."

"Last time it was I who suffered at his hands," Scrofulous Bai said. "We must guard against that happening again...at all costs."

"Last time nobody had any weapons and that's why we suffered at his hands. This time we'll have axes galore and of course we'll not be the ones to suffer."

"Now, even if that Ma man were a Buddhist deity with three heads and six arms, he would not be able to defeat us."

"Even mighty heroes and stout upstanding fellows would not be able to clear this hurdle." Lu the Lackey added.

The two men talked as they ate. When Lu the lackey had finished three bowls, he stood up, took a sip of tea and wiped his face. Then he sat down again for a moment before finally getting to his feet and bidding him farewell.

"Where shall we meet tomorrow?" Scrofulous Bai asked.

If you want to know what happens next, please read the following chapter.

18

Scrofulous Bai invites guests for a drink,
And Cheng Zimin hatches a dastardly plan.

Let us continue to relate how Lu the Lackey ate dinner at Scrofulous Bai's home and was just standing up to say goodbye when Scrofulous Bai asked where they should meet the following day.

"Tomorrow at noon I'll summon Sanbao Headsplitter, Siguan Bloodspitter, Eely Mudskipper and Scabby Crabby, to meet us at the Yidongtian teashop," Lu the Lackey replied. "You can talk to them there in person. In the afternoon I'll invite Cheng Zimin."

"I'll wait for you at Yidongtian, then" said Scrofulous Bai.

"Which restaurant shall we go to in the evening?" Lu the Lackey asked. "I'll make the arrangements in advance."

"I suggest Zhengxinglou on Fifth Avenue, the food and drink are good, and it's not too expensive."

"That sounds like an excellent idea. Until tomorrow!" He

stood up, left through the front door and took a rickshaw all the way to his own modest dwelling, where he got out of the rickshaw and paid the fare. Of him entering the house and retiring for the night we shall say no more.

Let us proceed to relate how when it came to the following day, Lu the Lackey got up at the crack of dawn and when he had washed and brushed his hair, he departed the house and went straight to the home of Sanbao Headsplitter. There, he was told that Sanbao Headsplitter had already left to go to a tea party. From there, Lu the Lackey went to see Siguan Bloodspitter. He entered through the door of the tiny house that also acted as a tailor's shop and went directly up to his small attic room. He saw Siguan Bloodspitter lying on the floor with a thin mat beneath him, and a cotton blanket barely covering his massive bulk. Both hands supported his head like a pillow and he was loudly snoring away. Lu the Lackey stooped over him and shouted his name in his ear. Siguan Bloodspitter opened his eyes in panic, coughed a couple of times when he saw it was Lu the Lackey, and spat out a mouthful of phlegm.

"Brother Lu, why have you come so early?"

"It's not early, it's almost nine o'clock."

Just as he was saying this, the clock downstairs in the tailor shop struck nine.

"Rise and shine, rise and shine, it's already nine o'clock," Lu the Lackey chuckled.

Siguan Bloodspitter yawned and sat up. "Crash!" He banged his head on the low sloping ceiling above him.

"This attic room is awful," he complained. "I bang my head like that all the time. It really is just too awful!"

"I'll go downstairs and wait for you in the reception room," Lu the Lackey told him. "Come down when you're ready."

He got up, being careful to duck his head, climbed down

the steep, ladder-like steps, and waited in the room downstairs, chatting for a while with the tailor's assistant. After a short time Siguan Bloodspitter climbed down from his attic room, and he and Lu the Lackey left the house and walked straight over to the Yidongtian teashop.

"What do you want, coming over at the crack of dawn and waking me up like that?" Siguan Bloodspitter asked.

"I have nothing to report except that tonight Boss Bai would like to invite you for dinner."

"Why does he want to treat me again? We are all of one family. There is no need for these formalities."

"This is just as it should be. The imperial court does not send forth hungry soldiers," he said, mimicking Scrofulous Bai.

The two men talked as they walked, and before they knew it, they had arrived at Pakhoi Road. On the street corner, in the distance, the lone figure of Sanbao Headsplitter could be seen, buying cigarettes from a kiosk. Lu the Lackey had a keen eye. Having recognized Sanbao Headsplitter from a distance he cried out to him. Sanbao Headsplitter heard someone call him and turned around to see who it was.

"Bruvver Lu! Good mornin! Where ya off ta now, mate?" He asked.

"I have just been to your house but they told me you were out on business, so I was on my way to the teashop to see if you were there. By sheer luck I've bumped into you here instead."

"Bruvver Lu, why ya lookin' for me? What is occurring?"

"I came looking for you for no other reason than we haven't seen each other for such a long time."

"I am unwurvvy!" Sanbao Headsplitter said with a chuckle.

"In fact," Siguan Bloodspitter piped up cheekily, "he has been looking for you for no other reason than he wants to invite you to dinner."

Sanbao Headsplitter said, "Oh, so you've recognized vat Gweedy Guts, yours twuly, is 'specially fond of eatin'."

"That's right. I've come to invite you to dinner." Lu the Lackey said, choosing to ignore Sanbao Headsplitter's quip.

"Why'd ya want to invite me ta dinner? And why would ya' put ya'self to va trouble of coming to ask us in person?"

"A good question!... Boss Bai will be the host," said Lu the Lackey.

"Bruvver Bai is too kind," Sanbao Headsplitter replied. "Ver is no need for vat, vough, we are all of one family. It's all in a day's work and not a big deal. Where ya boaf off ta now?"

"We're going to Yidongtian for a cup of tea," replied Lu the Lackey. "Why don't you come with us? Brother Bai will be there too."

The three of them made their way to Yidongtian together. They walked up the central staircase and saw Scrofulous Bai sitting there with a number of other thugs having a tea party. The three of them darted over to the table to take their seats. Everyone exchanged greetings and the waiter poured tea for them and handed out napkins.

"Brother Bai, why ya being so courte'us as to invite us for a meal again?" Sanbao Headsplitter asked. "We are all of one family and there's really no need for vat. You are just too kind, but in va end, you are exerting unnecessary energy wiv litwl reward."

"Even though people might know each other well," Scrofulous Bai replied, "there should never be any ambiguity when it comes to social etiquette. That is how it should be."

It turns out that Sanbao Headsplitter's words were said to emphasize the fact that he hadn't eaten and to give thanks before the event. In this way, the matter was fixed and could not be changed, thus giving rise to the situation where Scrofulous Bai really had no choice but to invite him to dinner. This is an old trick of the Shanghai ruffian. But I digress, enough of this idle chatter.

Let us proceed to relate how Scrofulous Bai told Lu the Lackey to go and look for the rest of the gang, Scabby Crabby and Eely Mudskipper.

"If I want to track them down," Lu the Lackey suggested, "I'll have to go to the Chaoyanglou. They hold a tea party there every day."

"Don't forget to do it though!" Scrofulous Bai implored him.

"Such a small matter. How could I possibly forget?"

"What is the time now?" Scrofulous Bai changed the subject.

Lu the Lackey replied that it was about noon, so Scrofulous Bai suggested they go for lunch. He got to his feet and invited Sanbao Headsplitter and Siguan Bloodspitter along, too. Sanbao Headsplitter thanked him, but, as required by etiquette, he politely declined, by saying that he wouldn't dream of disturbing him.

"No need to stand on ceremony, we are all of one family."

"Vat being the case, if we eat a meal togevver at noon, ver will be no need ta eat dinner tonight. Let's forget aw' about it."

"When you are invited to enjoy a meal like this," Scrofulous Bai said, somewhat irritated, "why take everything so seriously? Just accept the invitation and have done with it!"

"But it is such an expense!" Sanbao Headsplitter replied with a chuckle.

Scrofulous Bai ignored him and paid the tea bill, then the four men made their way together down the staircase.

"Where shall we go for lunch?" Lu the Lackey asked.

"Let's go to Zhengxinglou!" Suggested Scrofulous Bai. "While we are about it, we can write some invitations for the meal this evening."

Lu the Lackey agreed this was a good idea and the four men walked over to Kwangtung Road. When they arrived at the restaurant, the waiter came forward to greet them. The four men took their seats and the table was laid with cups and chopsticks.

"What would you like to order today gentlemen?" The waiter asked.

Scrofulous Bai asked his friends what sort of wine they would like. Siguan Bloodspitter was the first to reply. "I won't be drinking wine…" pausing for effect and sympathy, he then continued, "…on account of my cough."

Sanbao Headsplitter was asked the same question. He wasn't so fussy and said he would drink whatever was given to him.

Scrofulous Bai settled on two *jin* of his favourite Shao-Hsing Huadiao yellow wine. The servant shouted out the order then asked what they would like to eat.

Scrofulous Bai ordered a few dishes — chicken, duck, fish and meat — and the four men tucked in voraciously. When they had finished eating, the bill was paid and they reserved a table for the evening and wrote the invitations. Lu the Lackey gathered up the completed invitations and the four men left Zhengxinglou and arranged to meet again a little later. Sanbao Headsplitter and Siguan Bloodspitter left first. Scrofulous Bai told them: "This evening, I invite you to come a little early."

"If you don't come we'll just have to invite you again," said Lu the Lackey sneakily.

The two men nodded their heads. "We wouldn't dream of putting you to any trouble," said Sanbao Headsplitter. "We'll certainly be there on time."

"Brother Lu, you go to see Cheng Zimin," said Scrofulous Bai. "I'll make my own way to Zhengxinglou."

Lu the Lackey took out the invitation cards and chose a few to give to Scrofulous Bai, saying: "Please do make you own way, but take a few of these invitations with you to distribute."

"You'd better go to see Cheng Zimin now. It's already three o'clock."

Lu the Lackey said goodbye to Scrofulous Bai, and went straight to the opium house. When he arrived, he found that Cheng Zimin was not yet there, so he took a seat and called the assistant to light an opium lamp for him.

"Cheng Zimin been in?" he inquired.

On hearing he was asking after Cheng Zimin, the assistant looked him up and down, while lighting the lamp. "You came here yesterday, didn't you?" He said with a knowing smile, and told him that Cheng had not yet been in. Looking at the clock, he added, "It's after three o'clock, though, so he should be here soon."

Lu the Lackey lay down on the couch and smoked opium to while away the time. After a short time he heard a hacking cough outside and knew that that must be Cheng Zimin.

"Brother Cheng, I'm here," he shouted out as he got up to greet him.

Holding a small teapot in his hand, Cheng Zimin walked through the door and saw Lu the Lackey.

"How long have you been here?" Cheng asked.

"Not very long," Lu replied. "I've only just arrived."

Cheng Zimin coughed a few times more and lay down on the couch. The assistant lit the opium lamp and as usual filled a few pipes for him. Cheng Zimin took a couple of drags to satisfy his craving, then picked at a few snacks with his fingers.

"How is that matter progressing?" He asked.

"As far as the matter is concerned, when Brother Bai heard that you, such a distinguished patriarch, were willing to help, he was absolutely delighted." Then he seized the opportunity to broach the question of the dinner invitation. "This evening he would like to invite you to the Zhengxinglou on Fifth Avenue."

As he said this he delved into the folds of his jacket and brought out a red invitation card which he respectfully presented to Cheng Zimin. Cheng took it in his hand and read it.

If you want to know what happens next, please read the following chapter.

19

Ma Yongzhen is put in mortal danger as an evil trap is set,
And Scrofulous Bai gives vent to his anger as revenge is taken.

Let us proceed to relate how Lu the Lackey presented the invitation to Cheng Zimin and Cheng took it in his hand and read it.

"How many people are invited this evening?" He asked.

"Not that many," Lu the Lackey replied. "But we are all of one family, and would be greatly honored if you would grace us with your presence."

"If you have something to do now, please go on ahead and I shall follow on behind." Cheng Zimin said by way of a reply.

"I haven't got anything important on, so let's just go together."

Cheng Zimin agreed with a nod, then looked at the invitation and noticed it said seven o'clock. It was already past that time, so he took a few last puffs of the pipe, and walked out of the opium house together with Lu the Lackey. They took two rickshaws to

Kwangtung Road, got out at Zhengxinglou, paid the fare and walked inside. The waiter came over to welcome them.

"Scrofulous Bai invited us," Lu the Lackey told him. "Have the other guests arrived?"

"They have indeed, sir," the waiter said, and led them to a private room.

Scrofulous Bai saw Cheng Zimin enter the room and stood up to welcome him. The waiter brought over some tea and Scrofulous Bai informed him that all the guests were now present and the banquet could begin.

In no time at all the banquet was laid out and Scrofulous Bai invited Cheng Zimin to sit in the seat of honor. Then, Lu the Lackey, Siguan Bloodspitter, Sanbao Headsplitter, Ah Bao, Little Big Number Nine, Eely Mudskipper, and Scabby Crabby — that band of brothers — took their places. Scrofulous Bai sat in the host's seat and poured a round of drinks.

Altogether, including him, there were nine present. They scoffed the food down like a pack of greedy wolves and tigers. No sooner did a plate of food arrive than it was picked clean. In the end every plate was finished off and not a morsel of food remained, while the table itself was scattered all over with debris, just as if a typhoon had hit it.

"Brother Cheng, that Ma man has been thoroughly unruly and has been bullying our fellow brethren," Scrofulous Bai began. "Today it is a rare treat for us all to be gathered here today. We must find a way to teach that Ma man a lesson and dispel the hatred that is held within our hearts."

"That Ma man's reckless behavior is now truly out of control," added Lu the Lackey, "and we in the brotherhood have all lost face. Today we must find a way to reprimand him so we don't lose face again. My brothers, what do you think? Is this not the case?" As he said this he filled a glass to express his resolve.

The assembled crowd heard what he said and having eaten and drunk their fill at Scrofulous Bai's expense, shouted their approval in cacophonic disorder.

"Not so fast!" Cheng Zimin said, putting something of a dampener on things. "This problem can't be solved with words alone. What is more, that Ma man has considerable personal strength and more than one hundred disciples. He is certainly not one of the uninitiated who can be easily intimidated."

Everyone heard what Cheng Zimin said and looked at each other in dismay, not uttering a word. Scrofulous Bai looked at this despondent scene and in his mind he was far from willing to accept what Cheng was saying, but he knew it would be a mistake to lose his temper now. So he addressed him formally, "Brother Cheng, we invite you to think of a way to deal with this."

"As far as this matter is concerned, I think it would be best," Cheng posited, "to choose a time when that Ma man is off his guard, and to blind his eyes with a bag of quicklime, so that when it comes to make our attack, there will be nothing for us to be afraid of."

Scrofulous Bai heard this, clapped his hands with glee and shouted out in approval. Everyone else echoed him.

"That Ma man drinks tea every day in a small teashop at the foot of Sinza Bridge," Lu the Lackey told them. "Perhaps we should wait there for him to arrive and make our move then and there."

"That being the case, let's strike tomorrow," said Scrofulous Bai.

"If we are going to do it tomorrow," Cheng Zimin warned, "we must make arrangements tonight. I'll go back and talk to my people and tell them to take their axes to Sinza Bridge and lie in wait tomorrow."

Everyone agreed that they would act the following day, and after hearing Cheng Zimin's wise words, they suddenly all felt very brave. They had drunk Scrofulous Bai's wine and eaten his food, so of course they would feel obliged to volunteer for this.

"That bag of quicklime is crucial to our plan," said Lu the Lackey.

"In which case that crucial part of the plan must be given to you, Brother Lu," suggested Siguan Bloodspitter.

"Yes indeed," agreed Scrofulous Bai. "This task should be entrusted to Brother Lu."

Lu the Lackey saw that everyone was in agreement, and concurred that it was his bounden duty to see it through. Thereafter, they finished off the food and thanked Scrofulous Bai with one voice, before each going their separate ways.

When it came to the following day, Scrofulous Bai's band of misfits waited in the vicinity of Sinza Bridge and the Axe Head Gang set themselves up in a nearby teashop with their axes at the ready. After a short time, Ma Yongzhen arrived and by curious chance, on that particular day, he had ridden there on his horse alone. He entered the teashop, and as usual the waiter brought over some noodle soup. As he was wiping his face with a hot towel in preparation to eat, Lu the Lackey took the chance to conceal himself behind him, and waited for Ma to reveal his face again. When he did so, Lu the Lackey suddenly took aim and threw the bag of quicklime directly in his eyes.

...a doom-filled cloud of dust arose.

Ma Yongzhen shut his eyes in terrible pain and realized he had fallen into a trap. He was going to retaliate, but unfortunately it was all too late, as Sanbao Headsplitter, Siguan Bloodspitter, Scabby Crabby and Eely Mudskipper had already charged forward to launch their attack. Ma Yongzhen was overcome with fury and although he had lost his eyesight, the strength of his limbs had by no means diminished, so he raised his fists and intercepted his attackers, hitting out in all directions. As they fought, tables, and stools flew all over the room. As soon as he saw his henchmen had successfully mounted their attack, Lu the Lackey slipped off to call in the Axe Head Gang. On hearing the news, with axes in hand, they rushed from their hiding place over to the teashop.

Ma Yongzhen could be seen with his fists in the air, randomly hitting out in confusion, as if he had gone quite mad. Although Ma Yongzhen's eyesight was murky, his sense of hearing was as keen as ever, and he could make out every little sound. From this he knew that this morning he had come to grief, but nevertheless, with all his strength he began to attack at random, like a tiger released from its cage — if he came across anyone, he bit them. Before the Axe Head Gang came forward, it had been up to that pitiful duo Sanbao Headsplitter and Siguan Bloodspitter to lead the attack. They were upfront with their brethren, being pummelled by Ma Yongzhen, and were frozen to the spot, unable to move an inch. After a short time, Ma Yongzhen gradually began to feel the strain, and he could hear the sound of men all around had somewhat diminished. He thought to himself that the gang of thugs had probably retreated and had paused their attack. He used the backs of his hands to wipe his eyes, one after the other, and it was just then that the Axe Head Gang surrounded him and rushed forth to mount their first attack. Totally regardless of any consequences for themselves, they came forward and hacked at him indiscriminately for all their lives were worth. Straightaway, Ma Yongzhen was able to grab hold of one of the gang, who was thrown into such a panic that he lost control of his axe, and threw it up in the air. Shortly afterwards the axeless axeman was able to make a lucky escape when Ma Yongzhen's arm became a target and was hacked off by the gang.

Although he had now lost an arm and was in excruciating pain, he continued to come forward and fight, and was not in the slightest bit afraid. Ma Yongzhen continued to lash out, but by now his whole body was covered in blood. The few bystanders, looking on at this scene of carnage, grew into a huge crowd and eventually Ma's six closest disciples got to hear of it. They rushed over together to the small teashop at Sinza Bridge, where they saw the crowds gathered outside. When they heard that their master was in trouble they were overcome with panic and pushed their way through the spectators at the door. Like a ferocious six-headed tiger they stepped into the small teashop as a group, and saw where Ma Yongzhen was lying on the floor, still taking a beating. On seeing this, the six disciples rushed forward as one, with a feeling of great pain within their hearts. When the Axe Head Gang saw that reinforcements had arrived, they abandoned Ma Yongzhen and began fighting with the disciples. On realizing their master had suffered at the hands of this axe-wielding mob, the six men became so angry that they were emboldened to risk everything. Summoning up more strength than they had ever needed to before, they made their attack, without a thought for their own safety. No matter what weapons they encountered, they fought with the Axe Head Gang until they had utterly defeated them. The gang members scurried away, clutching their heads in their hands, and scattering in all directions as if someone had smeared oil on the soles of their feet. In just a short time they had vanished without trace. The six disciples helped Ma to sit up, and with one voice shouted, "Master!"

On hearing his disciples' voices, Ma Yongzhen bemoaned his fate with tears rolling down his cheeks. One of their number asked how he had fallen into the trap, so Ma Yongzhen told them how he had just finished wiping his face with a towel when Lu the Lackey threw a bag of lime in his eyes, and how he had then been attacked with axes and lost an arm. Just as the master and, his six disciples were talking, the police, who had heard news of the situation, arrived to quell the disturbance. They saw that the attackers had fled, while the gravely injured victim was still present. An ambulance rushed Ma to hospital, and the police did their best to assess the situation by collecting witness statements all round, before the onlookers went their separate ways. They then returned to the police station to make their reports so that the case could be heard in court the following day. Because Ma Yongzhen was a famous strongman and was a person of some renown on the Shanghai Bund, the news of the attack spread like wildfire and when Ma Yongzhen's new disciples got wind of it they all rushed over to learn more. A normally peaceful Sinza Road was full of excitement and panic. But enough of this idle chatter.

Let us continue to relate how the Axe Head Gang had been beaten off by Ma's disciples, and ran away to the Yidongtian teashop on Pakhoi Road, where they rushed up the central staircase to find Scrofulous Bai. Boss Bai had already heard the news and was so happy he could not help dancing with joy. He was thinking to himself that now Ma Yongzhen was dead he could sleep peacefully, entirely free from woes, and his prestige at the tea parties would reach new heights. As he had smashed Ma Yongzhen's power, he could now conduct himself as he pleases, behave recklessly, and do exactly what he wants. But the heavens uphold justice. Good and evil both have their reward, and in the end the villain will always get his comeuppance. Under such circumstances, how could there possibly be a good outcome for Scrofulous Bai?

If you want to know whether Ma Yongzhen lives or dies, please read the following chapter.

20

In the hospital mortal wounds cannot be repaired,
And hearts are broken as Ma's soul returns to whence it came.

Let us continue to relate how Ma Yongzhen fell foul of Boss Cheng and Boss Bai's dastardly plot to throw quicklime in his eyes to blind him, then beat him black and blue, ending up with the Axe Head Gang hacking off one of his arms, and afterwards how Ma was saved by his disciples and pulled to safety, escaping with his life and not dying from the wounds that were inflicted on him. The police station got wind of the incident and sent detectives to the scene to quell the violence and disperse the crowds. Ma Yongzhen was rushed to hospital in an ambulance, but by the time he arrived he had slipped into unconsciousness.

After receiving medical treatment he came to, but the doctor warned everyone that he had lost a lot of blood due to his severed arm, and the situation was grave, indeed. If he had been a normal person, he would certainly have stopped breathing by now. Alas and alack! But because Ma Yongzhen was possessed of remarkable physical strength, his injuries may not prove fatal after all. On awakening, Ma Yongzhen called for his disciples, who were already by his side.

"Master, what instructions do you have for us?" The disciples asked as one.

"I am badly hurt," Ma Yongzhen said through gritted teeth. "It looks like there is no hope for me. Quickly, go and fetch Chai…" Having said these few words he sank back into unconsciousness. Those round about called to him a few times and he awoke again.

"Has Chai Jiuyun arrived yet?" Ma asked them.

"We have sent someone to fetch him. Wait a short while and he will be here."

Ma Yongzhen said nothing. He closed his eyes and ground his teeth together as if he found the pain too excruciating to bear. After a short while, Chai Jiuyun arrived. He stepped into the room and saw Ma Yongzhen asleep in bed, having lost an arm, all covered in blood. On seeing him like this, Chai Jiuyun could not help his brave and noble eyes, like those of a heroic tiger, from shedding tears. For someone like Ma, with such consummate talent, to meet with this sort of suffering and pain, the more he thought about it, the more tragic he felt it to be. Ma Yongzhen woke up. He visibly swallowed, as if he were about to say something, and his disciples by his side called out to him, "Master Ma, Uncle Chai is here."

As soon as he heard that Chai Jiuyun had arrived, Ma tried to sit up, but how pitiful it was to see that without his arm he was simply unable to support himself, and he slumped straight back down onto the bed. Moments later, with his head propped up on a pillow, he was turned on his side so that he could speak to Chai Jiuyun:

"I am so glad you are here. If you had come any later, I fear you would not have seen me alive."

As he said this, that heroic nature for which he was celebrated could be seen no more, and his eyes were filled with tears of sadness and grief. On hearing what Ma Yongzhen said, Chai Jiuyun swallowed his tears, forcing himself to bear with the situation, and trying not to cry.

"Brother Ma," he said, "don't be like this. Although you have been attacked by a mean and petty mob, you shall find that heaven helps the worthy. It is best not to..." He got as far as this, and it was as if something got stuck in his throat and he was unable to continue. Then, with a high-pitched whimper, he began to weep. The tears flowed down his cheeks without cease and the front of his gown became soaked with tears.

Although Ma Yongzhen had lost his sight, he could still hear everything clearly.

"Brother Chai, don't cry for me. I, Ma Yongzhen, did indeed desire to come to Shanghai...but I did not want to die here." As he said the word "die", his voice faded considerably and from that moment on it continued to become less and less distinct. All that could be made out were the stilted words: "Brother...Chai... in the end...you must...take...*revenge*...for me." Of these words, just one, "revenge", rang out clear and true. Chai Jiuyun swore to Ma that his attackers would certainly be punished. Then Ma called for his six disciples to approach.

"Master," they said in unison.

When they had all gathered round, he spoke. "When I'm dead, prepare my coffin, deal with it hastily and do not go to too much expense. In the future you must listen to Uncle Chai's instructions. Uncle Chai is your leader now. You must be as faithful to him as I have always been. One day you must take revenge for me, and Scrofulous Bai must..." The remaining words were inaudible. After a while he spoke again: "You, my six closest disciples, followed me from Shandong all the way to Shanghai, with the hope of establishing yourselves in this city. Unfortunately, it has come to this. Before long my little sister Ma Suzhen will arrive in Shanghai. You must tell her the circumstances of how I met with harm. Tell her…let her know… so she may take revenge."

Ma Yongzhen got as far as this and drifted again into unconsciousness, while blood began to flow freely from his wound. Just then the doctor entered the room in a state of alarm.

"Everyone out, now," he told them. "The patient is in no state to be talking to anyone!"

Chai Jiuyun and the six disciples had no choice but to leave, and waited in a room close by. When evening came, the doctor came to see them.

"The patient's condition has improved and the bleeding has stopped," he told them. "In all likelihood there is no longer anything to worry about." When this diagnosis circulated amongst them, Chai Jiuyun and the disciples were overjoyed.

"You wait here," Chai addressed the disciples. "I must go home, but I shall return early tomorrow morning. Be sure to take good care."

Having said goodbye to the disciples, he returned home and went to bed.

At midnight he heard a loud, heavy knocking at the door, as if someone were banging heavily on a drum, and he got out of bed to see what all the commotion was about.

"There is someone here from the hospital," his servant called up from below. On hearing the word "hospital" Chai Jiuyun immediately rushed downstairs.

"What has happened?" He asked the messenger in alarm.

"Uncle Chai, Master Ma has taken a turn for the worse, please come as quickly as you can."

On hearing this, Chai Jiuyun instructed his servants to lock the doors and he and the messenger left together. Fortunately, the weather was fine. They found two rickshaws and were able to rush with all haste out of the Chinese city. In no time at all they arrived at the entrance to the hospital, paid the fare and walked through the front gates. On entering the ward they could see Ma Yongzhen lying in bed, already struggling to speak. When he heard Chai Jiuyun's voice, Ma called out as best he could.

"Brother Chai, how I have suffered. That Scrofulous..." he said nothing more. Then, calling out in despair one last time—a wordless cry—he ascended up to the heavens.

After Ma Yongzhen's death, Chai Jiuyun shed countless tears. He called on the disciples to keep guard over the body, while he hurried home to fetch two hundred silver dollars. As soon as it was light, at the first opportunity, he went to find a coffin so Ma Yongzhen could be laid within. All funeral arrangements were put in place. When the 107 disciples got wind of the news, they came to escort the coffin, and Buddhist monks and Daoist priests were hired to perform the funereal five-plum-blossom ritual. They then joined the procession, and offered up prayers. Bustling crowds were everywhere, as the coffin was escorted along the streets to the Shandong Native-Place Association. When the ceremony was over, all the disciples—more than one hundred men—gathered together and swore to take revenge.

Later on, Ma Suzhen dreamed a dream, and came to Shanghai to seek news of her brother. She met with Chai Jiuyun, convened a meeting at the Shandong Meeting House, and held a public memorial service for Ma Yongzhen. Later on, Ma Suzhen took revenge for her brother by slaughtering her enemies in broad daylight. All of this and many other events besides would occur at a later date. This volume has been dedicated to the telling of the true story of Ma Yongzhen, but no doubt there have been many inadvertent omissions. Now, I hope you will allow this author to take some rest, to gather his strength and to enliven his spirits before he continues to record *The Adventures of Ma Suzhen*. This will tell how a heroic woman took revenge for her brother in Shanghai. Fair reader, please wait calmly and do not be too impatient to learn more, for now yours truly, Zhu Dagong, must bid you farewell. Until we meet again, adieu!

"MA YONGZHEN'S SHANGHAI": AN ESSAY

Abbreviations

MYZ (Ma Yongzhen)	*Murder in the Maloo:*
	A Tale of Old Shanghai
MSZ (Ma Suzhen)	*The Adventures of Ma Suzhen*
NCH	*North-China Herald*

Murder in the Maloo: A Tale of Old Shanghai, is set in Shanghai in the years 1878, when Ma Yongzhen arrived in the city, and 1879, when he met his tragic death at the hands of rival gangsters. Ma Yongzhen was an historical figure and his murder was perpetrated in the Yidongtian teashop on 13 April 1879. The following excerpt from an English-language newspaper tells of the discovery of his body by a "foreign" constable:

> The constable entered the teashop, and found it deserted by those interested in its management. Not a single individual was to be found downstairs, and proceeding in to the upper room facing the street he there discovered Moh Yung-ching [Ma Yongzhen] with his numerous wounds bleeding profusely... From the severity of the wounds and the quantity of blood on the floor, it was a matter of wonder that Moh Yung-ching had survived so long.[5]

---

5   "The Murder in the Maloo" in *The North-China Herald* (22 April 1879), p. 393.

The great metropolis of Shanghai is where most of the action takes place in the book. In the first chapter, the journey from Ma Yongzhen's hometown in Shandong Province is briefly described, but is simply included for the purpose of plot development. By the end of Chapter One, Ma has already arrived in Shanghai, and this is where the locus of the action becomes central to the telling of the story. From this point on, the city plays an important role in the narrative, with the authors, Qi Fanniu and Zhu Dagong, often going out of their way to feature famous Shanghai landmarks, or to refer in detail to the topography of the city.

The City of Shanghai

In the early 1920s, the Qing dynasty (1644-1911) was within living memory for most residents of Shanghai, including some children, but a lot had changed between the time of Ma's death in 1879 and the publication of the MYZ book in 1923. Perhaps the biggest change in Shanghai, and in China itself, was that the Chinese empire had ceased to be, and a republic had been established in its place in 1912. Two books illustrate well some of the changes that occurred between the 1870s and 1920s: first, a four-volume publication on Shanghai written by Ge Yuanxu 葛元煦 (n.d.), *Huyou zaji* 滬游雜記 (*Miscellaneous Records of Wanderings Around Shanghai*) first published in 1876 (two years before Ma Yongzhen arrived in Shanghai) and reprinted several times in the 1870s and 1880s; and second, a modern-style guidebook, *Shanghai zhinan* 上海指南 ("Guide to Shanghai: a Chinese Directory of the Port") published in 1920 (with a preface dated 1918).[6] The latter publication follows the general format

---

6   Ge Yuanxu 葛元煦 and Yuan Zuzhi 袁祖志, *Huyou zaji* 滬游雜記 (Miscellaneous Records of Wanderings Around Shanghai) (Shanghai, 1876). *Shanghai zhinan* 上海指南 ("Guide to Shanghai: a Chinese Directory of the Port") (Shanghai: Shanghai yinshuguan, 1920) [preface dated 7th Year of Republic [1918].

and layout of modern 20th century guidebooks, with its roots in its international counterparts published since the 19th century. Ge Yuanxu's book should be seen as a precursor to this, and was written in a style aimed at the educated Chinese elite, with the inclusion of much poetry, and short literary vignettes known as *biji* 筆記 (literary notes), which had been popular among scholars for centuries. The 1920 guidebook should certainly be seen as being closely related to the earlier example, as there are many things that can be found in both. However, the literary quality of Ge's book is not matched by the 1920s publication, and it is this that sets them apart. Together, the content of both books shows how much Shanghai changed between the time of Ma's death in 1879, and when the publication of MYZ was being considered by Qi Fanniu and Zhu Dagong in the early 1920s.

One example of the big changes that occurred in Shanghai that was clear to all, concerned the traffic on the streets. The introduction of rickshaws, new to the city in the mid-1870s, changed the face of Shanghai. Before their arrival, horses and donkeys, carriages of various kinds drawn by beasts of burden, sedan chairs, and wheelbarrows conveyed the people of Shanghai from place to place, and these continued to be used alongside the increasingly popular rickshaw after its arrival in China. This hand-drawn vehicle had been introduced from Japan, and the derivation of the modern English-language name "rickshaw", was a Japanese word, "Jinrikisha" 人力車 (Human-powered cart).[7] That being said, these vehicles are more commonly referred to in writings of the time as *Dongyangche* 東洋車 (carts of the eastern oceans, effectively, "Japanese carts"). This is the case both in fiction like MYZ and in the nonfiction writings of

---

7   In the 19th century, English-language sources also used the name "jinriksha". See "The Murder in the Maloo" in *The North-China Herald* (22 April 1879), p. 393.

authors such as Ge Yuanxu.[8] In MYZ they are further described as "iron-tired Japanese carts" and the narrator comments on how uncomfortable taking a rickshaw was during the 1870s, as the *huangbaoche* (a type of modernized rickshaw, with rubber tyres and improved suspension) was not yet in use.

The two rickshaw pullers who play a part in the story, with their iron-tired rickshaws, are said to be from the Jiangbei region (also called Subei). In both instances, they are made to appear unsophisticated, and even quite stupid. This plays into the prejudice against people from Jiangbei that was so widespread in Shanghai during the Republican Era, something that could be seen even until quite recently. As noted by the late Emily Honig, "More than any other occupation, rickshaw pulling was associated with and symbolized the status of Subei people in the Shanghai labor market."[9] Their status was low, and they were known for taking on menial jobs that were both physically demanding and badly paid. Little Big Number Nine, Scrofulous Bai's stableboy, who is made to look foolish by talking to a horse in Chapter Nine, is also from the Jiangbei region, and, due to his lowly status, taking care of horses at the most basic level, is subject to the same prejudice as the rickshaw pullers in the story.[10]

Most of the action in MYZ takes place in Shanghai's International Settlement, with brief excursions into the French Concession, where the Jing'an Temple is located, and Scrofulous

---

8   "Dongyangche" 東洋車, in Ge Yuanxu 葛元煦 and Yuan Zuzhi 袁祖志, *Chongxiu Huyou zaji* 重修滬游雜記 (Miscellaneous Records of Wanderings Around Shanghai, Revised) (Shanghai, 1888), n.p. See also the caption to a lithograph in *Dianshizhai huabao* 點石齋 畫報 (Dianshizhai Pictorial) (1884), vol. 1, p. 30.

9   Emily Honig, "The Politics of Prejudice: Subei People in Republican-Era Shanghai," *Modern China* 15, no. 3 (1989), pp. 245-246.

10   Emily Honig, "The Politics of Prejudice: Subei People in Republican-Era Shanghai," *Modern China* 15, no. 3 (1989), pp. 243-274.

Bai has his home; and to the Chinese city, where Chai Jiuyun lives. These were Shanghai's three main administrative areas during the 1920s and had developed out of the original Chinese walled city and various foreign settlements formed in the 19th century, following Shanghai's rise as a Treaty Port after the Opium War of 1839-1842. It is perhaps surprising that none of the action in the story takes place on, or near the Bund, the riverside location that was so central to Shanghai's identity, from the time it came into being after the Opium War, into the 20th century, and throughout the Republican period.

Even though Shanghai was a vibrant city in the 1870s, full of comings and goings, and there were many places one could go to enjoy oneself, the modern nightclubs, dance halls and entertainment venues for which Shanghai became so famous in the later 1920s, were not yet in evidence during the time when MYZ is set. For example, The New World "entertainment resort", at the corner of Thibet Road and Bubbling Well Road, wasn't established until 1914, and its competitor, The Great World, situated at the intersection between the International Settlement and the French Concession, didn't open until 1917.[11] These multi-functional entertainment palaces became central to the story of Shanghai in later years, and often appear prominently in fictional works of the 1920s and 1930s. Much social interaction outside the

---

11   The Great World opened on Bastille Day, Sunday, July 14, 1917, to attract as many customers from the French Concession as possible. Yang Jiayou 楊嘉祐, *Shanghai laofangzi de gushi* 上海老房子的故事 (Tales of the Old Buildings of Shanghai) (Shanghai renmin chubanshe: Shanghai, 2006), p. 291-292. The Great World was imitated, in both name and design, in other major Chinese cities such as Wuhan and Ningbo (and in Singapore in 1929), and there were as many as four entertainment "worlds" in Shanghai by 1933: the Great World, the New World, the Small World and the Daqian World. Such entertainment venues were described in an illustrated gazetteer of the time as "amusement resorts that cater to those of moderate means". Zhou Shixun 周世勳 (ed.), Zhu Shunlin 朱順麟 (photos.), Li Qiyu 李啟宇 (tr.), *Shanghai shi da guan* 上海市大觀 ('The Greater Shanghai') (Shanghai: Meishu tushu gongsi, 1933), n.p.

home before that time, took place in "teashops" and restaurants.[12] Depending on what sort of teashop it was, and its size, these were places where people went to visit friends, drink tea, or alcohol, eat snacks, or attend banquets, and to watch Chinese Opera, or other forms of entertainment, both large- and small-scale. They were also the preferred meeting places for Shanghai's gangsters, as can be seen throughout the story of MYZ. The euphemistically termed "tea parties" were where gangsters discussed their criminal business, and the Shanghainese term *chijiangcha* 吃講茶 was a sort of unofficial gangland court that took place in the teashops.

The Six Avenues

In the International Settlement, teashops and restaurants shared the same area as the brothels and courtesan houses, which were situated in the lanes and alleyways off the six long "avenues" that led from the Bund to the Race Club, from east to west. The first of the six avenues, Shanghai's main thoroughfare, Nanking Road ("The Maloo"), was actually designated "Da malu" (Grand Avenue) in Chinese, rather than "Yi malu" (First Avenue).[13] The next two roads in the numbered sequence, Second Avenue, Kiukiang Road, and Third Avenue, Hankow Road, do not feature in MYZ. However, Fourth Avenue, Foochow Road is central to much of the action. Both of the courtesan houses visited by Ma Yongzhen and Chai Jiuyun, are situated close to Foochow Road (one off Swatow Road and the other off Fuhkien Road). Early in the story, it is at a teahouse on Foochow Road that Ma meets Poxy Fang. It was also the location of the Da Qingguan, a documented restaurant, where Ma and Chai ate, drank and played a finger-

---

12 The name "teashop" can be found in English-language sources of the 1870s and has been adopted here. Sometimes the term "tea garden" is used to describe larger establishments, which were effectively theaters.

13 The name "Da Malu" was also given to the Rue du Consulat in the French Concession.

guessing game, before making their drunken way to Hua Baoyu's courtesan house.[14] It was at the top of Foochow Road that the poet Yuan Zuzhi, a well-known literary figure of the time, built his Weeping Willow Terrace and gardens. This is the place in Chapter Four where Ma lifts the massive stone *ding* tripod. Fifth Avenue, Kwangtung Road is where the Yanleyuan restaurant is found, and is also the location of the Zhengxinglou, to which Cheng Zimin is invited by Scrofulous Bai. For our purposes, the Yidongtian teashop is the most significant of all Shanghai teashops, as this was the place where the historical Ma Yongzhen met his grizzly end. A discrepancy between the true story and MYZ should be noted at this point. Clearly, in the NCH article, "The Maloo" refers to Nanking Road (and this can be corroborated by other newspaper reports of the time), but in both MYZ and MSZ the Yidongtian teashop is said to be situated on Sixth Avenue, Pakhoi Road. The reason for this discrepancy is unclear. It will not trouble us here, as the actual location of the teashop makes no difference to the telling of the story, or its outcome.

The Yidongtian had always been a famous teashop, and according to Ge Yuanxu's book, was the oldest in Shanghai:

> The first of the teashops was Yidongtian. At that time, when the avenues opened, teashops were as numerous as trees in the forest...[15]

---

14   This is another example where MYZ may have got things wrong. According to a 1920 guidebook, Da Qingguan was actually situated on Kwangtung Road. See *Shanghai zhinan* 上海指南 (Guide to Shanghai: a Chinese Directory of the Port) (Shanghai: Shanghai yinshuguan, 1920 [preface dated 1918]), *Yi* 乙 (B) *Yinshidian* 飲食店 (Food and Drink Establishments), p. 10a.

15   See "Huyouji lüe" 滬游記略 (A Summary of Wanderings Around Shanghai) in Ge Yuanxu 葛元煦 and Yuan Zuzhi 袁祖志, *Chongxiu Huyou zaji* 重修滬游雜記 (Miscellaneous Records of Wanderings Around Shanghai, Revised) (Shanghai, 1888), vol. 1, p. 24a. Lishuitai, a grand three-story tea garden, was established in the first year of the reign of the Tongzhi emperor (1862), sixteen years before the story of MYZ is set.

The Death of Ma Yongzhen

Reports of Ma's murder and the trial that followed, appeared in the Chinese newspapers, and the events are recounted in great detail over a number of days. English-language reports are fewer, but those that were published, are of significant length and are remarkably detailed. One takes up almost a page-and-a-half of dense text in this large-format newspaper, while another, though shorter, is still not insubstantial. In the *North-China Herald* (NCH), the location of the teashop where Ma died is described but not named: "Great excitement prevailed Sunday in the Maloo and neighbourhood, occasioned by a murderous outrage at a native teashop near the Racquet Court."[16] In another NCH report, the location is described in a little more detail, but still not named: " …the teashop…is at the west corner of the entrance to the theater on the north side of the Mall, between the Mixed Court and the Racquet Court…"[17]

For reasons best known to the authors of MYZ, in their version of the story, Ma Yongzhen is murdered in a small unnamed teashop, and Yidongtian is adopted instead as the place where Scrofulous Bai holds his gang meetings and entertains friends. In the *Shenbao* reports, it is specifically stated that the Yidongtian teashop was the place where Ma was murdered, remembering that this teashop was in fact on "The Maloo" (Nanking Road). In MYZ and MSZ, the authors, Qi Fanniu and Zhu Dagong, site it on Pakhoi Road, and, according to them, it wasn't even the place of Ma's murder.

> …The incident of the Boxing Master, Ma Yongzhen gravely injured in a stabbing by horse traders in the Yidongtian Teashop.

---

16 "Summary of News" in *The North-China Herald* (15 April 1879), p. 346.
17 "The Murder in the Maloo" in *The North-China Herald* (22 April 1879), p. 393.

The horse traders Gu Zhongxi, Ma Lian, and others, held a grievance against Ma Yongzhen and the day before yesterday at 4 o'clock arranged to meet for peaceful negotiations. Three horse traders were the first to arrive and the remaining group went upstairs to find a place to sit. As soon as Ma Yongzhen took his seat a bag of quicklime was thrown into his eyes to blind him. He immediately stepped back to protect himself, hitting out in front of him, but missing his target. At which point he was promptly stabbed with a sharp blade, receiving wounds from head to foot, but still had some hope of struggling free. Then a sharp blade hacked off his right foot, so that the bone was cut clean through. Then his left foot was severed, leaving only the skin attached, and he fell to the floor. Then someone hacked twice at his arm. Just then, Gu Zhongxi could be heard to give orders to the rest of the gang, telling them to make a run for it: "Don't worry about me, you take care of yourselves!" On hearing his voice, Ma seized a wooden stool and threw it, striking Gu on the head, and causing blood to flow...[18]

According to the NCH reports, this dispute was over money owed for a horse, which Gu Zhongxi had sold to Ma.[19] A fictional source, *The Nine-tailed Vixen* (a story that may be based on reality) suggests this was part of a protection racket that had been set up

---

18   "Quanshi shangbi xiqing" 拳師傷斃細情 (The Details of the Murder of a Boxing Master) in *Shenbao* 申報 ("The Shun Pao") (15 April 1879).

19   "The Murder in the Maloo" in *The North-China Herald* (22 April 1879), p. 393.

by Ma.[20] Another bone of contention between the two men can be found in various versions of a tale concerning a young child. In one, Ma accused Gu of kidnapping his child servant, something that Gu denied. According to the story in *The Nine-tailed Vixen,* the child ran away from Ma in Shandong after being beaten with a horsewhip, and, after a chance meeting with Gu, had taken up with him, before they left together for Shanghai.[21]

The Chinese report tells of the retrieval of a Japanese sword from the lodgings of the attackers by the police.[22] The NCH is more specific, and confirms that it was this Japanese sword, belonging to Ma Jian, that inflicted Ma Yongzhen's fatal injuries. The deadly nature of Japanese "samurai swords", with their devastatingly sharp blades, would account for the severity of Ma's wounds as described in the reports. The two English-language reports, based on various sources (no doubt to some extent including the Chinese-language press), tell the reader many details that are not available in the Chinese versions (and vice versa). These include a list of injuries that are only hinted at in the Chinese article above, and were presumably

---

20   Menghua Guanzhu 夢花館主 (Master of the Hall of Floral Dreams) [Jiang Yinxiang 江薩香], *Jiuwei hu* 九尾狐 (The Nine-tailed Vixen) in *Wan Qing xiaoshuo daxi* 晚清小說大系 (Compendium of Late Qing Fiction) vol. 11 (Taibei: Guangya chuban youxian gongsi, 1984). The version of the Ma Yongzhen story told in this book appears in chapters 26 to 30.

21   Menghua Guanzhu 夢花館主 (Master of the Hall of Floral Dreams) [Jiang Yinxiang 江薩香], *Jiuwei hu* 九尾狐 (The Nine-tailed Vixen) in *Wan Qing xiaoshuo daxi* 晚清小說大系 (Compendium of Late Qing Fiction) vol. 11 (Taibei: Guangya chuban youxian gongsi, 1984).

22   The weapons recovered after the death of Ma Yongzhen were a Japanese sword, a smaller sword, two daggers, and a handgun. See "Chuxun zanren quanshi an" 初訊攢刃拳師案 (Initial Hearing in the Case of the Knifing of a Master Boxer) in *Shenbao* 申報 ("The Shun Pao") (16 April 1879).

taken directly from a transcript of the doctor's report.[23] Rather surprisingly, the throwing of the quicklime in Ma's eyes to blind him, is not mentioned in the English newspapers. In all Chinese-language accounts, factual or fictional, this is considered to be an important detail, as it was this dirty trick that incapacitated Ma, who, under normal fighting conditions, was widely considered to be indestructible. The stool thrown by Ma, as mentioned in the Chinese report, hit its target with great precision, despite Ma having been blinded by the quicklime.

> [A policeman found]…Koo Ching-chee [Gu Zhongxi] with his face downwards on the pavement close to the teashop door. He was moaning hideously, with the object apparently conveying of the impression that he had been attacked and ill-used and was not the aggressor. His face was certainly covered with blood, but when he was examined only a small wound was found on his forehead, and concluding from the course of events that the ruse he was playing was not likely to succeed he feigned intoxication.[24]

The hospital to which Ma was taken is also mentioned in the newspaper reports. The Gutzlaff Hospital (*Tiren yiyuan* 體仁醫院) was on Ningpo Road, to the west of the scene of the crime,

---

23 "Over each eye he had a deep longitudinal cut, the skin of the nose was sliced off, his left elbow joint and left hip joint cut into, the bone of the same thigh split longitudinally and cut through about four inches below the joint by an oblique cut; the bone of the same leg was split longitudinally three inches below the knee, and the ankle cut into, leaving the foot hanging by the back tendon. The right knee joint, with the bone below, was split longitudinally, and the ankle joint of the same leg opened by a straight cut. Both his feet were removed by Dr Jamieson, and his other injuries attended to; but…[in the end] he succumbed to his injuries." "Summary of News" in *The North-China Herald* (15 April 1879), p. 346.
24 "The Murder in the Maloo" in *The North-China Herald* (22 April 1879), p. 393.

and Ma was rushed there in a rickshaw, but succumbed to his wounds the same night.[25]

Ma the Man

Ma Yongzhen was known as a martial artist, performing strongman, equestrian performer and horse trader. To some extent these are all reflected in MYZ, which presents themed chapters focusing on different aspects of his life in Shanghai. The slogan "He has trodden on both shores of the Yellow River and has fought with his fists in the capitals north and south," is introduced in Chapter One and features again in Chapters Six and Eight, each time with slight variations. This is a phrase that was often associated with Ma, and versions of it appear in a number of writings in which his story is told, including the lengthy late-Qing work of fiction, *The Nine-tailed Vixen*. In two articles written decades after the event, it is said that the slogan was specifically used to draw a crowd to Ma's street performances, and this is its function in MYZ too.[26]

Much of the content of the chapters is thematic, and introduces the reader to a variety of aspects of Shanghai life in the 1870s, as colored by the experience of the authors from the standpoint of the 1920s. There are two visits to opium halls in Chapters Thirteen/Fourteen and Chapter Seventeen. There are visits to courtesan houses in both halves of the book, in Chapter Three and Chapter Fifteen. There is a visit to Lungwha Temple

---

25 "Quanshi chiku" 拳師吃苦 (The Suffering of a Boxing Master) in *Shenbao* 申報 ("The Shun Pao") (14 April 1879).

26 For example, the slogan is quoted in Qian Jibo 錢基博, "Jiji yuwen bu, Ma Yongzhen" 技擊餘聞補，馬永貞 (Supplementary Anecdotes on the Martial Arts, Ma Yongzhen) in *Xiaoshuo yuebao* 小説月報 ("The Short Story Magazine") vol. 5 no. 7 (25 October 1914), p. 1. See also Yi Yi 乙乙, "Ma Yongzhen, Yilu suibi" 馬永貞，乙盧隨筆 (Ma Yongzhen, Yi Lu Random Notes) in *Xiaoshuo xinbao* 小説新報 (New Fiction) vol. 2 no. 8 (1916), pp. 4-11.

and Pagoda, in spring when the peach trees are in bloom, which lays much emphasis on poetic themes. There are three occasions when the action is based around fighting: Chapter Ten, with a gang fight in a teashop, Chapters Nineteen/Twenty in which Ma is fatally attacked by Scrofulous Bai's stooges and the Axe Head Gang, and Chapter Seven. The latter, in which Yellow Beard challenges Ma to a "friendly" bout, is the only example in which elements of anything approaching "martial arts writing" can be found. In the MYZ version of the story, the fight begins with a sort of mid-air arm wrestle and continues in this vein for a while, until it becomes gradually more lively as the action progresses, and eventually a number of specific martial arts moves are introduced: "Black Tiger Steals the Heart," "The Iron Eagle Pounces on the Tiger," "The Hungry Wolf Swallows the Lamb," and "The Bee Enters its Nest." It is with these moves that Ma topples Yellow Beard three times at the purpose-built arena erected near the Jing'an Temple. This is the only place in the novel where named martial arts moves occur, and a relative lack of combative content means the book cannot rightly be classed as a "martial arts" story, despite it being advertised on its front cover as a *jiji xiaoshuo* 技擊小説 (literally: "martial arts work of fiction"). This is somewhat different to the MSZ book, which does feature martial arts moves in several chapters, though it too should never rightly be described as a conventional martial arts novel, despite also being published as a *jiji xiaoshuo*.

In the account of Ma's life found in *The Nine-tailed Vixen*, this fight is presented rather differently, but still involves the grasping of hands. It is presented as a contest of strength between the two men, squeezing each other's hands as hard as they can, to see who will be the first to submit. Needless to say, Yellow Beard is unable to bear the pain of Ma's vice-like grip, and it is Ma who emerges victorious.[27] In this version of the story, the two strongmen walk hand-in hand from the Bund in the east to Nichengqiao by the Race Club and back.

> ...Yellow Beard then reached out and grasped Ma Yongzhen's hand, and they began to walk shoulder to shoulder, while secretly using their strength [to squeeze each other's hands]. From the Bund they walked to the foot of Nicheng Bridge, Yellow Beard allowing Ma Yongzhen to keep hold of his hand all the way. At first, it was impossible to decide who was the winner and who the loser. But on the return journey, from Nicheng Bridge to the Bund, as they neared the Racquet Court, Ma Yongzhen gradually began to increase the pressure of his grip. Yellow Beard felt that he could bear it no longer, but still thought it best to reluctantly persevere...[28]

In the version of the Ma Yongzhen story described in MYZ, Ma's enemy, Yellow Beard is identified simply as a foreign strongman, of no specific nationality. One clue as to his origins, however, is that during the first fight in Chapter Ten, he runs off to the "Big Striking Clock" to report the disturbance, rather than to one of the police stations in the International Settlement. The "Big Striking Clock" was the name given by the locals to the

---

27   Menghua Guanzhu 夢花館主 (Master of the Hall of Floral Dreams) [Jiang Yinxiang 江蔭香], *Jiuwei hu* 九尾狐 (The Nine-tailed Vixen) in *Wan Qing xiaoshuo daxi* 晚清小説大系 (Compendium of Late Qing Fiction) vol. 11 (Taibei: Guangya chuban youxian gongsi, 1984), chapter 27, p. 213.

28   Menghua Guanzhu 夢花館主 (Master of the Hall of Floral Dreams) [Jiang Yinxiang 江蔭香], *Jiuwei hu* 九尾狐 (The Nine-tailed Vixen) in *Wan Qing xiaoshuo daxi* 晚清小説大系 (Compendium of Late Qing Fiction) vol. 11 (Taibei: Guangya chuban youxian gongsi, 1984), chapter 27, p. 213.

French Municipal Police headquarters, in the French Concession, due to the presence of the clock placed high up on the front face of its domed clocktower, as depicted in *Dianshizhai huabao* and *Shenjiang shenjing*, and described in Ge Yuanxu's book.[29] It must be assumed, then, that Yellow Beard was envisioned by the authors of MYZ as French. Indeed, in *The Adventures of Ma Suzhen* (written by the same authors), he is specifically said to be a "French Hercules".[30] Elsewhere, in different accounts, Yellow Beard is described variously as Russian, Belgian, or Dutch, or as an "English policeman". It is the latter description that appears in the *Nine-tailed Vixen*, and in the illustrations to one edition of that book, Yellow Beard can be clearly seen wearing a police uniform similar to the type worn by the police of the International Settlement in the early 20th century.[31]

It is Yellow Beard's defeat in the martial arts contest, together with the humiliation suffered by Scrofulous Bai when he gets drunk and makes a fool of himself at the Yileyuan restaurant — incidents that don't mean much to Ma when they take place — that are ultimately responsible for Ma's downfall, something that is predicted by Lu Shouji in Chapter Five. The other fights that take place in the story, at the end of the first half, and later in

---

29 See "Faguo jieqi" 法國節期 (The French Public Holiday) in *Dianshizhai huabao* 點石齋 畫報 (Dianshizhai Pictorial) (1884), vol. 2, p. 64. "Fa xunfu fang" 法巡撫房 (The French Police Station) in Zunwenge Zhuren 尊聞閣主人 (Master of the Zunwenge) [Ernest Major] and Wu Youru 吳友如, *Shenjiang shengjing tu* 申江勝景圖 (Wondrous Scenes of Shanghai) (Shanghai: Shenbao guan 1884), part 2, pp. 52-53. Reprint published by Taipei, Guangwen shuju, 1981. See also "Da zimingzhong" 大自鳴鐘 (Big Striking Clock) in Ge Yuanxu 葛元煦 and Yuan Zuzhi 袁祖志, *Chongxiu Huyou zaji* 重修滬游雜記 (Miscellaneous Records of Wanderings Around Shanghai, Revised) 4 *juan* (Shanghai, 1888), vol. 1, p. 12b.

30 Qi Fanniu and Zhu Dagong (attrib.) and Paul Bevan (tr.), *The Adventures of Ma Suzhen: An Heroic Woman Takes Revenge in Shanghai* (Palgrave Macmillan, 2021), p. 71.

31 Menghua Guanzhu 夢花館主 (Master of the Hall of Floral Dreams) [Jiang Yinxiang 江蔭 香], *Jiuwei hu* 九尾狐 (The Nine-tailed Vixen) (Suzhou: Jiaotong tushuguan minyoushe, 1918), chapter 5.

the attack in which Ma Yongzhen meets his death, are simply brawls, and are not choreographed in such detail as the martial arts contest. The first of these brawls ends in stalemate, but throughout the second half of the book, Scrofulous Bai's hatred grows, until at the end he is given the opportunity to take his revenge, with the aid of the deadly Axe Head Gang.

Shanghai Gangs

Ma Yongzhen was a gangster, and an emphasis on Shanghai gangland culture can be seen throughout the book. This begins with the introduction of the minor character, the merchant, Zhao Lianyu, who had taken up with the *Qing bang* 青幫 (Green Gang). In 1878, the Green Gang, a well-known, historical underworld organization, was only in its infancy. As mentioned by Brian G. Martin, Shanghai "...emerged as a centre for the modern Green Gang...in the decades of the 1880s and 1890s,"[32] and the famous Green Gang boss, Du Yuesheng 杜月笙 "Big Ears Du" (1888-1951) was born towards the end of that time. This is another of the many examples in MYZ where chronology and historical accuracy are conveniently skimmed over by the authors, in order to tell their story in the most direct way possible, and to hold maximum appeal for their readership. Though not mentioned in the text, it was widely known that the Green Gang's main business interests were in the trafficking and sale of opium and in prostitution.

Opium Houses

Opium was a problem for the authorities in Shanghai, before, after, and throughout the forty-year period that is the focus here. Despite the efforts of various anti-opium organizations, the

---

32   Brian G. Martin, *The Shanghai Green Gang: Politics and Organized Crime, 1919-1937* (Berkeley, Los Angeles, London: University of California Press, 1996), p. 28.

drug was still much consumed by people at all levels of society. The following, from Ge Yuanxu's book, shows how normalized extravagant and luxurious opium houses had become for the wealthy elite in the late 1870s:

> Shanghai's opium houses are the finest in all under heaven. Their layout is clean and elegant, with tea bowls and opium lamps, not one that is not most finely wrought. In the beginning, the most famous was Mianyunge, its windows, doors and lattices displaying pierced ornamental carving of the very highest workmanship. Others, such as Nanchengxin and Beichengxin, are the finest and most spacious. Zuileju and Qingliange have food and victuals that surpass those served in restaurants. The interiors are furnished with tables and chairs that are mostly made of *hongmu* wood, inlaid with marble, and are all of the finest quality.[33]

The unnamed opium houses in MYZ situated in the International Settlement, to which Poxy Fang and Cheng Zimin go in Chapter Thirteen and Chapter Seventeen respectively, are certainly not as luxurious as the establishments named in this passage. Cheng is no doubt aware of the relatively low status of his favourite haunt, but clearly finds its surroundings meet his needs as the leader of the Axe Head Gang. In the other opium-smoking scene, in conversation with Chai Jiuyun, Poxy Fang actually names one of the establishments mentioned in the above passage in Ge's book, Nanchengxin. This was a luxurious,

---

33 See "Yan guan" 烟館 (Opium Houses), Ge Yuanxu 葛元煦 and Yuan Zuzhi 袁祖志, *Chongxiu Huyou zaji* 重修滬游雜記 (Miscellaneous Records of Wanderings Around Shanghai, Revised) 4 *juan* (Shanghai, 1888), vol. 2, pp. 11a and 11b.

high-class opium house in the French Concession, and was one of Shanghai's most famous. It appeared in an 1884 collection of lithographs by the famous commercial artist Wu Youru 吳友如 (1840-1893), published by Ernest Major (1841-1908), owner of the *Shenbao* newspaper. In the scene depicted in the print, marble inlay, as mentioned in Ge's description above, can be seen in every piece of furniture in the room, and is echoed in what appear to be four mounted and framed marble wall panels, probably representing the four seasons.[34] Nanchengxin is mentioned by Ge together with its sister establishment, Beichengxin, and Poxy Fang recognizes the first of these as being a purveyor of fine quality opium. Even so, Poxy Fang considers the high-class *chandu* opium that he smokes in his favorite haunt, to equal that found in high-class establishments. From the way they are described in MYZ, both Poxy Fang's and Cheng Zimin's preferred hideouts are laid out with just the bare essentials, and they and their guests appear to be the only customers present on each occasion. In MYZ, the place that most closely resembles the elegantly furnished establishments mentioned in Ge's book, is not an opium house at all, but is Hua Baoyu's courtesan house in Puqing Li, with its fine furnishings and *hongmu* furniture.

In Chapter Three, the suggestion that an electric bell had been installed in Hua Baoqin's establishment at this early date, and was used to announce the arrival of guests, is fanciful. Even an opium house as prestigious as Nanchengxin didn't adopt electric lighting until the 1890s, having previously used gas, and the Pinyulou shuchang 品玉樓書場 (Pinyulou Storytelling Hall), a high-class courtesan establishment, did not have electricity

---

34 Zunwenge Zhuren 尊聞閣主人 (Master of the Zunwenge) [Ernest Major] and Wu Youru 吳友如, *Shenjiang shengjing tu* 申江勝景圖 (Wondrous Scenes of Shanghai) (Shanghai: Shenbao guan 1884), part 2, pp. 8-9. Reprint: Taipei, Guangwen shuju, 1981.

installed until 1894.[35] It should be noted that the first electricity was not available in Shanghai at all until 1882, three years after Ma's death.[36] Electric doorbells were only in worldwide use after 1913.[37]

Yuan Zuzhi: a Shanghai Poet

In chapter four, Ma Yongzhen lifts the stone *ding* incense burner. It is from this time on, due to the attention he attracts while engaging in this feat of strength, that Ma decides to expand his prestige by taking on more disciples. This display ostensibly takes place in the garden of the poet Yuan Zuzhi 袁祖志 (1827-1898), grandson of his even more famous grandfather, Yuan Mei 袁枚 (1716-1798), who was considered to be among the greatest poets of the Qing dynasty. Yuan Zuzhi was a well-known figure in Shanghai, and worked in the city as a local government official before becoming an editor of the *Xinbao* 新報 newspaper.[38] He was a renowned poet, and frequent contributor of poetry and other writings to other publications, including the newspaper, *Shenbao*.[39] In reality, Yuan built his *Yangliu loutai* 楊柳樓臺 (Weeping Willow Terrace) on Foochow Road in 1881 (two years after the death of Ma Yongzhen), and the terrace and its gardens are the subject of much discussion and poetry writing in *Shenbao*

---

35 Ye Xiaoqing, *Popular Culture in Shanghai, 1884-1898* (Doctoral thesis. The Australian National University, 1991), p. 91.

36 According to James Carter, electricity in Shanghai began at 7.00, on July 26, 1882. See The first days of electric Shanghai – The China Project Accessed 15 August 2023.

37 Doorbells Transformed – The Doorbell Museum (electrachime.net) Accessed 31 August 2023.

38 Rudolf G. Wagner, *Joining the Global Public: Word, Image, and City in Early Chinese Newspaper* (Albany: State University of New York Press, 2012), p. 64.

39 As noted by Yeh, the first poems in *Shenbao* appeared in the second issue (30 April 1872) and ended in 21 March 1890. Catherine Yeh, *Shanghai Love: Courtesans, Intellectuals, and Entertainment Culture, 1850-1910* (Washington: University of Washington Press, 2006), p. 368n50.

that year, and throughout the 1880s and 1890s. Yuan's poet friends are just the sort of people who are the brunt of the joke in MYZ, but in fact they were some of the best-known men of letters in Shanghai. Yuan was particularly renowned for his *Zhuzhi ci* 竹枝詞 (Bamboo Branch Lyrics), and it was through his poetry that he gained something of a celebrity status.[40] His fame meant that his appearance in MYZ, was not the first time he was satirized in fiction in the years after his death. He appeared under the name Hou Aochu, grandson of Hou Shiweng, in a serialized story, *Ershi nian mudu zhi guai xianzhuang* 二十年目睹之怪現狀 (Strange Happenings Witnessed over a Period of Twenty Years), by Wu Woyao 吳沃堯 (1866-1910) in the magazine *Xin Xiaoshuo* 新小説 (New Fiction), which was edited by the important intellectual leader and reformer, Liang Qichao 梁啓超 (1873-1929), and published in book form in 1909.[41]

> Shu Danhu...took a horse and carriage to Fourth Avenue and stopped opposite the Parsee Gardens, in order to discuss matters with Hou Aochu, a grandson of that Hou Shiweng who appears in the novel *Pinhua baojian*.[42] This Hou Aochu was editor of some sort of newspaper or other. When he caught site of Danhu, he squinted at him with eyes half closed, smiling that sort

40   For more on Yuan Zuzhi see Catherine Yeh, *Shanghai Love: Courtesans, Intellectuals, and Entertainment Culture, 1850-1910* (Washington: University of Washington Press, 2006), pp. 197-198.

41   As noted by Duncan M. Campbell in Qian Zhongshu and Duncan M. Campbell (ed. / tr.), *Seven Essays on Art and Literature* (Leiden: Brill, 2014), p. 212n4.

42   The Bosi huayuan 波斯花園 (literally, "Persian Gardens", but in this case, "Parsee Gardens") refers to the area around the Zoroastrian Temple (built in 1866) and cemetery on Fuzhou Lu. For more on Zoroastrianism in China see Takeshi Aoki, "Zoroastrianism in the Far East" in Michael Stausberg and Yuhan Sohrab-Dinshaw Vevaina (eds.), *The Wiley Blackwell Companion to Zoroastrianism* (West Sussex: Wiley Blackwell, 2015).

of smile that is not really a smile at all...[43]

Yuan Zuzhi was a highly respected figure in the Shanghai literary world, who in addition to his books about Shanghai, wrote several important books that relate his experiences on his trips abroad to Europe and America.[44] Several articles concerning his foreign travels appeared in *Shenbao,* particularly in 1883. Back home he continued to write about Shanghai and by 1888 was responsible for editing the revised edition of Ge Yuanxu's much read, *Huyou zaji.* The events of April 1879, when Ma met his death, are likely to have been well known to Yuan Zuzhi and his circle, as it was big news in Shanghai at the time, and was reported extensively, for several days, in *Shenbao,* a newspaper to which Yuan and his friends contributed. In Ge's book, Yuan's poems, and those of his associates, appear in volume three of the four-volume set, and often take as their subjects the same assorted everyday themes as the *biji* entries found elsewhere in the book.[45] All aspects of the city are discussed, often very briefly in just two or three lines, and are on miscellaneous themes: teashops, gardens, rickshaws, temples (including Lungwha and Jing'an), police stations, termites, newspaper companies (*Xinbao* and *Shenbao*), courtesans, the Western calendar, and a list of things that were forbidden in the International Settlement, to name just a few. In the fourth and final volume, information can be found

---

43 Wu Jianren 吳趼人 [Wu Woyao 吳沃堯], *Ershi nian mudu zhi guai xianzhuang* 二十年目睹之怪現狀 (Strange Happenings Witnessed over a Period of Twenty Years) (Shanghai Shijie shuju, 1923) *juan* 6, chapter 66, p. 1a. *Pinhua baojian* 品花寶鑒 (A Precious Mirror for Ranking Flowers) was an early homoerotic novel written by Chen Sen 陳森 (active 1823-1849).

44 See for example, Yuan Zuzhi, *Yinghai caiwen jishi* 瀛海採問紀實 (A Record of Things Collected and Explained from Beyond the Oceans).

45 For a good example of Yuan's poems in this book, see Cangshan jiuzhu 倉山舊主 (Old Master of Cang Mountain) [Yuan Zuzhi], *Hubei shijing* 滬北十景 (Ten Scenes of the Foreign Concessions), vol. 4, pp. 7b-8b.

of the type that would be expected in a standard guidebook: extensive information on shipping timetables, routes and prices for ferries; the tides; addresses for shops of all sorts; banks and financial institutions; and the consulates of various countries. There are also lists of things that one might not expect to find in a typical guidebook: "Famous Calligraphers and Painters", plus their place of origin, their courtesy name (*zi* 字), and what type of calligraphy and painting they specialized in; a list of actors from five famous Shanghai "tea garden" theaters, and the acting roles for which they were best known; and "Famous Female Singers from Each of the Storytelling Halls" and the titles of the stories with which they were most associated. These performers were the highest class of courtesan in Shanghai, and were skilled in all aspects of the arts.[46] This list is found at the very end of Ge Yuanxu's book. At the beginning of both the 1876 and 1888 editions, there is a preface written by Yuan, in which he observes how Shanghai had prospered over a twenty- or thirty-year period, an extract from which reads as follows:

> I once consulted the Shanghai city gazetteer, in which it is recorded that the city during the Ming dynasty stretched from Huating to the sea, and was but a small province. In our own dynasty, because the waters of the Liu River estuary at Taicang silted up, the situation changed so that seagoing ships entered and departed via Wusong. As a result, the city gradually

---

46   *Shuhua mingjia* 書畫名家 (Famous Calligraphers and Painters), : Ge Yuanxu, *Huyou zaji* 滬游雜記 (Miscellaneous Records of Wanderings around Shanghai), 4 *juan* (Shanghai, 1876), vol. 4, pp. 3a-4b; *Tianxian, Yongni, Liuchun, Xin Dangui, Jiuxiang, wu chayuan zhuming juese* 天仙詠霓留春新丹桂九香五茶園著名脚色 (Famous Actors from the Five Tea Gardens, Tianxian, Yongni, Liuchun, Xin dangui, and Jiuxiang), vol. 4, pp. 25b-28a. *Ge shuchang zhuming nü changshu* 各書場著名女唱書 (Famous Female Singers from Each of the Storytelling Halls), vol. 4, pp. 28a-28b.

became more prosperous, until, in the final years of the reign of the Daoguang Emperor, the five Treaty Ports opened for trade. China and foreign countries began to do business with one another, and Shanghai became a magnificent sight to behold. In recent years, increasingly more paddle steamers have made their way here. From the outer seas and the Yangtse River, the city has become accessible from all sides. People who have come to Shanghai include those from the eighteen provinces within the Great Wall, and the twenty-four countries beyond the seas. Oh, yes! It is flourishing indeed! Not since the birth of mankind has there been a place as perfect and complete as this.[47]

Yuan Zuzhi's admiration for Shanghai, as reflected in this encomium, can also be seen in the books he and his colleagues wrote about the city. Certainly Ge Yuanxu's book is written from the point of view of someone who is immensely proud of the city he called home. His aim, and that of his fellow contributors to the book, including Yuan, was to introduce all aspects of Shanghai to the curious intellectual visitor. This includes descriptions of famous sights and some of the new buildings and infrastructure that made Shanghai the most modern Chinese city at the time.

Courtesans

The red light district was a constant in the history of Shanghai. In the 1920s and 1930s prostitution was rife and this was the

---

47 Yuan Zuzhi 袁祖志, Xu 序 (Preface) in Ge Yuanxu 葛元煦 and Yuan Zuzhi, *Chongxiu Huyou zaji* 重修滬游雜記 (Miscellaneous Records of Wanderings Around Shanghai, Revised) 4 *juan* (Shanghai, 1888), n.p., and Ge Yuanxu, *Huyou zaji* 滬游雜記 (Miscellaneous Records of Wanderings around Shanghai), 4 *juan* (Shanghai, 1876), pp. 1b and 2a.

chief reason Shanghai became popularly known as the City of Sin. Back in the 19th century, the pastime of visiting courtesan houses was considered a perfectly respectable part of everyday life for the upper echelons of male society. It was so much part of Shanghai entertainment culture that information about courtesan houses could be found in books like Ge's that were written for the convenience of gentlemen travelers to the city. In Ge Yuanxu's book there is much about courtesans. It is interesting to compare this with the later 1920 guidebook, *Shanghai zhinan*, as it too includes sections on courtesan houses and brothel culture, something that is clearly important for the understanding of at least two chapters in MYZ. Some may think it surprising to find such information in a mainstream guidebook from the 1920s, but even guidebooks from later years continued to introduce aspects of prostitution and courtesan culture in the same way, listing the different types of brothel, and those who worked in them, plus the prices for the various services offered (such as tea, food, and entertainment in the form of music and song).

Yuan Zuzhi was himself deeply involved in courtesan culture and was notoriously romantically involved with one courtesan in particular, Li Sansan. He wrote poems about her, and as a result of Yuan's patronage and the attention of other gentlemen admirers, she became widely known, not just in Shanghai, but further afield.[48]

There are two scenes in MYZ that take place in courtesan houses. In the second half of the book (as written by Zhu Dagong), Chai Jiuyun and Ma Yongzhen visit Hua Baoyu in Puqing Li, situated off today's Fujian Zhong Lu. This is the scene in Chapter Fifteen, in which Ma and the maid Ah Hong find it difficult to understand

48   For more on Li Sansan see Catherine Yeh, *Shanghai Love: Courtesans, Intellectuals, and Entertainment Culture, 1850-1910* (Washington: University of Washington Press, 2006), pp. 198-199.

each other, as discussed on pages 214-215. In Chapter Three, in the first half of MYZ (written by Qi Fanniu), a visit is made to Hua Baoqin's establishment in Qunyu Fang off Swatow Road, where Zhou Lianyu and Ma Yongzhen go at the invitation of Chai Jiuyun and become involved in games of *penghu* 碰和 and *wahua* 挖花. According to Andrew Lo, during the 19th century *penghu* was just another name used to refer to *maque* 麻雀, the game commonly known today as *majiang* 麻將 or *mahjong*.[49] This is confirmed by what is found in the above-mentioned 1920 *Shanghai zhinan*, at the end of which can be found an introduction to the Shanghai and Suzhou languages, written for the benefit of Chinese visitors to Shanghai. This introduction takes the form of a list of terms with brief definitions, one of which refers to the game of *penghu*. This explanation reads quite simply:

Penghu: to play mahjong. A game for four players
鬥麻雀牌也。以四人為一局.

This definition of the term was given in the year when the writing of MYZ was in progress, so it gives some sort of guide as to what the writer, Zhu Dagong may have had in mind when referring to this game in the third decade of the 20th century. The game is referred to in a number of works of popular fiction from the 19th and early 20th centuries. These include chapters in, *The Nine-tailed Vixen*, and *Qinglou meng* 青樓夢 (The Dream

49   Andrew Lo, "China's Passion for *Pai*: Playing Cards, Dominoes, and Mahjong" in Colin Mackenzie and Irving L. Finkel (eds.), *Asian Games: The Art of Contest* (New York: Asia Society, 2004), p. 20.

of the Green Chamber).[50] The other game mentioned in MYZ is *wahua* (scooping out flowers), which could be played with cards or tiles. Andrew Lo identifies this game as still being played in Ningbo, Zhejiang Province, today.

> The basic set of twenty-one cards is multiplied six times to form a deck or 126 cards. Half of the cards are called *wu hua pai* (cards with no flowers) and half are called *hua pai* (cards with flowers)...Each player takes twenty cards, and the idea is to form sets of two cards.[51]

This was the game of choice for Hua Baoyu, who was put off by the complexities of Mahjong.

Zhou Fenglin: Performer of Female Roles

In MYZ, the enthusiastic reaction of those present at Ma's performance when he lifts the *ding* in Yuan Zuzhi's garden—his disciples, Yuan's poetic guests, and passersby—is compared to the applause given to one of the most famous Kunqu Opera performers of the late Qing and early Republican eras, Zhou Fenglin.

50   Menghua Guanzhu 夢花館主 (Master of the Hall of Floral Dreams) [Jiang Yinxiang 江蔭香], *Jiuwei hu* 九尾狐 (The Nine-tailed Vixen) in *Wan Qing xiaoshuo daxi* 晚清小説大系 (Compendium of Late Qing Fiction) vol. 11 (Taibei: Guangya chuban youxian gongsi, 1984), chapter 2, pp. 8-9 and chapter 60, pp. 492-493. Yu Da 俞達, *Qinglou meng* 青樓夢 (Dream of the Green Chamber) in *Wan Qing xiaoshuo daxi* 晚清小説大系 (Compendium of Late Qing Fiction) vol. 3 (Taibei: Guangya chuban youxian gongsi, 1984), chapter 45, pp. 297-298.
51   Andrew Lo, "China's Passion for *Pai*: Playing Cards, Dominoes, and Mahjong" in Colin Mackenzie and Irving L. Finkel (eds.), *Asian Games: The Art of Contest* (New York: Asia Society, 2004), p. 224.

> Of the surrounding onlookers, not one was not
> cheering and shouting his praise, just as if he were a
> great star performer, like that famous player of female
> roles, Zhou Fenglin when he sang "Jumping the Wall",
> from the *Romance of the Western Chamber*, on the Kunqu
> Opera stage.

Xixiang ji 西廂記 (The Romance of the Western Chamber) was
originally a northern-style play written by Wang Shifu 王實甫
(1250-1337?) during the Yuan dynasty (1271-1368) and "Jumping
the Wall" is the part in that story where the young man Zhang
Sheng jumps over the wall of the Pujiu Temple to meet with Cui
Yingying, a beautiful young woman with whom he has fallen
in love. Zhou Fenglin's southern-style version was performed
in the manner adopted by exponents of Kunqu Opera, a form
of sophisticated Chinese sung drama that first became popular
during the Ming dynasty (1368-1644). Zhou was a performer of
dan female roles and will have taken the lead role of Cui Yingying
in this play. He is one of the famous actors listed at the back of
Ge Yuanxu's book, and appears there as number four in the list
of sixty-two famous Kunqu and Peking Opera performers. In
this list, Zhou is said to be famous for playing four female roles
(Cui Yingying not among them). They are: Lady Tian in *Butterfly
Dream*; Princess White Flower in *The Phoenix Mountain*; Lady Zou
in *Cut the Hair In Place of the Head*; and Wang Zhizhen, the nun
in *Jade Hibiscus*.[52] Zhou was very much a celebrity figure, and the
following newspaper report describes him in glowing terms:

---

52   *Hudie meng Tian shi* 蝴蝶夢田氏, Lady Tian's aria from *Butterfly Dream*; *Fenghuangshan
gongzhu* 鳳凰山公主; Princess Baihua from *The Phoenix Mountain* (also known as
Baihuaji 百花記); Lady Zou in *Gefa daishou zoushi* 割髮代首鄒氏, from *The Romance of the
Three Kingdoms*; *Yu Furong Wang Zhizhen* 玉芙蓉王志貞, Wang Zhizhen, the nun in *Jade
Hibiscus*.

Fenglin is from the town of Suzhou. His figure is lithe and slender like the willow, and he is both handsome and intelligent. In singing and other performing skills he holds the crown amongst all performers in the Kunqu troupe of Shanghai's Garden of Three Elegances.[53]

Sanya yuan 三雅園 (The Garden of Three Elegances) was Shanghai's first public Chinese Opera theater and was established in 1851.[54] It was a Beijing-style "tea garden", catering for tea drinkers and diners, with a prominent stage for entertainment. Some of the larger teashops and restaurants that appear in MYZ, such as Yidongtian and Yileyuan, would also have been multi-level performance venues of this type. The five grand theaters listed in Ge Yuanxu's book, as the venues at which the sixty-two listed actors (including Zhou Fenglin) performed, were largely responsible for the rise in popularity of *Haipai* 海派 (Shanghai-style) Peking Opera during the late 19th century.[55]

The Mas on Stage and Screen

A "modern" stage version of *Ma Yongzhen* was mounted by the *Minmingshe* 民明社 (People's Cry Society) at the *Xiao wutai* 笑舞臺 (Laughter Stage) in 1923. This sort of spoken drama had little to do with *kunqu*, as performed by Zhou Fenglin, or other forms of

---

53 "Zeng lingren Zhou Fenglin" 贈伶人周鳳林 (Presented to the Actor Zhou Fenglin) in *Shenbao* 申報 *("The Shun Pao")* (10 April 1882).

54 Li Xiao, *Chinese Kunqu Opera* (Shanghai: Long River Press, 2005), pp. 237-239.

55 *Tianxian Chayuan* 天仙茶園, established in 1875 and situated on Fuhkien Road at the corner of Kwantung Road; *Yongni Chayuan* 詠霓茶園; *Liuchun Chayuan* 留春茶園; *Xin dan'gui Chayuan* 新丹桂茶園, originally established (as *Dangui*) in 1867 at the corner of Kwangtung Road and Hoopeh Road. A second theater was built at the corner of Foochow Road and Hoopeh Road in 1883 and named the "New Dangui"; and *Jiuxiang Chayuan* 九香茶園.

Chinese Opera that took place in local tea gardens. The Laughter Stage mounted *wenmingxi* "Civilized Drama" productions, a form of modern Western/Japanese-inspired spoken drama that became part of the popular cultural scene of Shanghai. Two of the main figures involved in this play were Zheng Zhengqiu 鄭正秋 (1889-1935) and Zhang Shichuan 張石川 (1890-1954). Later, in 1927, both men were central to the production of a film, *Shandong Ma Yongzhen* 山東馬永貞 (Ma Yongzhen of Shandong), made by their own Mingxing yingpian gongsi 明星影片公司 (The Star Motion Picture Producing Co, Ltd.).[56] The film is now lost, but a few stills survive, published in magazines of the day, most notably in an issue of the film company's souvenir magazine *Mingxing Tekan* 明星特刊 (Mingxing Special) that was devoted to it.[57] *Shandong Ma Yongzhen* was directed by Zhang Shichuan and the screenplay was written by Zheng Zhengqiu. They were two of the most prominent figures working in the Chinese film world in the 1920s, and established the Mingxing film company with others in 1922, the year before the books MYZ and MSZ were published. By 1927, when they came to make *Ma Yongzhen of Shandong*, they had already produced thirty-five films.[58]

Ma Yongzhen and Islam

Ma Yongzhen's cultural origins in his hometown in Shandong province were as a Hui Muslim. This religious aspect of Ma

---

56   Even though Mingxing released 193 feature films (143 silent, 50 sound), only twenty-five have survived. See Huang Xuelei, *Shanghai Filmmaking: Crossing Borders, Connecting to the Globe, 1922-1938* (Leiden: Brill, 2014), p. 19.

57   *Mingxing Tekan* 明星特刊 (Mingxing Special) no. 28 (1 December 1927).

58   A newspaper advertisement for *Shandong Ma Yongzhen* recognizes it as Mingxing's thirty-sixth production. *Shenbao* 申報 ("The Shun Pao") (4 December 1927), front page. For more about the film and drama, see the essay, "Ma Suzhen: A Hero of the Women's Realm", in Qi Fanniu and Zhu Dagong (attrib.) and Paul Bevan (tr.), *The Adventures of Ma Suzhen: An Heroic Woman Takes Revenge in Shanghai* (Palgrave Macmillan, 2021), pp. 105-127.

Yongzhen's life is significant. It rarely finds its way into fictional accounts but is well-known among modern scholars. It is also recognized in contemporary newspaper reports. In MYZ, after Ma's death, Chai Jiuyun goes to buy a coffin to lay Ma to rest; in MSZ, Ma Suzhen takes her brother's body back to Shandong for burial. Both of these accord with Han Chinese traditional burial customs, but, in fact, as we are told in a *Shenbao* report, the reality was that Ma Yongzhen's nephew, Ma Changchun asked to take charge of his body following his death, and sought permission from the court authorities to have his body moved to the Muslim cemetery in Shanghai.[59] This is also mentioned in one of the English-language reports: "A nephew of the deceased made an application for the body, explaining that he wished to wrap it in cloth and bury it in the ground."[60] Unlike the Chinese report, this doesn't explicitly state that Ma was a Muslim, but later, in the same report, it does point out that all of Ma's assailants were: "It also transpired during the inquiry that Koo Ching-chee [Gu Zhongxi] and Moh-lee [Ma Lian], as well as the other men suspected of being concerned in the fight are Mahomedans [sic]."[61] "Ma" is one of the most common family names found among Hui Muslim people in China. Traditionally, the Hui people have their own customs, their own cuisine, their own dress, and Ma Yongzhen was a great exponent of Hui martial arts.

Afterlife

Looking back at all the different versions of the story of Ma Yongzhen, it may well be that his true life story is now lost to

---

59 "Quanshi shangbi xiqing" 拳師傷斃細情 (Specifics Concerning the Mortal Wounding of a Master Boxer) in *Shenbao* ("The Shun Pao") (15 April 1879).

60 "The Murder in the Maloo" in *The North-China Herald* (22 April 1879), p. 393.

61 "The Murder in the Maloo" in *The North-China Herald* (22 April 1879), p. 393.

us forever. Apart from the newspaper reports published after his death, and a few articles telling of his performances as a strongman, the details of his life are all lost. Piecing together the details of the life of an historical figure who is best known because of his death, is no easy matter. This hasn't stopped people using the bare bones of what is known about him to construct their own widely differing stories, throughout the 20th century. And there are many of these. Throughout the 1930s, 40s, and 50s Ma continued to be seen as the hero of theatrical productions of all sorts, from a rerun of the *wenmingxi* version, with some of the original actors, to local Shanghai opera, *Huju* productions. These were followed by films, beginning with a 1962 remake of Zhang and Zheng's 1927 film.[62]

The heyday of the Ma Yongzhen film was during the 1970s. In the past fifty years he, his fictional sister, Ma Suzhen, and even their mother, have appeared in leading roles in martial arts films and TV series well over a dozen times. In the most recent example, *Ma Yongzhen zhi Zhabei jue* 马永贞之闸北决 ("Ma Yongzhen: Duel in Zhabei", dir. Xu Jun 徐俊, 2020), the screenplay is written so that almost every aspect of his life is retold.[63] This action-packed martial arts film bears no relation whatsoever to what we know about the historical figure. But does this really matter? It could be argued that this rewriting of his story simply carries on a tradition that stretches back to the earliest stories based on his life, in film and popular fiction, and indeed can be seen in the fanciful "historical romance" that is *Murder in the Maloo: A Tale of Old Shanghai*.

---

62 *Ma Yongzhen of Shandong* (*Shandong Ma Yongzhen*, dir. Hoh Ban, 1962).
63 Some examples include: *The Avenger* (*Chou*, dir. Florence Yu Fung-Chi, 1972); *A Brave Girl Boxer In Shanghai* (*Shanghai tan Ma Suzhen*, dir. Yu Han-Hsiang and Fu Ching-Hua, 1972); *Ma Yongzhen The Boxer from Shantung* (*Ma Yong Chen*, dir. Chang Che, 1972); *Queen of Fist* (*Shandong laoniang*, dir. Lung Chien, 1973); *Ma Yongzhen: Duel in Zhabei* (*Ma Yongzhen zhi Zhabei jue*, dir. Xu Jun, 2020).

A NOTE ON LANGUAGE

Quotations and Sayings

As was common in Chinese fiction before the introduction of the "New Literature", following the New Culture Movement and the protests of May Fourth 1919, a number of quotations and sayings arc used by the authors throughout MYZ, to punctuate the dialogue and help develop the plot. Excerpts can be found from sources as diverse as *Lunyu* 論語 (*The Analects*) of Confucius and the *Daodejing* 道德經, the Tang dynasty *shi* 詩 poetry of Wang Changling 王昌齡 (698-756), and the Song dynasty *ci* 詞 lyrics of Ouyang Xiu 歐陽修 (1007-1072). All quotations that appear in the book are well-known, and have been much quoted elsewhere, and there is no doubt the authors expected their readers to recognize them immediately on reading them.

Quotations from philosophical or poetic sources are often found grouped together in the same chapter, or part of a chapter. For example, in the introduction to the second half, in Chapter Eleven, a number of quotations follow in quick succession within the first few lines. The first is from the *Daodejing*: "It has been said since ancient times that the soft can overcome the hard and the weak can conquer the strong," and goes on to quote from *The Analects* of Confucius: "A little impatience can ruin truly great plans."[64] Both sentiments seem to admonish Ma Yongzhen for

---

64   D. C. Lau, *Tao Te Ching* (London: Penguin, 1963), Book Two LXXVIII, p. 85. Lau's translation reads: "...that the weak overcomes the strong, and the submissive overcomes the hard..." William Edward Soothill, *The Analects, or the Conversations of Confucius with his Disciples and Others* (London, New York, Toronto: Oxford University Press, 1937 [1910]), Book XV, Chapter XXVI, p. 170. Soothill's translation reads: "The Master said, Plausible words confound morals, and a trifling impatience may confound a great project."

his impatience, and use of force with regard to his ambition to become number one among the gangsters of Shanghai, which ultimately leads to his downfall.

Other sayings from early Chinese philosophical sources found throughout the book include, in addition to quotations that are commonly attributed to Confucius himself, one that is said to be by his grandson Zisi 子思 (c.483-402BC): "In the south the ambience is soft and gentle; in the north the ambience is hard and strong."[65] This is pertinent to the discussion of Ma's travels from Shandong in the north to Jiangnan in the south in Chapter One. Another well-known quotation by the Confucian scholar, Xunzi 荀子 (c.316- c.235BC), is used in the same chapter to describe Ma Yongzhen's progress in martial arts training as a young man, and how he came to surpass his master in skill: "Blue comes from the indigo plant but it is bluer than the plant itself."[66]

The phrase "Within the Four Seas All Men are Brothers," is another quotation from The Analects, and is one that is directly relevant to the book's main themes, gangs and gangsters.[67] In this context, the term "brothers" is taken to mean the "brothers-in-arms" of Shanghai's gangland culture. Likewise, the phrase "we are all of one family", which is repeated many times in the

---

65　The origins of this phrase can be found in the Zhongyong 中庸 (Doctrine of the Mean). Sima Qian 司馬遷 (145?-86? BC) was the first to suggest that Zisi was the author of the Zhongyong but it has been doubted ever since and is widely rejected by modern scholars. See Zhongyong chapter 10 in Xie Bingying 謝冰瑩 et al. (eds.), Xinyi sishu duben 新譯四書讀本 (A Four Books Reader, Newly Interpreted) (Taipei: Sanmin shuju, 2002 [1987]), pp. 32-33.

66　Translation by Watson. Burton Watson (tr.), Hsün Tsu: Basic Writings (New York: Columbia University Press, 1963). Chapter 1, p. 15.

67　William Edward Soothill, The Analects, or the Conversations of Confucius with his Disciples and Others (London, New York, Toronto: Oxford University Press, 1937 [1910]), Book XII, Chapter V, p. 117. Soothill's translation reads: "…all within the four seas are his brothers."

second half of the book, reflects the existence of brotherly ties between gangsters in underworld Shanghai. Gangster-related language can be found throughout the book. Another stock phrase often used in gangland feuds, as a defense when accused of wrongdoing, is: "In days gone by we have had nothing to complain about; there has never been any hatred between you and me." Variations on this theme can be found in many writings that focus on the world of Jianghu.

The subject of a secret language used by underworld gangsters, also rears its head in MYZ. We never get to discover what this is, however, as the narrator tells us:

> *Unfortunately, fair reader, this author does not understand the inner workings of Jianghu — that underworld of traveling fighters, and wanderers of rivers and lakes — so is unable to write this jargon down for you to see. All I can do is leave it blank. I beg the reader's forgiveness for this. Even Ma Yongzhen dared not say those words out loud.*

There are also passages relating to Ma Yongzhen's equestrian skills. For example, with reference to him as being comparable to the sage of horses from the Spring and Autumn Period (770 BC to 481 BC), Bo Le 伯樂 in Chapter One, and later in the same chapter with regard to Ma's use of *xiangma* 相馬 (horse physiognomy), as originally devised and practiced by Bo Le. Another example of a saying with an equestrian theme in the same chapter, is taken from the great epic, *Sanguo yanyi* 三國演義 (Romance of the Three Kingdoms): "Southerners ride boats and northerners ride horses." This was said by the warlord Liu Bei 劉備 (161-223) to Sun Quan 孫權 (182-252), when he happened to spy a small boat among the waves. In the original, Sun Quan takes this comment as a personal slight and promptly mounts his horse to show off his equestrian skills.[68] Young Master Dong Jiguang quotes this to show his admiration for the horsemanship of Ma and his disciples.

There are some very deliberate references to poetry, which show the author, Zhu Dagong, in lyrical mood. These appear mainly in Chapter Fourteen, when Ma Yongzhen visits the Lungwha Temple and Pagoda at Chai Jiuyun's invitation. Here can be found quotations from, or references to, the poetry of Ouyang Xiu, Wang Changling, and Zhou Bangyan 周邦彥 (1056-1121).[69] These are all on the theme of Spring, some with a festive flavor, and others that display nostalgic sentiments. In MYZ, these passages are rarely direct quotations, and more often than not, just hint at the poem in question. A good example of this is when Ma alludes to a poem by Zhou Bangyan with the line: "At this time of year, while far from home, I should regret allowing time to pass in vain." The original line to which (the apparently now learned and poetic) Ma is referring: 正單衣試酒，恨客里、光陰虛擲, translates more literally as: "It is now the season to change into light clothes and sample fine wine. I regret residing in a foreign land, where time flows by without purpose."[70] The subtitle of Zhou Bangyan's poem "Qiangwei xie hou zuo" 薔薇

68 Luo Guanzhong, *Sanguo yanyi* 三國演義 (The Romance of the Three Kingdoms) (Shanghai: Shanghai guji chubanshe, 2001), Chapter 54, p. 385.

69 Wang Changling 王昌齡, "Guiyuan" 閨怨 (A Young Wife's Regret) in *Quan Tang shi* 全唐詩 (Complete Tang Poems) *juan* 143, no. 25 (Beijing: Zhonghua shuju, 1960), vol. 2, p. 1446. Ouyang Xiu 歐陽修, "Yu dai hua" 御帶花 in Tang Guizhang 唐圭璋 (ed.), *Quan Song ci* 全宋詞 (Complete Song Lyrics) (Beijing: Zhonghua shuju, 1965), vol. 1, p. 144. Zhou Bangyan 周邦彥, "Liu Chou•Qiangwei xie hou zuo" 六醜•薔薇謝後作 (Six Uglinesses•Composed after the Wild Roses have Faded) in Qian Hongying 錢鴻瑛 (ed.), *Zhou Bangyan ci shangxi* 周邦彥詞賞析 (An Appreciation of the Lyric Poems of Zhou Bangyan) (Zhengzhou: Zhongzhou guji chubanshe, 1988), p. 144.

70 Zhou Bangyan 周邦彥, "Liu Chou•Qiangwei xie hou zuo" 六醜•薔薇謝後作 (Six Uglinesses•Composed after the Wild Roses have Faded) in Qian Hongying 錢鴻瑛 (ed.), *Zhou Bangyan ci shangxi* 周邦彥詞賞析 (An Appreciation of the Lyric Poems of Zhou Bangyan) (Zhengzhou: Zhongzhou guji chubanshe, 1988), p. 144.

謝後作 (Composed after the Wild Roses have Faded) alludes to a poem by the Tang dynasty poet Du Mu 杜牧 (803-853?), "Liu zeng" 留贈 ("Presented on Departure"), which includes the line *Qiangwei hua xie ji guilai* 薔薇花謝即歸來 (When the wild roses have faded I shall return).[71] This adds poignancy to Ma's uncharacteristically impassioned declaration, as he briefly thinks of his Shandong home. There are many other historical and literary allusions scattered throughout the book, some of which are explained in the text and others that for want of space have been left to the readers' imagination.

---

71   Du Mu 杜牧, "Liu zeng" 留贈 (Presented on Departure) in *Quan Tang shi* 全唐詩 (Complete Tang Poems) *juan* 524, no. 23 (Beijing: Zhonghua shuju, 1960), vol. 8, p. 5994.

CHANGES TO THE TEXT

The edition used for this translation of *Ma Yongzhen Yanyi*, published in Shanghai by Zhonghua Tushu jicheng Gongsi is a good example of the type of cheaply produced popular fiction that was printed in large numbers during the first decades of the 20th century. With books of this type, quality control was not foremost in the publishers' minds, so inevitably there are a number of places in the text where errors and discrepancies appear, some minor, and others that are really quite significant. As a result, in an effort to make the story work in the English language, some changes and corrections have been made to the original text, and these appear below.

Perhaps the most notable discrepancy in the main text concerns the location of the Yidongtian teashop, the place where the historical Ma Yongzhen was murdered. In the NCH newspaper reports it clearly states that the teashop was on "The Maloo", i.e., Nanking Road. However, in both MYZ and MSZ the Yidongtian is situated on Sixth Avenue, Pakhoi Road. Consequently, in this translation, Nanking Road is not mentioned with regard to the teashop, and when Yidongtian is referred to, it is on Pakhoi Road.

Another major discrepancy occurs in Chapters Three and Four, when Zhao Lianyu introduces himself to Ma Yongzhen at the Race Club, and invites him to visit a courtesan house at the invitation of Chai Jiuyun. By Chapter Four, the character of Zhao Lianyu has somehow made a clumsy metamorphosis into Chai Jiuyun. It is as if between the two chapters the author completely forgot about Zhao, and from this juncture, Chai Jiuyun becomes one of the central characters in the story. In this translation, the decision has been taken to make Chai Jiuyun the main subject, right from the moment he meets Ma in the courtesan house, at which point Zhao fades into the background to become just another of Chai's party guests.

Another glaring error, which again highlights the slapdash nature of the original editing, can be seen in Chapters Five and Six. In the story as it appears in the published book, it is Lu Shouji who warns Ma of the problems that he thinks will arise if foreigners are allowed to become involved in the planned martial arts tournament. Somewhere along the way, when the book was written or edited, a change was made to the story, and this is no doubt the reason that some of the arguments and plot lines in this chapter (and in other chapters) do not always follow in logical and reasonable order. A hint as to what this major change might have been, can be found in the title of Chapter Six, the second line of which reads: "An Old Woman Sends a Letter Urging Caution". Leaving aside the fact that in Chapter Five, Lu Shouji (a man) has already warned Ma Yongzhen about the problems of Westerners getting involved, no old woman appears at anytime, anywhere in the story, and no such letter is sent or received. This is an example of the poor continuity that is found, sometimes in less glaring ways, throughout the book. Lu Shouji's warning proves to be true (even though what he wants Ma to guard against is not made fully explicit) as the outcome of the contest with Yellow Beard is directly linked to Ma Yongzhen's murder at the end of the story.

The wording of other chapter headings can also be a little haphazard. Sometimes the content of the chapter, as shown in the caption, is not what actually takes place in the chapter. For example, the bird that is retrieved from Dog-eared Gao, which is mentioned in the title of Chapter Two, doesn't actually appear until Chapter Three. In cases such as this, the decision has been made to leave the titles as they are, even if the title and text of the chapter differ in content. It should be further noted with regard to chapter titles, that Chapter Ten does not even appear in the index. This is a minor error, but again illustrates well the rather careless approach to editing adopted by the publishers.

The book is formed of two halves, each written by a different author. The first half is said to be written by Qi Fanniu and the second by Zhu Dagong. There does not appear to be any scheme that assigns numbers to chapters according to the principles of yin-yang theory or numerology, as can be seen in some works of fiction of the late Qing dynasty. Originally the chapter numbers ran from 1 to 10 in each half of the book, but for the avoidance of any confusion, in this translation the chapters are numbered from 1 to 20.

There are a number of errors with regard to the names or major and minor characters. In Chapter One, Young Master Dong Jiguang is referred to incorrectly as Nao Jiguang, and a little later on as Ye Jiguang. On each occasion this occurs only once. In this translation his name appears as Dong Jiguang throughout.

Likewise, Wang Desheng, one of Ma Yongzhen's favourite disciples, appears in the book under a variety of different names: Ding Desheng, Peng Desheng, and Zhao Desheng. Again, in each case, the errors occur only once. In this translation this important character appears throughout under the name Wang Desheng. Two other similar examples are when the courtesan Hua Baoqin is wrongly referred to as Hua Baosheng in Chapter Five, and when Sanbao Headsplitter's Chinese name appears as Kaitou Sanbao 開頭三保, rather than Kaitou Sanbao 開頭三寶, in Chapter Eleven.

In Chapter Eight, Ma's Scrofulous Bai's children come to warn him that his horses have been taken ill, and shout out, "Daddy, come home quickly!" The scene continues with the words "...this made Yongzhen jump," but of course Ma Yongzhen is nowhere to be seen, and this should read "...this made Scrofulous Bai jump." This discrepancy has been appropriately addressed.

Deliberate Changes for the Sake of Continuity
There is a tendency to be deliberately approximate with the use of numbers in the book. Rather than specifying a single number when required, often two adjacent numbers appear, "five or six horses", or "six or seven disciples", as in the following passage: "Ma Yongzhen received this news and bought five or six fine horses there and then...He took with him six or seven of his disciples..." This is all rather vague and doesn't offer much help to the reader in understanding what is going on. There are, after all, only six disciples at this point and they have in their possession six horses between them. In most cases in this translation, such instances have been altered so that only one number appears in each instance: "six horses" and "six disciples".

Also with regard to Ma's disciples. When he takes on new followers, he is said to receive 108 disciples, but logically this number should be inclusive of, not only his existing disciples, but also Ma himself, as the whole point of this part of the story is that his followers are given the names of the 108 outlaws in *The Water Margin*. Logically, it would follow that Ma would take on the name of Song Jiang, leader of the bandits, though, that name is actually assigned to one of his followers. In this translation, rather than going along with the suggestion that he takes on 108 disciples, as can be found in the original text, it is made clear that this number, 108, is the final number, inclusive of Ma and his long-standing disciples. The following short paragraph has been added by the translator to make this clear to the reader: "On this day, Ma Yongzhen accepted 101 disciples, and together with his established followers and himself, this brought his band of brothers to the number 108, the same number of outlaws as appear in *The Water Margin*."

Most chapters begin with the phrase "Let us continue to relate…" (or "Let us proceed to relate"), and occasionally it also appears at other points in the story. This is the English translation used for the terms *Que shuo* 卻說, or *Hua shuo* 話說 (說話 *Shuo hua* in Chapter Fifteen), and follows the same pattern found in my translation of *The Adventures of Ma Suzhen*. Only once (in Chapter Five) does the opening phrase of a chapter appear as *Dang jiang* 當將. All these phrases have much the same meaning and have been translated in the same (or a similar) way throughout.

When Chai Jiuyun and Ma Yongzhen visit Hua Baoyu in Puqing Li, there is much hilarity due to a series of misunderstandings caused by Ma's inability to understand the local language of Shanghai as spoken by the maid Ah Hong, and likewise, her failure to understand Ma's northern accent when he speaks Shandong-style Mandarin. With this in mind, in this translation Ah Hong has been given a strong regional accent to at least give the impression that her way of speaking is difficult to understand. To do this, Geordie, scouse, a Scottish dialect, or other regional British accent might have been used, but I have chosen to use cockney, for the simple reason that as a Londoner I am more familiar with cockney than any other UK regional accent. There are other short episodes in the book where the authors chose to use a version of the local Shanghai language rather than Mandarin, such as in Chapter Eight when Lu the Lackey is speaking to Scrofulous Bai. In this case, I have chosen to translate his speech into standard English, otherwise, for the sake of continuity, everything Lu the Lackey says throughout the book would have to appear in cockney (even when, as is mostly the case, the original is written in standard Mandarin) and that would certainly affect the readability of the book. In Chapter

Eighteen, another character, Sanbao Headsplitter speaks cockney on the few occasions he is assigned a speaking role.

Place Names
The translation follows the pinyin system of Romanization, except in the following place names, which use the English versions of the names as they were known at the time when the original book was written.

Baxianqiao is Pahsienjiao
Beihai Lu is Pakhoi Road
Fujian Lu is Fuhkien Road
Fuzhou Lu is Foochow Road
Guangdong Lu is Kwangtung Road
Nanjing Lu is Nanking Road
Shantou Lu is Swatow Road
Xinzha Lu is Sinza Road
Hubei Lu is Hoopeh Road

Names of Characters
At certain points, to improve the flow of the story, some of the names of individual characters have been changed. This includes the changing of some family names.

"Bai Laili" 白癩痢 has become "Scrofulous Bai".
"Han Gaotou" 韓高頭 has become "Headman Han".
"Jiuqiu Shitiaoman" 九鰍十條鰻 has become "Eely Mudskipper".
"Kaitou Sanbao" 開頭三寶 has become "Sanbao Headsplitter".
"Liu Sanzi" 劉三子 has become "Poxy Fang".
"Lu Ah Gou" 陸阿狗 has become "Dog-Eared Gao".
"Pao Longtao" 跑龍套 has become "Lu the Lackey".
"Sixie Yilaituan" 四蟹一癩團 has become "Scabby Crabby".

"Tuxue Siguan" 吐血四官 has become "Siguan Bloodsplitter".
"Xiaoda Jiuzi" 小大九子 has become "Little Big Number Nine".

APPENDIX

Original Preface to *Ma Yongzhen yanyi* (Ma Yongzhen: an Historical Romance) [*Murder in the Maloo*]

Since ancient times, the states of Yan and Zhao have been known as places where heroes of profound thought have expressed themselves through tragic song. Gao Jianli plucked his zither by the Yi River, and the man of Chu crossed the river and danced with sword in hand. From ancient times to the present day, the ambience of northern parts has been hard and strong. With heroes and champions to the east of the mountains, and heroes and champions to the west of the mountains. I had never heard of fine men of great talent south of the Yangtse River. But, in fact, since the time of Zhao She of the Ma clan of Fufeng, in each generation there have been those who have come down to us. In the martial sphere, there were father and son, Ma Sheng and Ma Chao of the Western Liang; in the civil sphere, there were the brothers "White Eyebrows" Ma Liang and Ma Su. During the Jin, Tang, Song, and Yuan dynasties, there were simply too many to enumerate. When it came to the time of the Ming dynasty, the Chongzhen emperor lost the throne, and Wu Sangui, later of Yunnan, invited the Qing army through the Shanhai Pass, to snatch the leadership and the mandate of the Han away. At that time there was Ma Sanbao, who guarded the palace gates and fended off the enemy, dying a hero's death. Ma was a truly remarkable man, and for a period of one thousand autumns there were none who could equal him. Up to now, though, those who have delighted in discussing the workings of government departments, and who revel in imparting all they know, have not spoken of him. Those who talk of green rivers and blue mountains; the fisherman and woodcutter chatting idly; of sitting 'mid mountain ranges, the rivers and the streams; facing towards the setting sun by the old ferry crossing, they smile when they talk of Ma Sanbao's martyred spirit. There are none who do not' open their mouths to laugh and clap their hands; who push back their hats to reveal their foreheads, and getting to their feet, their spirits in energetic mood, esteem and revere him without end. As for Ma Yongzhen of Shandong from that dynasty, he is much the same. Yongzhen excelled at rearing horses. From the very beginning he possessed an authority that shook the world, and the status of one who holds tight to honesty and integrity. Those who had heard of him or seen him, knew he was not like the old nag that stumbles at the first hurdle, but like a dragon horse that could leap and bound for one thousand *li*. Those who had dealings with him knew that he was not like the chariot driver of Yan Zi, Prime Minister of Qi, who was overly proud of the chariot he drove, but like Wang Heng and Zhang Bao who rode their horses to the front and back of General Yue Fei.

If you are not blessed with consummate skill, how can you reach the Spring River. Ma's reputation grew until he was known all around and by 1845 his true nature began to be made clear. Occasionally he would talk of the Way. Always proud and excited, he was articulate, able to exert himself, full of vitality, and possessing of a manner that was both brave and vigorous. From this it can be seen that Ma Yongzhen was an extraordinary man indeed. What a pity it is that there are no books dedicated to the telling of his story. With the passing of the years and months he has become a forgotten hero. How can it be that his name should fade into obscurity? My friend Luzhuang Yunqi is a man of great moral integrity and unwavering character. He is fond of the ancient and devoted to the curious. He has published this book especially for the benefit of later generations so that they may offer a myriad libations to their ancestors. Those worthy men who talk of Shanghai often recall Ma Yongzhen, so henceforth his name shall be remembered forever.

Preface written in the Ancient Liaotian Pavilion by Chen Dongfu of Chongming in the high summer of the *xingyou* year [1921].

BIBLIOGRAPHY

Books

Bao Tianxiao 包天笑, *Shanghai chunqiu* 上海春秋 (Annals of Shanghai) (Shanghai: Shanghai guji chubanshe, 1991).

Cao Xueqin 曹雪芹, Gao E 高鶚, *Honglou meng* 紅樓夢 (The Dream of the Red Chamber) 2 vols. (Shanghai: Shanghai guji chubanshe, 1988).

French, Paul, *The Old Shanghai A-Z* (Hong Kong: Hong Kong University Press, 2010).

Ge Yuanxu 葛元煦 and Yuan Zuzhi 袁祖志, *Huyou zaji* 滬游雜記 (Miscellaneous Records of Wanderings Around Shanghai) 4 *juan* (Shanghai, 1876).

Ge Yuanxu 葛元煦 and Yuan Zuzhi, *Chongxiu Huyou zaji* 重修滬游雜記 (Miscellaneous Records of Wanderings Around Shanghai, Revised) 4 *juan* (Shanghai, 1888).

Henriot, Christian, and Nöel Castelino (tr.), *Prostitution and Sexuality in Shanghai: A Social History, 1849-1949* (Cambridge: Cambridge, 2001).

Huang Xuelei, *Shanghai Filmmaking: Crossing Borders, Connecting to the Globe, 1922-1938* (Leiden: Brill, 2014).

Lau, D. C., *Tao Te Ching* (London: Penguin, 1963).

Lu Eting 陸萼庭, *Kunju yanchu shigao* 昆劇演出史稿 (Notes on the History of Kunju Opera Performance) (Shanghai: Shanghai wenyi chubanshe, 1980).

Lu Hanchao, *Beyond the Neon Lights: Everyday Shanghai in the Early Twentieth Century* (Berkeley, Los Angeles, London: University of California Press, 2004).

Luo Guanzhong, *Sanguo yanyi* 三國演義 (The Romance of the Three Kingdoms) (Shanghai: Shanghai guji chubanshe, 2001).

Martin, Brian G., *The Shanghai Green Gang: Politics and Organized Crime, 1919-1937* (Berkeley, Los Angeles, London: University of California Press, 1996).

Martin, Steven, *The Art of Opium Antiques* (Chiang Mai: Silkworm Books, 2007).

Menghua Guanzhu 夢花館主 (Master of the Hall of Floral Dreams) [Jiang Yinxiang 江蔭香], *Jiuwei hu* 九尾狐 (The Nine-tailed Vixen) (Suzhou: Jiaotong tushuguan minyoushe, 1918).

Menghua Guanzhu 夢花館主 (Master of the Hall of Floral Dreams) [Jiang Yinxiang 江蔭香], *Jiuwei hu* 九尾狐 (The Nine-tailed Vixen) in *Wan Qing xiaoshuo daxi* 晚清小説大系 (Compendium of Late Qing Fiction) vol. 11 (Taibei: Guangya chuban youxian gongsi, 1984).

Qi Fanniu 戚飯牛 and Zhu Dagong 朱大公, *Ma Suzhen lixian ji* 馬素貞歷險記 (The Adventures of Ma Suzhen) (Shanghai: Zhonghua tushu jicheng gongsi, [January] 1923).

Qi Fanniu 戚飯牛 and Zhu Dagong 朱大公, *Ma Suzhen quanzhuan* 馬素貞全傳 (The Complete Story of Ma Suzhen) (Shanghai: Guangji shuju, 1929).

Qi Fanniu 戚飯牛 and Zhu Dagong 朱大公, *Ma Yongzhen yanyi* 馬永貞演義 (Ma Yongzhen — An Historical Romance) (Shanghai: Zhonghua tushu jicheng gongsi, [October] 1923).

Qi Fanniu and Zhu Dagong (attrib.) and Paul Bevan (tr.), *The Adventures of Ma Suzhen: An Heroic Woman Takes Revenge in Shanghai* (Palgrave Macmillan, 2021).

Qian Hongying 錢鴻瑛 (ed.), *Zhou Bangyan ci shangxi* 周邦彥詞賞析 (An Appreciation of the Lyric Poems of Zhou Bangyan) (Zhengzhou: Zhongzhou guji chubanshe, 1988).

Qian Zhongshu and Duncan M. Campbell (ed.) *Seven Essays on Art and Literature* (Leiden: Brill, 2014).

Quan Tang shi 全唐詩 (Complete Tang Poems) 12 vols. (Beijing: Zhonghua shuju, 1960).

Shanghai zhinan 上海指南 [增訂十一版附上海地圖名表] (Guide to Shanghai: a Chinese Directory of the Port). [11th edition (revised)] (Shanghai: Shanghai yinshuguan, 1920) [preface dated SeventhYear of Republic [1918]].

Shi Nai'an, Luo Guanzhong and Sidney Shapiro (tr.), *Outlaws of the Marsh* (Beijing: Foreign Languages Press, 2003).

Soothill, William Edward, *The Analects, or the Conversations of Confucius with his Disciples and Others* (London, New York, Toronto: Oxford University Press, 1937 [1910]).

Tang Guizhang 唐圭璋 (ed.), *Quan Song ci* 全宋詞 (Complete Song Lyrics) 5 vols. (Beijing: Zhonghua shuju, 1965).

Wagner, Rudolf G., *Joining the Global Public: Word, Image, and City in Early Chinese Newspaper* (Albany: State University of New York Press, 2012).

Watson, Burton (tr.), *Hsün Tsu: Basic Writings* (New York: Columbia University Press, 1963).

Wen Kang 文康, *Ernü yingxiong zhuan* 兒女英雄傳 (The Tale of Heroic Sons and Daughters) (Shanghai: Yandong tushuguan, 1925).

Wilkinson, Endymion, *Chinese History: a Manual* (Cambridge, Massachusetts: Harvard University Asia Center, 2000).

Wu Liang, translated by Wang Mingjie, *Old Shanghai: a Lost Age* (Beijing: Foreign Language Press, 2001).

Wu Jianren 吳趼人 [Wu Woyao 吳沃堯], *Ershi nian mudu zhi guai xianzhuang* 二十年目睹之怪現狀 (Strange Happenings Witnessed over a Period of Twenty Years), 8 *juan* (Shanghai: Shijie shuju, 1923).

Wue, Roberta, *Art Worlds: Artists, Images, and Audiences in Late Nineteenth-Century Shanghai* (Hong Kong: Hong Kong University Press, 2014).

TRANSLATED BY PAUL BEVAN

Xie Bingying 謝冰瑩 et al. (eds.), *Xinyi sishu duben* 新譯四書讀本 (A Four Books Reader, Newly Interpreted) (Taipei: Sanmin shuju, 2002 [1987]).

Yang Jiayou 楊嘉祐, *Shanghai laofangzi de gushi* 上海老房子的故事 (Tales of the Old Buildings of Shanghai) (Shanghai renmin chubanshe: Shanghai, 2006).

Ye Xiaoqing, *Popular Culture in Shanghai, 1884-1898* (Doctoral thesis. The Australian National University, 1991).

Yeh, Catherine, *Shanghai Love: Courtesans, Intellectuals, and Entertainment Culture, 1850-1910* (Washington: University of Washington Press, 2006).

Yu Da 俞達, *Qinglou meng* 青樓夢 (Dream of the Green Chamber) in *Wan Qing xiaoshuo daxi* 晚清小説大系 (Compendium of Late Qing Fiction) vol. 3 (Taibei: Guangya chuban youxian gongsi, 1984).

Zhang Henshui 張恨水, *Tixiao yinyuan* 啼笑因緣 (Fate in Tears and Laughter) (Shanghai: Sanyou shushe, 1947).

Zhou Shixun 周世勳 (ed.), Zhu Shunlin 朱順麟 (photos.), Li Qiyu 李啟宇 (tr.), *Shanghai shi da guan* 上海市大觀 ("The Greater Shanghai") (Shanghai: Meishu tushu gongsi, 1933).

Zunwenge Zhuren 尊聞閣主人 (Master of the Zunwenge) [Ernest Major] and Wu Youru 吳友如, *Shenjiang shengjing tu* 申江勝景圖 (Wondrous Scenes of Shanghai) (Shanghai: Shenbao guan 1884). Reprint: Taipei, Guangwen shuju, 1981.

Articles in Books Newspapers, Journals and Magazines

[Advertisement] *Minguo ribao* 民國日報 ("The Republican Daily News") (August 1924), p. 7.

"Bei Nicheng bang tianping gongjun" 北泥城浜填平工竣 (Works to Level Out the North Nicheng Creek are Complete), in *Minguo ribao* 民國日報 ("The Republican Daily News") (25 October 1920), p. 11.

"Bei Nichenghe yi wanquan tianping" 北泥城河已完全填平 (The Levelling Out of North Nicheng Creek is Complete) in *Shibao* 時報 ("Eastern Times") (25 October 1920), p. 5,

Bevan, Paul, "The Legends of Ma Suzhen and Ma Yongzhen: From Shanghai Silent Film to Hong Kong Martial Arts Cinema," in Feng Lin (ed.), *Film History and Development of Screen Culture in and Beyond Greater China* (Routledge, Forthcoming).

Bevan, Paul, "Ma Yongzhen: 'He Fought with his Fists in the Capitals, North and South'," in *Arts of Asia* (Summer 2023), pp. 48-54.

"Faguo jieqi" 法國節期 (The French Public Holiday) in *Dianshizhai huabao* 點石齋畫報 (Dianshizhai Pictorial) (1884), vol. 2, p. 64.

"Fa xunfu fang" 法巡撫房 (The French Police Station) in Zunwenge Zhuren 尊聞閣主人 (Master of the Zunwenge) [Ernest Major] and Wu Youru 吳友如, *Shenjiang shengjing tu* 申江勝景圖 (Wondrous Scenes of Shanghai) (Shanghai: Shenbao guan 1884), part 2, pp. 52-53. Reprint published by Taipei, Guangwen shuju, 1981.

Honig, Emily, "The Politics of Prejudice: Subei People in Republican-Era Shanghai." *Modern China* vol. 15, no. 3 (1989), pp. 243-274.

Liang, Samuel Y., "Where the Courtyard Meets the Street: Spatial Culture of the Li Neighborhoods, Shanghai, 1870–1900" in *Journal of the Society of Architectural Historians* (2008) 67 (4), pp. 482-503.

Lo, Andrew, "China's Passion for *Pai*: Playing Cards, Dominoes, and Mahjong" in Colin Mackenzie, and Irving L. Finkel (eds.), *Asian Games: The Art of Contest* (New York: Asia Society, 2004), pp. 216-231.

Mingxing tekan 明星特刊 (Mingxing Special) no. 28 (1 December 1927).

"The Murder in the Maloo" in *The North-China Herald* (22 April 1879), p. 393.

Qian Jibo 錢基博, "Jiji yuwen bu, Ma Yongzhen" 技擊餘聞補, 馬永貞 (Supplementary Anecdotes on the Martial Arts, Ma Yongzhen) in *Xiaoshuo yuebao* 小説月報 ("The Short Story Magazine") vol. 5 no. 7 (25 October 1914), pp. 1-4.

"Quanshi chiku" 拳師吃苦 (The Suffering of a Boxing Master) in *Shenbao* 申報 ("The Shun Pao") (14 April 1879).

[Shao] Zuiweng [邵] 醉翁 [Runje Shaw], "Ji zuowan Xiao wutai zhi 'Ma Yongzhen'" 記昨晚笑舞台之 "馬永貞" (Yesterday Evening's "Ma Yongzhen" at the Xiao wutai) in *Shenbao* 申報 ("The Shun Pao") (13 November 1923), p. 18.

"Summary of News" in *The North-China Herald* (15 April 1879), p. 346.

Xu Xueqing, "The Mandarin Duck and Butterfly School", in Kirk A. Denton and Michel Hockx (eds.), *Literary Societies in Republican China* (Lanham, MD: Lexington Books, 2008), pp. 47-78.

Yi Yi 乙乙, "Ma Yongzhen, Yilu suibi" 馬永貞, 乙盧隨筆 (Ma Yongzhen, Yi Lu Random Notes) in *Xiaoshuo xinbao* 小説新報 (New Fiction) vol. 2 no. 8 (1916), pp. 4-11.

"Zeng lingren Zhou Fenglin" 贈伶人周鳳林 (Presented to the Actor Zhou Fenglin) in *Shenbao* 申報 ("The Shun Pao") (10 April 1882).

Internet

The first days of electric Shanghai—The China Project, Accessed 15 August 2023.

Doorbells Transformed—The Doorbell Museum (electrachime. net), Accessed 31 August 2023.

ACKNOWLEDGEMENTS

To begin with, I'd like to thank three individuals who have not been directly involved in the production of this book, but have each been of great help to me over the years: Professor Michel Hockx, for his constant encouragement during my career; Professor Margaret Hillenbrand, at the University of Oxford, for her belief in me and for her continual support; and Professor Bernhard Fuehrer, formerly of the School of Oriental and African Studies (SOAS), London who has been a great inspiration to me since my studies at graduate level. Next, I thank those who have helped directly with areas of specialist inquiry relating to the book: Dr Lars Laamann for his helpful comments to do with matters concerning opium; Dr Rachel Silberstein for her suggestions concerning 19th century cloth dyes and clothing; Dr Helen Wang for her invaluable expertise with regard to Chinese money; and Professor Andrew Lo for his expert help with matters relating to Chinese games.

I am grateful to the staff of SOAS Library, and the Bodleain Library, Oxford, for their help in accessing research materials. Thanks to Jiyeon Wood of SOAS library for her initial interest in a popular *nianhua*-style print showing Ma Yongzhen, which prompted me to look into his story more deeply. With further regard to this print, I am particularly indebted to Frances Wood for unwittingly introducing me to it in the first place. Little did I know when teaching a class on the history of the book at SOAS (the items having all been chosen by Frances) that this print would lead me down such an interesting avenue of research. The starting point for all the work I've done on Ma Yongzhen since then, was this popular print. Thank you to the SOAS Special Collections for their kind permission to reproduce a detail of this print on the cover of the book.

I would also like to offer my warm thanks to Jessica Harrison-Hall, Head of the China Section at the British Museum, for inviting me to write the essay, "Ma Yongzhen: 'He Fought with his Fists in the Capitals, North and South" for the magazine *Arts of Asia* published to coincide with the British Museum's 2023 exhibition, "China's Hidden Century."

Special thanks also to Graham Earnshaw and the team at Earnshaw Books for all their hard work in preparing the book for publication.

I am grateful to my friends for their patience in listening to me talk about the book and my work in general, and for their encouragement with both: Jon Banks, Howard Benge, Leandro Espinoza, Miguel Lawrence and "The Confabulists." Thanks also to my brother Jason for his help with all IT issues, and also my sister Hannah and nephews Django and Ben. This book is dedicated to the memory of my mother and father, Fern Bevan (1925–2021) and Hubert Graham Llewelyn Bevan (1915–1996).

About the Translator

Paul Bevan is a Sinologist, historian, researcher and literary translator. From 2020 to 2023 he worked as Departmental Lecturer in Modern Chinese Literature and Culture at the University of Oxford. Before that, from 2018 to 2020, he was Christensen Fellow in Chinese Painting at the Ashmolean Museum, Oxford. His research focuses equally on the visual arts and literature, and concerns the impact of Western art and literature on China during the Republican Era and the late Qing dynasty, particularly with regard to periodicals and magazines. Paul's first book, *A Modern Miscellany – Shanghai Cartoon Artists, Shao Xunmei's Circle and the Travels of Jack Chen, 1926-1938*, Leiden: Brill, 2015, was hailed as "a major contribution to modern Chinese studies"; his second, *'Intoxicating Shanghai': Modern Art and Literature in Pictorial Magazines during Shanghai's Jazz Age* was published by Brill in 2020. John A. Crespi's review calls attention to the translations imbedded in the book: "Featured within the book's densely informative analyses are translations of four modernist short stories. [These] in themselves contribute significantly to modern Chinese literary studies...". These four short stories are: "The Girl in the Inky-Green Cheongsam", and "Camel, Nietzscheanist and Woman" by Mu Shiying, "Hai Alai Scenes" by Hei Ying, and "Attempted Murder" by Liu Na'ou.

Printed in Great Britain
by Amazon